M000087168

Patriote Peril

Thomas Thorpe

Black Rose Writing
www.blackrosewriting.com

© 2011 by Thomas Thorpe

All rights reserved. No part of this book may be reproduced, stored in a retrieval system or transmitted in any form or by any means without the prior written permission of the publishers, except by a reviewer who may quote brief passages in a review to be printed in a newspaper, magazine or journal.

The final approval for this literary material is granted by the author.

First printing

All characters appearing in this work are fictitious. Any resemblance to real persons, living or dead, is purely coincidental.

ISBN: 978-1-61296-066-1

PUBLISHED BY BLACK ROSE WRITING

www.blackrosewriting.com

Printed in the United States of America

Patriote Peril is printed in Times New Roman

Cover art by Historic Canadian Scenery, National Archives of Canada.

To Linda
For roads less taken . . .

Other Books in the Darmon Series

Patriote Peril

Chapter One

Elizabeth gazed across the valley.

Her eyes searched a carpet of swaying pine trees below the veranda of her sister's cabin. Situated high on a rim overlooking Humphrey's Valley, the porch offered an unobstructed view out to jagged peaks far beyond the basin. She could not imagine a more isolated spot within the Costigan Mountains of New Brunswick Colony, ninety miles northwest of Halifax.

A tiny speck raced across the canyon floor.

Elizabeth squinted at a carriage making its way between grassy hummocks.

Her husband, two sisters and their spouses left hours earlier to see Grand Falls on the Saint John River, thirty miles north. Elizabeth had looked forward to the trip, but awoke in the morning with a splitting headache and begged to be left behind. Instead, she spent the day inside a darkened room, listening to four servants going about their duties.

The carriage plunged forward, lurching, bouncing and spewing clouds of dust into the air before diving under tree cover.

Elizabeth's eyebrows knitted.

The vehicle hove into view again, careening toward her side of the valley.

Without a driver.

Near the base of the rim, its two horses did not pause. The conveyance sped up a rising trail at breakneck speed, precariously swinging the closed passenger compartment back and forth. The transport barreled around a curve, disappearing under an overhanging ledge.

Elizabeth hurried down three steps and dashed along a path to the front of the lodge.

She stood at the edge of the road, heart pounding louder than the gently rustling grasses on the hillside. Agonizing seconds passed while a bucolic landscape seemed to mock her concern.

She strained on tiptoe to catch a glimpse of the approaching carriage.

Earth began to tremble.

Vibrations grew to shaking, drumming sounds became pounding that intensified to a deafening roar.

Terrified horses burst into view.

Lathered animals tore headlong at her, spraying pebbles in all directions.

The horrific image blasted past.

Elizabeth sprang after, bounding over a rutted path and choking back dust, she chased the vehicle as it rumbled down a narrow road leading to the corral. Frantically avoiding rocks and crevices, she threw her head back and caught a glimpse of the carriage already circling in front of the paddock fence.

By the time she reached the perimeter, a stable hand had rushed from the barn to grab the reins and slow the coach to a stop.

A door on the left side swung loose. Elizabeth grabbed the swaying handle and peered inside an empty compartment. A sticky substance stuck to her palm. Her eyes widened at the brownish smear.

Blood!

She swallowed hard, fighting queasiness rising within her stomach. She turned to the stable hand. "Peter, saddle a horse for me. Tell the servants to send for help. I must find out what happened."

The young man, not yet twenty, hesitated. "Ma'am, it might be Indians. You'd not be safe riding out there, especially being unfamiliar with the territory and all. Better wait 'til we call for soldiers from the garrison at Fredericton."

She squeezed the handle again to keep from shaking. "I can't sit here until help arrives. My family may be somewhere bleeding to death."

"But, what could you do for them?"

"I must go! Hurry!"

Peter trod heavily into the barn and returned a few minutes later with a gray mare saddled for western riding. Elizabeth did not hesitate to climb up. She adopted the New World riding custom with proficiency owing to years of horsemanship on their estate in Kent. There, she took pride in an ability to ride better than most men.

Seconds later, her horse charged up the road. She took small comfort to be out of his sight before throwing up, and barely heard the stable hand call out, "Keep to the green, ma'am!"

Two hours of riding uncovered neither family nor threat from Indians.

There was just enough time to reach Grand Falls and return to the lodge before darkness. Visions of bloodied bodies sprawled along the road assaulted Elizabeth's mind. Danger in the frontier was always close at hand, but now, she stood on the verge of being left alone and helpless in a foreboding wilderness.

She retreated to thoughts of life in Southern England. Unlike this secluded world, she and her two sisters, Emily and Victoria lived among friends and countless acquaintances. They grew up attending family gatherings and society balls. That is, until her youngest sister, Victoria married Richard Hudson and announced their intention to move to British North America.

"Why must you go to such a dangerous place?" Elizabeth pleaded.

"Richard should stop looking for greener pastures," William, her husband, warned.

Victoria remained committed. "During the war, when the Royal Navy was deprived of wood from the mainland, Richard said that Canadian forests were a Godsend. Now, immigrant settlements are springing up everywhere. It's 1831, and there's money to be made in the booming timber industry."

"But where will you live?" Emily persisted.

"We've an option to purchase one thousand acres of Crown land in New Brunswick Colony," Victoria said. "We'll build our own residence."

Six months following the wedding, they departed London Dock for a new life in Canada.

Two years later, Elizabeth received an invitation to spend a summer at the Hudson's newly completed Lodge overlooking Humphrey's Valley.

At Grand Falls, Elizabeth found only an empty clearing. She paused within a wooded area, listening to the water's roar, as it hurtled and twisted against the rocks, then widened into a huge slide before plunging into a gorge a hundred feet below. Trees stirred in the late afternoon breeze and sunlight filtered through branches creating shadows of watching figures.

Anxiously, she searched for a sign of human presence, trampled earth or a broken branch, but nothing tainted the pristine wilderness. Foliage around the perimeter seemed to close in around her. She tried to come up with alternatives for her relations' whereabouts. An absence of carriage tracks and footprints suggested her family never made it to the overlook. The last sight of wheel ruts came just before crossing a twenty-foot-wide creek, a few miles back on the road.

Maybe, Richard impulsively took them to see some other attraction.

Further search would have to wait until morning. By then, help might arrive.

Elizabeth's mount plodded back toward the Lodge. Chilling breezes permeated long shadows, not far ahead of darkness. A lonesome bird cried eerily through the stillness.

Once more, her mind wandered, reliving their holiday abroad.

The Atlantic voyage took four weeks. No servants accompanied them, and Elizabeth quickly came to appreciate the sacrifices she would make in this demanding country. She also endured bouts of seasickness, counting each day until the pitching deck would settle down.

Victoria and Richard came to Halifax to meet their arrival.

"Well, we actually made it!" Elizabeth announced, arriving at the foot of the gangplank.

After a moment's teary-eyed hugging, the sisters stepped back to size up each other.

"Lizzy, you've changed your hair!" Victoria remarked.

"Emily did it. I was useless on board, *mal-de-mer* had me at the railing every day."

"Yes, she was a limp rag most of the trip," Emily smiled. "I cut it close for minimal upkeep. It may not be stylish, but Elizabeth is always the practical one. We hadn't done each other's hair since the summer I met Charles."

Victoria added her approval. "I love the tight curls."

From Halifax, overland travel took them to the town of Moncton across Northumberland Strait from Charlottetown on Prince Edward Island. The rowdy settlement of spruce log buildings epitomized the western frontier. Noisy dancehalls, street brawls and gunfire greeted the visitors, and kept them awake most of the night. Elizabeth squeezed William's arm, glad to be free of the place when they moved on.

The next night, they found accommodation at the seacoast village of Newcastle, well known for its fishing industry. Markets for Newcastle cod burgeoned worldwide. Commerce in lumber also thrived, exemplified by brand new buildings all around.

Late the following day, they arrived at Hudson's Lodge. Elizabeth paused in amazement at the two-story, sixteen-room, live oak building five hundred feet above the valley floor, completely staffed with housekeeping, cooking and stable personnel.

The three couples got along tremendously. Strange animals provided game, which William, Charles and Richard took pleasure in pursuing for their evening table. At night, they played games, indulged in serious conversation or simply rested on the verandah taking in the view. Colorful wild flowers grew everywhere. For a while, Elizabeth enjoyed the primitive, yet wondrous world, but a need to be home grew with each passing day.

Elizabeth reined her horse upon reaching the stream.

Carriage tracks entered the water on the far side, but did not emerge on the other. The gently flowing brook measured no more than a foot deep with places where the bed of rocks lay only an inch below the surface.

A glint upstream caught her eye, halfway across the river.

She dismounted, hiked up her skirts and sloshed up to the

winking object. Gingerly, she reached into icy water and picked up a shiny coin, a fourteenth century gold franc! Emily religiously carried such a rare object from an event years past. She would never have let it out of her sight unless it was dropped to provide a clue.

"They've been kidnapped!" she gasped.

There was no time to search further. Darkness would soon be upon her, and clouds billowing over the dimly lit mountaintops signaled a gathering storm.

Elizabeth rode in twilight by the time she started down a gentle slope into Humphrey's Valley opposite Hudson's Lodge.

She glanced up at heavy clouds covering most of the valley.

From a far ridge, thick columns of smoke rose. They looked denser than the gentle wisps of a fireplace or campfire.

She urged her horse on.

Within ten minutes, Elizabeth reached the last section of trail beneath the valley rim. Smoke hung heavy in the air.

By the time her horse climbed to the top, glowing embers danced within a suffocating haze.

The silhouette of a huge mound of irregular spikes jumped out at her. A pile of rubble stood in place of the lodge. Ugly black timbers and red cinders smoldered in the gloom. The entire two-story structure, her sister's home, had burned to the ground.

"God help us! God help us! Please God, help us!"

Her shaking hands dropped the reins. Elizabeth dismounted.

On fragile legs, she stepped cautiously through a myriad of floating embers and empty stillness. An eerie silence transformed the once comforting haven into a horrifying scene.

"Peter... Andrew... Sarah," she called out weakly for the servants until a mouthful of ashes caused violent coughs to ravage her throat. Waves of queasiness overcame Elizabeth.

She paused unsteadily, clutching both arms, digging nails into flesh above her elbows to keep from running terrified into the brush.

What was left of the stable seethed in the distance. She swallowed resolutely with a mouth tasting like wool and forced her reluctant feet down the path to the stable, scattering debris with each tentative step.

A sudden scurrying jerked her head into the air. Her foot caught on a charred timber, pitching the startled woman forward onto black earth.

Covered with soot, she lay curled into a ball as sobs wracked her body. She squeezed her eyes shut to erase the spectacle. Soft moaning sounds spilled from her mouth while she rocked back and forth.

After a time, her pounding heart subsided. Eyelids parted and sight focused on a darkened log. A rounded object stood out near one end.

A charred human skull.

She screamed into unconsciousness.

A bit later, the dimly lit scene flashed back into mind. With a reluctant sigh, her eyes returned to the skeleton. Charred pieces of servants were all that remained of the lodge's inhabitants. *Why? Was it an accident or a deliberate act?* Whoever caused this tragedy might still be nearby. He could be watching her. Panic welled. The uneasy feeling replaced shock numbing her brain. She had to get back down the mountain. She sat up.

A hundred feet away, the horse whinnied.

Someone might be waiting for her.

It was darker now. Gnarled tree remnants and fallen timber merged into a black outline underneath a hazy violet sky. Amid the ebon silhouettes, she struggled to her feet on legs that felt like lead weights.

She decided to sneak up on whoever held her mount.

Carefully, she placed a step softly on the earth and counted every footfall toward the mare, each one softly crunching in the gloom.

A twig snapped.

She froze.

A dark form rose amid the pile of rubble to her right. Boards clattered to the ground around the specter, sending ashes swirling into the air.

With a terrified shriek, Elizabeth flung herself headlong toward her ride. She leaped onto the animal's back and kicked its ribs mercilessly. The steed bounded off perilously, sensing her terror, and stampeded down the trail. She pressed her head against its neck and clung for dear life.

Elizabeth did not catch a breath until she had crossed the valley floor.

In the dark of night, her horse slowed to a walk.

She had to make sense of the situation. She could only pray that help was on the way. Hopefully, Peter started for Fredericton before the fire broke out.

Her worst fear had come true. She was alone in this alien country, consumed by a vast territory that cared not if she lived or died.

With her family lost and no idea whether they were alive, the best chance would be to ride to Newcastle and seek help from local law enforcement. Tomorrow, they could all return to the desolate scene.

She took a deep, shaky breath. Tears overflowed.

Lightning flashed, thunder roared. Cold raindrops began pummeling the frightened refugee. She rode on into the night.

Chapter Two

Elizabeth had never endured such a driving downpour. Every inch of clothing was soaked, and bone-chilling cold permeated aching muscles. Frantically, she searched for the safe haven of Newcastle. Hours of pushing through muddy morasses in total darkness finally ended on the banks of the *Miramichi River*.

At the late hour, streets of Newcastle were deserted, but at the far end of a flooded town square, a shaft of light pierced the night. Above the window, a small sign said 'Hotel'.

Inside, a dozing clerk reluctantly roused at her pleas and raised an eyebrow at the sight of an unescorted woman in disheveled condition. For three shillings and a signature, she got a room with no questions. Elizabeth always carried a small purse containing twenty pounds and the recent addition of a rare gold coin.

A sagging bed, well-worn bureau and small chipped table under a blackened oil-lamp seemed like paradise compared to the onslaught outside. With shaking fingers, she fumbled with the lock to bolt an aged door. Dripping, she undressed to flop on the bed. For ten minutes she lay shivering on the bed, while tears streamed down icy cheeks. Her exhausted body finally settled down, but sleep did not come. Her mind would not stop worrying whether her family still breathed somewhere.

Elizabeth arrived at the Sheriff's office just after daybreak.

Constable John Thomas listened to her bizarre account, slowly shaking his head.

"I'm sorry to say, Mrs. Darmon, we've received no word from Hudson's Lodge regarding the events you described," he observed behind a cluttered desk. "I've known Richard Hudson for over a year and can't imagine why anyone would want to kidnap him."

"What about an Indian uprising of some sort?" Elizabeth persisted.

The sun-tanned and unshaven man of fifty smiled from his chair leaning against the wall.

"There haven't been hostilities in this area for years. *Malecite* and *Abnaki* tribes are quite peaceful, and the *Micmac's* of Nova Scotia have become sedentary. Only the *Iroquois* up on the Saint Lawrence occasionally raid campsites for food, but I doubt they'd travel one-hundred miles to inflict such harm on the Lodge or its residents."

"But, who would do such a thing?" Elizabeth's voice rose with frustration.

He fingered a small wooden carving. "Oh, I suppose an Acadian might resent Mr. Hudson's holdings. They're descendants from the original French settlers and live in wooded areas along the rivers, but they're an illiterate bunch and usually keep to themselves."

His eyes narrowed. "It's possible renegades from the south, particularly Americans forayed into the territory. Resentment still lingers from the war back in 1815, and arguments over our boundary with Maine continue since it became a state in 1820."

"Do you think the two incidents are related?" Elizabeth voiced her worst fear. "Could an attack on the carriage be part of a larger plan that included destruction of the Hudson holdings in Humphrey's Valley?"

Constable Thomas' brow furrowed. He put down the figurine and hunched forward. "It's a decided coincidence, to be sure. Mr. Hudson may have enemies, but I'd rather believe the fire was an accident or the act of a local hoodlum; perhaps someone with too much drink. There's no telling what goes on in the back woods. Survival away from well established towns can be precarious."

Elizabeth squeezed the arms of her chair, wondering how the man could dismiss these attacks so casually? She must push for some type of action. "When will you inspect the area?"

He sighed. "I'm afraid we're stuck here until the rain lets up. It won't be easy to track your family now, but when the weather clears, I'll take a few men up to Dawes Creek and start from there. I can't promise anything. We don't have a lot of law enforcement people here in Newcastle. Besides two deputies who provide night watch, there are only a few shopkeepers on-call for emergencies."

Elizabeth nodded.

Richard told them that many towns lacked lawmen. By the Act of Provincial Government of 1793, a regional Justice of the Peace appointed a local townsperson constable. An innkeeper by trade, John Thomas passed the propriety of his tavern, Black Bear on to his son while he served a five-year term of legal oversight. Fees for serving warrants, escorting prisoners and attending court in Moncton did not provide much of an income for an honest man dedicated to ensuring peace in the village.

On the fourth day, weather finally improved. Constable Thomas, Elizabeth and seven townspeople rode over a muddy landscape to Dawes Creek, where she had last seen carriage tracks. Four of the new 'deputies' split into pairs to search for clues upstream and down, while the rest rode on to the Lodge. A local doctor, Samuel McHenry accompanied them to reclaim the servants' bodies for burial.

Doctor McHenry picked among the ruins for some time before approaching the Constable with an outstretched palm held flat. "See these shot balls? I pulled them from the victims' remains. They were each killed by small arms fire."

Elizabeth looked up from smoldering wreckage a few feet away. "Small arms fire? What does that mean?"

"It means that someone murdered the servants prior to setting the fire," Thomas answered. "From the dispersion of the bodies, I doubt each one knew what happened to the others. An individual probably crept up, fired his pistol, then looted the household and later, burned the buildings to cover his crime."

His gaze scanned piles of charred wood before returning to the doctor. "Have you accounted for all the servants named by Mrs. Darmon?"

The other man shook his head. "No. It appears the stable hand is missing."

"Then he's our primary suspect," Thomas replied grimly.

"But how do you know he wasn't away when all this happened?"

Elizabeth protested. "I asked him to ride to Fort Fredericton and seek help."

Thomas agreed it was a possibility, but maintained his conjecture was more likely. He dispatched the remaining two deputies to Fort Fredericton and Moncton to seek word of the missing Peter McDougall.

Two more hours of inspection gave no further insight. There was nothing left to do, but return to Newcastle and wait for news from the search parties.

A week passed. Despite her anxiety, Elizabeth became familiar with the village while she waited for word from the Constable.

An elderly couple named Bambridge who lived in a small cottage overlooking *Miramichi* Bay, befriended the lonely, frightened Englishwoman. They insisted she stay with them. Accommodations proved meager by Elizabeth's standards, but she was grateful for the company and helped pass the time assisting in household chores. These tasks made it difficult to keep up her appearance, but she gradually adjusted to a less stylish lifestyle and took pride in a growing self-reliance.

On the eighth day, upstream trackers returned to the Constable's office.

Elizabeth received a summons and rushed to join them, biting a lip with an expectation of the worst news.

Inside the law office, John Thomas and two exhausted deputies shifted uncomfortably while she took a seat to hear their findings.

"We followed the Dawes northwest to where it joins the Saint John and flows south to the Bay of Fundy," Deputy Amos reported. "At *Petit Sault*, we came across news of McDougall. The town constable confirmed a man by that name checked into the town's only hotel a week ago. "Two days later, a cleaning woman found his body in an upstairs room."

"Oh no!" Elizabeth gasped. "Poor lad."

The deputy looked at Thomas, who nodded for him to continue. "They found a small wound at the base of his skull, suggesting a pistol used at close range."

"Just like the servants," Thomas interjected.

The lawman pressed on. "The constable's inquiries showed the only known visitor to be a dancehall girl named Beatrice. A guest saw her knocking on his door the night prior to the murder. Now, she's missing. They presume she left town after committing the crime, but a day's ride north and south failed to turn up her trail."

Elizabeth shook her head. "Do you think Peter was part of a sinister plot, which required his elimination once his role was completed?"

The deputy glanced at the other tracker. "It's possible, ma'am."

"He could be innocent," she suggested. "Maybe, fearing implication, he kept to himself awaiting news of the fire. The dancehall girl might have been a night's indulgence. The whore took advantage of the situation, killed him and stole whatever he brought from the Lodge."

"One thing's certain," Constable Thomas growled. "The man didn't come to Petit Sault to alert the townspeople of the missing carriage or destruction of the Lodge. He made no attempt to speak with anyone. The fact he remained holed up tells me he feared the authorities."

The deputy nodded. "But, was he on his own or waiting to be contacted by the kidnappers?"

Elizabeth shifted restlessly.

"If both events were part of a coordinated plan, what was the motive? Surely the Hudson's were not a threat to anyone. Is there so little law enforcement in the Colony that any decent citizen can be attacked?"

"Now wait a minute," Thomas objected. "It's true the Colonial Office gives us little resource to control a large unsettled territory, but local authorities are present in every town as agents of the Crown and good citizens usually notice newcomers in the area."

The remark did not soothe her.

"So, what's your explanation?" she retorted. "My family was forcibly taken from their carriage. I would hardly call that simple robbery. At the same time, a servant goes berserk, killing everyone and burning down the Lodge, only to be done in by a dancehall woman who leaves no evidence of any stolen property. Are we just to write it off as a consequence of frontier living?"

The Constable reddened. He stood from his chair and held up a hand. "Mrs. Darmon, I can't explain this tragedy, but I assure you we'll not rest until these outlaws are brought to justice.

"The crimes do appear to be the work of determined perpetrators. I've asked Deputy Amos to enlist a tracking party to search north of Petit Sault to find this woman and, hopefully, a lead to the kidnappers. It's likely she fled across the Saint Lawrence to another Province."

He took a deep breath. "As to motive, I've given it some thought. There are several possibilities. Mr. Hudson isn't popular with local timber merchants. Ever since the Colonial Office appointed Thomas Baille resident commissioner, our prized timberlands have been auctioned off to outside interests. There's growing resentment, and a lot of people feel these new owners should be driven out.

"Another possibility is the growing agitation for independence in Lower Canada. There are many, especially among French Canadians, who support the idea of self-government-like the Americans. Protagonists in both Lower and Upper Canada are speaking out against British rule. A key issue is whether to continue sending our revenues abroad or keep them here. Both poor French farmers in Quebec and English merchants complain they're being exploited by the motherland.

"I've noticed that recent immigrants like Richard Hudson favor such radical ideas. It's possible a French Canadian by the name of Louis Joseph Papineau is behind this act. Papineau is a seigneur, who leads the *Patriote* Party. He is also the Speaker in the Lower Canada Assembly. He proposes elimination of the *Chateau Clique*, a group of English speaking merchants and clergymen, who were given land back in '91 after Canada was divided into two provinces. Papineau is one of many who favor independent states.

"Further west, a gentleman named William Mackenzie proposes a similar rebellion against the Family Compact of Upper Canada. As editor of the Colonial Advocate, he's very outspoken against Tory rule and now there's even talk he may become mayor of the Capitol at York. Perhaps this kidnapping is a political statement-a statement that Englishmen are no longer welcome to treat Canada as their backyard.

"Also, as I mentioned earlier, there are the Americans. Ever since the Erie Canal opened, they've been competing for European markets. They send goods down the Hudson River and out to sea instead of up the Saint Lawrence. The Canal at Welland bypasses Niagara Falls, and our ships can now travel from Lake Erie all the way to Europe without touching land. But, it's been difficult to ensure safe passage with Americans interfering every step of the way. I wouldn't be surprised to learn this crime was a stunt to create havoc among the timber owners."

Elizabeth winced at the antagonism displayed toward her homeland.

"Is there another revolution coming?"

"If I were you, I wouldn't stay here any longer than absolutely necessary," the Constable advised.

She let the suggestion pass. "I must be included in the search party."

The deputies shifted uneasily in their chairs. Thomas rolled his eyes. "Mrs. Darmon, conditions would not be suitable for a lady. The men must move quickly without regard to comfort, and who knows what awaits them should they find the villains. It's unthinkable."

Elizabeth rose to show defiance. "I'm accustomed to rude environments. I can ride with the best horsemen, and I'm the only one who can identify my family members. I'm not going to sit waiting for news any longer. This is a crime against my people, and I insist upon being present at its resolution!"

The Constable scratched his head dubiously, then sighed reluctantly. "If the search party agrees to let you join them and you accept the consequences, I won't stand in your way."

Elizabeth tipped her head with polite thanks to each deputy. She bid them good day and left to prepare for the morning's expedition.

As she proceeded down a wooden walkway to her temporary residence, her thoughts turned to Peter McDougall. The young stable hand got caught up in a devious plot and lost his life as payment. Elizabeth would never believe he was responsible for the kidnapping. He seemed genuinely concerned at the disappearance of her family. She did not agree with the premise he was a ruthless killer. What were his last words to her? *"Keep to the green, ma'am."*
What did he mean by that?

~

The search party rode out of Newcastle shortly after sunrise.

Elizabeth had little difficulty securing membership once she offered a pound sterling to each man for his inconvenience. Constable Thomas saw she was furnished with a mount, complete with bedroll and foodstuff. She purchased leather chaps, riding boots and a durable shirt with leather vest containing numerous useful pockets. The group consisted of four deputies and a *Micmac* Indian named Sequa. Two of the men were experienced hunters who would provide game for an extended journey. Amos took charge and would lead tracking of the missing woman once they reached Petit Sault, two days hence.

Riding through countryside did not prove to be difficult the first day of a one hundred twenty-mile journey until a gradual rise of inland mountains gave way to densely forested plateaus. Thereafter, the posse rode single file along a narrow winding path between tall tree trunks. The men seemed amiable enough, often conversing among themselves. They did not include Elizabeth in their discussions, respectful of her status, but she asked questions about the surroundings to draw them out.

They camped by a small brook that night. Elizabeth seated herself by the fire where she eagerly devoured deer meat carried from Newcastle. When the men finally doused the flames, she huddled under a coarse, woolen blanket, listening to the hoots of a distant owl. Every part of her body ached from the long ride. Eventually, fatigue provided entry into a deep, dreamless sleep.

The following morning, their trail passed through woods that hid the graceful panorama of hills and valleys. Elizabeth sensed their approach to the Saint John River. North of the river falls, a well-worn path meandered within twenty yards of swiftly moving water all the way to Petit Sault.

Five miles from the hamlet, they encountered an Acadian accompanied by his wife and young son. The sight put Elizabeth in mind of gypsies. The scruffy looking individual bore a large backpack and wore a tattered hat above a dark coat, which, combined with a long black beard gave a sinister look. His wife followed, dressed in simple tunic also carrying considerable gear. To the rear, the small boy herded a fully-grown pig along the path. They made no attempt to converse. Elizabeth moved her horse to one side, allowing them to pass. The woman flashed an appreciative smile and tramped on.

Petit Sault displayed thirty wood-framed buildings. Carved out of wilderness across the river from the northern tip of Maine, the settlement stood at a strategic junction of the Madawaska and St John Rivers. The Province's northern territory had not fully recovered from the Great Miramichi Fire of 1825, which destroyed thousands of acres of prime New Brunswick timber. As a result, the Governor encouraged lumbermen to pursue vast forests to the west in an area disputed with the United States, further heightening hostility between the two countries. Local taverns were often sites of tension between American and British timber men proclaiming their right to log in the disputed region.

Elizabeth looked forward to the amenities of a hotel room as their horses slowly trudged into town. Undergrowth encroached right up to the edge of the village where the path widened into a rutted main street. It wasn't hard to pick out the town jail, a somber grey building with barred windows.

The Constable did not have much to report once the six visitors crowded inside his office.

"Beatrice Canerci is still missing. McDougall was buried last week. Here are his possessions." The agent shoved a small pile across his desk to Elizabeth. It contained three shillings, a flint and several clumps of dried meat.

"Poor man didn't have much to show for his life," Elizabeth observed sadly. "But, there's nothing here to incriminate him for the fire at Richard Hudson's place."

The official nodded. "It's possible there were more belongings on his horse, but it was never found. The woman may have used his mount to make her escape."

~

After the search party spent a night in town, they left early the next day on a trail heading north.

The second day out, Samuel, one of the hunters, was thrown from his horse when it stepped in a rat hole. The rider landed against a tree trunk, breaking his left leg. They fashioned a splint, but the injured marksman writhed in pain and became delirious by nightfall. It was agreed to send John, the other tracker, back to Petit Sault with the victim. Elizabeth, Amos, Sequa and George-the remaining hunter-decided to ride on. John would catch up once he found medical attention for Samuel.

The remaining searchers set off toward the Saint Lawrence. Twenty miles from the river, they entered a clearing surrounding a small cabin. Smoke rose in a wispy column from its chimney.

All four riders dismounted fifty feet from the door and walked up to the rustic building.

A rough-hewn door opened slightly. Suddenly, a thunderous report echoed through the trees.

George clutched his neck and crumpled face-first to the ground.

Amos pushed Elizabeth behind a water trough and scrambled away while the occupant reloaded his musket.

She watched through frightened eyes as the deputy and Indian disappeared around the back of the structure. No sound came from inside. The front door remained closed, but she could not move. The watering trough did not provide much protection against bullets only ten feet from the entrance. She twisted to search for a way to retreat. Her vision fell onto a pool of blood forming next to George's motionless head. She closed her eyes tightly.

Interminable minutes passed. She listened to softly rustling branches of fir trees around the clearing's perimeter.

A second shot broke the stillness behind the cabin. Elizabeth threw herself flat on the ground, faced down, clutching handfuls of grass. Footsteps echoed inside the small house. The door opened. Amos appeared.

"All clear," he shouted.

Elizabeth pushed herself up. Brushing dirt from her leather chaps, she shook her head at George's lifeless form. Her legs felt uncertain, and her hands quivered.

She reached the doorway and paused before stepping into the cabin. A repugnant odor assaulted her nostrils. Bolstering her courage, she entered the dwelling.

On the floor of a single room, a large man lay next to the kneeling deputy. He resembled the Acadian she saw south of Petit Sault.

Sadly, Elizabeth regarded him. He probably tried to protect his home from intruders. The putrid smell, however, did not come from his body.

She surveyed the room.

In one corner lay the decaying body of a young woman.

Amos noticed the Englishwoman's stare and stepped over to the other lifeless form.

"Was she his wife?" Elizabeth asked, suppressing a shudder.

"No, I doubt this man would choose an English woman. Look at her make-up and clothing. Looks like a dancehall girl," Amos replied.

"Beatrice?" she gasped.

"Could be. She may have been ambushed, just as we were. The man probably fired on anyone approaching his cabin, then dragged bodies inside to search for valuables."

Elizabeth could not hold back quaking this time. She took a long breath and continued with a cracking voice. "Is there anything from the Hudson's Lodge-something she could have taken from Peter?"

They searched the premises and the Acadian's body, but found nothing familiar.

"What do we do now?" she asked weakly. "Do we wait here for John or should we continue on while there's still a chance of catching up to the kidnappers?"

The deputy considered her question for a moment.

"First we bury George and these two. By then, it'll be nightfall. That blasted Indian took off and probably won't be back. We'll be safe in this cabin 'til morning. It's less than an hour's ride to the Saint Lawrence. So, I propose we look along the shoreline for signs of cast off. If your five relatives and their captors took to the river, there should be tracks at water's edge. If we find something, we can decide whether to return to Newcastle or find a way across the water."

"Where would they go?" she wondered.

"The next major settlement is Quebec City, fifty miles upriver on the other side.

Around here, the Saint Lawrence is ten miles wide. We'll need a canoe to get across. If we can find one nearby, it'd be the best way to travel. It's a long way, but paddling is safer than hiking along shore. Iroquois aren't always friendly."

Elizabeth smiled gratefully at the man's determination. She suspected he would rather be on his own despite the need for her to identify victims.

"Thank you, deputy. I could never return to Newcastle without knowing the fate of my family."

Her words brought down the situation heavily on her shoulders. Tears filled her eyes.

"I can't bear this. I have to know what happened to them!"

Amos laid a hand on her shoulder. "We'll find them, ma'am. The kidnappers wouldn't have gone to all this trouble if they planned to do away with your husband and sisters."

"If only I'd gone with them to the Falls..." she whispered.

"It's not your fault. You're their only chance now. We'll keep after them."

"How can we? We're only two against ruthless criminals," she objected.

"I know this territory better than most. I won't stop 'til we find them. Then we'll get some help."

Elizabeth wiped tears from her face and managed a weak smile. "Did you know Richard?"

He nodded. "Met him once. Seemed a decent enough sort, although I've heard he's not much of a timber man. Maybe that's just sour grapes from the townspeople."

Elizabeth shook her head. "I've never understood why Victoria left everything to come to this desolate place so far from her family."

He grinned without taking offense. "Ma'am, if you'd grown up here, you'd realize this place is heaven on earth. Sure, it's hard at times, especially in winter, but the land's good. A man can find a place for himself without catering to some rich landlord. There's opportunity everywhere, and nowhere is there more natural beauty."

Elizabeth cast him a sheepish glance. "I guess you're right, deputy. I'm just homesick. I'd give anything to find my family and reclaim the life I used to know."

Chapter Three

Indians stood in a semi-circle around Elizabeth and Amos, preventing their escape. The English woman had never seen an Iroquois. Broad faced with long dark hair, they spoke in low, guttural tones she could not understand. Many were boys, dressed in buckskin breeches with beaded belts and moccasins. A few warriors held guns in addition to long knives.

"Get off your horse-slowly," Amos commanded. "This is a hunting party. They're not looking for trouble, but we must not appear threatening."

He dismounted, took three steps toward the oldest-looking brave and slowly voiced the same peculiar sounds. They conversed for a moment, then, he turned to her.

"I told them why we're here. I think we got lucky. They saw a dozen individuals camped on the riverbank a mile south of here six days ago. The band didn't make a campfire, but near midnight, two torches were lit and after a while, a boat with sails came to shore. Everyone boarded and the vessel sailed upriver."

"It's them!" Elizabeth exclaimed. "We have to follow their trail."

Amos went back to the two tallest natives who appeared to be in charge. Following a brief exchange, the Iroquois conversed among themselves. One shook his head and gestured fiercely toward the river. Two others joined in, raising their voices until the savage finally nodded at the deputy. One of the leaders shouted to a young brave who ran off into the trees.

"I've offered them our horses in exchange for a canoe. We can paddle up to Quebec and arrange passage back to Newcastle aboard a ship."

Moments later, two Indians came out from the brush carrying a fifteen-foot birch-bark canoe over their heads. They placed it in the water while Amos and Elizabeth unloaded supplies from their saddlebags and carried them to the boat. Another brave came over and handed the lawman two paddles and a sack. Amos raised a hand to the leader, who smiled slightly.

"We should be off before they change their minds," the deputy muttered. "It's a good bargain for them to get horses, but we're outnumbered. They could easily take everything we have, leave us stranded or worse."

He helped Elizabeth into the canoe and climbed in himself. One of the hunters shoved the boat off the rocky beach. Amos began steering the vessel away from shore. Elizabeth picked up the other oar, but when she tried to lift the heavy instrument over the side of the boat, it hit the edge and splashed into the water. She lunged for it, almost tipping them over. Amos shouted for her to wait. He circled the craft back to the floating implement.

Her cheeks blushed at the incompetence. Several young braves laughed at the miscue, while the tribe's leaders mounted their newly acquired animals.

Finally, they were underway. Amos demonstrated the proper stroke and with a little zigzagging, the boat made its way out into the river's swift current.

As they fell into rhythm, the deputy described what he knew about the great waterway.

Between the headwaters of the Great Lakes basin and the Atlantic Ocean, the Saint Lawrence was the largest known river in North America draining to the East coast. The fast-flowing current stretched seven hundred miles from Lake Ontario out to the Saint Lawrence gulf, where it widened to seventy miles across. Since its discovery by Jacques Cartier in 1535, explorers have commercially exploited the vital waterway to the western frontier.

By late afternoon, the shoreline had disappeared.

Elizabeth felt worn out. Her arms complained mercilessly fighting the choppy flow crossing their path. She expected passage to be a pleasure, gliding smoothly over water in the native bark. She could barely lift the paddle.

"Please can we rest awhile?"

The deputy looked over his shoulder and nodded.

"Not for long. Every minute we spend floating down river means more to make up tomorrow. We should reach the other side by nightfall. In the morning, we can keep close to shore where the current won't slow our progress."

"I'm sorry. It's just so difficult to keep up this pace," she replied meekly. "My arms feel like dead weight. Can you make it without my help?"

Amos sighed. He rummaged through the bag provided by the Indians and retrieved two strips of dried meat and some red berries. "Eat this. It will help restore your energy, "

The food had a strange taste, but she ate greedily. Arms still felt leaden, but that no longer concerned her. Dark clouds were forming to the north. In the late afternoon, water had become the color of gunmetal.

"Will it be safer on the other side?"

The deputy shrugged.

"Maybe. We'll have to deal with the French Canadians. They're suspicious of Englishmen, but usually mind their own business. There shouldn't be any problem with Indians. The Frenchies get along well with the Iroquois. I expect we'll mostly be ignored."

In twilight, Amos finally pulled the canoe onto a narrow gravel beach.

They made a fire and drank soup from dented metal cups before retiring. A damp wind off the river kept Elizabeth awake despite a need to rest.

Amos talked about the territory and his upbringing. He was born November 24, 1798, the oldest in a family of nine. Until age twelve, he lived with his brothers and sisters in a log cabin north of Fredericton near the Nashwaak River. Amos grew up in frontier country. Howling wolf packs put him to sleep at night and danger from Indians lay everywhere. He had very little schooling, learning more from Acadians in the woods than from books. His love for adventure came out of the constant threats.

In 1810, his father was appointed collector of the port of Saint John, and the family moved to the city. Shortly thereafter, war broke out in America and ships carrying thousands of loyalist refugees crowded into the harbor. Seeking a role in the conflict, Amos volunteered for service to the British Garrison at Nashwaak. He was assigned to carry dispatches throughout the province, including Newcastle where he met John Thomas. Although the Americans never invaded New Brunswick, Amos's knowledge of the countryside served him well.

After the war, he tried farming, but it did not satisfy his adventuresome nature. He returned to Newcastle and hired on as the Constable's deputy.

Elizabeth awoke to splashes of water hitting her face. She lay wrapped in a blanket, curled up at the base of a pine tree. A gentle rain fell during the night and by daylight branches overhead dripped wet. Her arms stretched out in cold dampness, accentuating aches from the day before.

Toward the river, Amos busily tended a campfire near the trunk of an even thicker spruce tree. Two fish rotated on a crude spit, while steam poured upward from a small metal pot resting on one end of a burning log. Elizabeth drew the blanket close around her shoulders and climbed to her feet. Surrounding their clearing, murky hollows between trees became sinister in the morning gloom, and the massive, flowing waterway did not appear friendly.

She crunched over to join him.

"Good morning. Are we going to spend a day here until the weather clears?" she asked hopefully.

He looked up at the overcast sky which had begun to drizzle.

"I should think not. The trail's cold enough without passing up a chance to close ground on that bunch. This bit of rain will hardly slow us down. There's shelter enough if we keep close to shore. Have some breakfast."

Food and warmth from the fire were welcome luxuries, but clouds and pale water worried Elizabeth. Drops began to fall harder, cutting visibility to less than a few hundred yards off shore.

They finished eating and packed belongings into the canoe.

Resigned to her fate, Elizabeth pulled the blanket over her head and took a position behind the deputy. It took extreme effort just to lift an oar. She started paddling in small strokes, grimacing at pain shooting up her arms. Soon, however, her limbs numbed in the wet misery as their craft wound its way upriver.

True to his word, Amos steered the craft within fifty feet of shore.

An hour of hard work passed.

Rain did not let up. Several inches of water sloshed in boat's bottom. Gradually, the canoe yawed more and more out into the river, and land faded behind a steady curtain of moisture.

Elizabeth concentrated on the deputy's back, mechanically repeating the rowing motion. It was agonizing to pull the slippery paddle when it hit the water with stinging splashes, but she persisted, making enough progress to keep the vessel on a westerly course.

Away from shore, the waves grew larger, tipping the canoe fore and aft with mounting force. The spray soaked her blanket and rainwater poured from her head in rivulets.

"Shouldn't we be closer to shore? This is getting us nowhere!" Elizabeth shouted.

There was no response from the rigid deputy in front of her. Wind and rain howled, drowning out her voice. Splashing waves jarred the boat with increasing force.

She looked around through eyes wide with alarm, suddenly realizing they were out of sight from the coastline. Convinced they had to put to land, she stood up and reached toward the lawman's shoulder to get his attention. An abrupt swell hammered the vessel's left side and flung her backwards. She groped wildly for a handhold, but pitched overboard, plunging into icy water. Elizabeth screamed, thrashing the frigid, swirling maelstrom. Her sounds were lost in the wind, and current pulled her under.

Her head broke the churning surface seconds later. The canoe was now twenty feet away. She spewed torrents of water from her mouth. "Amos, help! Help me. Please!"

The deputy did not turn.

A three-foot rise pulled her under again. She regained the surface, only to see the craft further off, disappearing into the gloom. Forcing herself not to panic, Elizabeth tried to float on her back, but the raging turbulence kept submerging her head. She could not keep above the waves. Frantically, she dove down and pried off her boots. Life now depended on a determined swim to shore. She remembered the canoe moved parallel to the coastline, so she struggled to her right across the flow. Current relentlessly carried downriver, but she hoped her effort would be enough to draw to shore before her strength gave out.

A steady pace was the only chance.

Elizabeth was not a good swimmer. Terrified of water in her youth, she spent family vacations at Brighton well away from shore. She endured bouts of seasickness over the years and, as an adult, avoided travel by ship whenever possible. Only by her marriage to William, an accomplished swimmer, did she overcome an abhorrence of water sports. Despite attempts to share his enjoyment of a lake adjoining their manor, she could never compensate for a lack of ability learned at a young age. At best, she could cross a stretch of one hundred feet at the price of complete exhaustion.

Elizabeth twisted in swirling fluid, gulping water and groping at the surface to keep her head in the air. Determined to develop some sort of rhythm, she could not imagine how some people could propel themselves smoothly and effortlessly without concentration. It seemed as if she made no progress at all.

The river tossed her up and down, more often under the surface than on top. She grew weaker and movements became more sluggish within the numbing cold.

Her thoughts wandered. Images of home in Kent danced in the distance with William sitting on the front steps patiently waiting her return. She wondered if they would ever be together again. Her vision grew hazy. Waters merged into a gray scene without variation or purpose. The effort became dreamlike. She imagined herself suspended high above the river looking down at a pathetic creature trying to imitate a fish. Why such urgency, such struggle, and such desperation? She welcomed the soothing detachment, floating away from the scene below.

An annoying nose itch refused to go away. Arms would not move to scratch it. Light increased behind the eyelids, forming colors; greens, browns and most of all, blue. Birds chirped around her.

Suddenly, she realized waves no longer tossed her like a rag doll. The river had not swallowed her up.

She was on land.

Sunlight's warmth bathed her body, and a cool breeze ruffled overhanging branches. She dragged her eyes open. She had made it to shore and collapsed a few feet from water's edge. The sky was clear, not a trace of clouds. She lifted an aching hand to touch her clothes. They felt soft and dry.

How long have I been lying here?

Weak and hungry, Elizabeth pulled herself up to a sitting position and looked around for the canoe. There was no sign of Amos in any direction; only peaceful sounds of ruffling leaves and distant birds. An uneasy feeling crept through her veins.

Why didn't he come back for me? Maybe the canoe capsized in the storm, and he drowned in the current.

Again, she found herself alone in a primitive world.

Elizabeth quelled self-pity and climbed to her feet. She had to find food.

Bare feet stepped gingerly over the densely forested riverbank. Each footfall in the tangled undergrowth reminded her of how ill-equipped she was to survive in the wilderness. She could not fish, hunt or prepare a small animal to eat. She would certainly starve without help from another human being. There was no choice but to work her way upriver in the hope of finding someone near Quebec City. Perhaps she could find tracks left by Deputy Amos before hunger overcame her.

A bush near the water displayed bits of red color among its leaves. Berries! They resembled raspberries, but lighter in color.

She tasted them, wrinkling her nose at their bitterness. No matter, she was not going to starve after all. Eagerly, she consumed handfuls of the strange looking fruit. Hunger satisfied, she returned to scrambling over roots and rocks scattered along the riverbank.

A few minutes later, fierce pain stabbed her stomach. She doubled over with piercing agony, barely able to breathe. Eyes teared, nearly blinding vision. The English woman squirmed on the ground, clinging to the earth, waiting for the spasms to pass.

A light flashed in the distance.

Elizabeth wiped blurring wetness from her eyes and squinted to see in the distance. Not fifty feet from shore, an empty canoe floated downstream. Was it their boat? Supplies might still be inside. She would have to swim to it, before it floated past.

Despite pain, she threw herself into the water, desperately splashing toward the wayward vessel. Shock of cold water made the ache in her stomach seem less bothersome.

Elizabeth gasped for air by the time she took hold of the meandering craft. It was nearly half-filled with water and the paddles were missing, but it was their canoe. Bundles they loaded the day before bobbed up and down, trapped within the conveyance's confines.

Holding on to one side, she paddled with her feet. The effort changed the boat's path enough to head it toward shore. Once her feet scraped bottom, twenty feet from land, she pushed the craft into calmer waters and onto sand.

She grabbed the sacks and staggered up to dry ground.

What happened to the deputy? Did he dock the canoe, and current swept the vessel away before he could secure it? Under normal circumstance, he would have retrieved the supplies. Or maybe, he encountered the kidnappers. Whatever the reason, fates provided her with the means to continue on.

Elizabeth felt better. She spent the rest of the day fashioning a paddle for the journey to Quebec City. She found a sturdy branch within the undergrowth and gathered shorter, thinner segments to break over a sharp-edged rock into one-foot lengths. Using strips of cloth torn from her dress, she tied the collection of sticks together with cross-pieces near the end of the two inch diameter limb. The Indian's leather pouch was stretched over the wide end and tied tightly at the neck.

She looked at her handiwork with satisfaction. It appeared rigid enough to serve her purpose.

Progress improved aboard the canoe over the next two days. The sky remained clear while the boat made its way upriver, keeping to calm waters near shore where the thick woods gave way to towering cliffs on the North side-cliffs without signs of life. On two occasions, tall sailing ships came into view heading east, presumably out to the Atlantic. They were too far away to acknowledge her frantic gestures. She paddled on.

Richard once told her Quebec City was a thriving seaport. It became a major trade center following James Wolfe's conquest in 1759 and once American threats ended after the war of 1812. Merchants exported fur, lumber and dry goods to European markets and, on return, Canadian provinces received impoverished immigrant families.

Mid-morning of the third day, Elizabeth ventured well out from shore. Her meager food supply was exhausted and she had to brave rougher waters if she hoped to be rescued.

Low hanging fog obscured vision beyond a few hundred yards, making it more difficult for a ship to spot the canoe, but having spent the night on a barren rocky shore, she was willing to take the risk.

The added effort to paddle against the flow downriver required more energy than she imagined. The pace of strokes to hold a steady position against the current quickly sapped her strength. *I can make it through this, I'm made of strong stuff.*

She began thinking of alternatives to lessen her plight when a huge, dark form loomed in the mist, less than a mile upriver.

Had she lost her mind?

Was there land out in the middle of the river?

An island!

The mass continued to take shape. Elizabeth let out a whoop of joy when she spotted man-made structures. The isle was inhabited. Food and shelter were at hand. Excitement gave her strength to close the remaining distance.

At last, the canoe bumped onto a rocky beach. She dearly hopped it would be the end of paddling for a long time.

From the beach, she climbed a small hill leading to a plateau, thirty feet above the river.

To her left, thick woods bordered an open field. Across the meadow, a two-story building stood with a high-pitched roof and open canopies on both sides. Dark forms dotted ground under these covers. Beyond, several smaller structures clustered along a fence.

She began walking toward the house.

Her view of the "forms" changed when she neared the compound.

Individuals crowded next to the white washed building. Some lay prone on the ground. Others huddled together in groups. At least fifty adults and children alike stood like statues. No one made a sound, and none of them paid her attention as she made her way to their midst.

The spectacle looked unreal.

She approached the nearest group, a poor lot dressed in peasant clothes. They appeared sickly. Faces grimaced, they stood or sat, staring out at the river, perhaps awaiting some anticipated arrival.

She walked over to a young woman holding a sleeping infant.

"Excuse me, ma'am. May I ask what is this place? Are you expecting someone?"

Instead of answering, the woman gestured toward the house.

Elizabeth nodded and moved in the direction of the dwelling, maneuvering around prostrated bodies. The number of incapacitated increased. By the time she reached the door, scarcely a spot existed to place one's foot. She winced at a sour smell permeating the air. Once or twice, she heard a voice muttering in low tone with a heavy Irish brogue.

She knocked at the entrance.

The door swung open.

A tall man wearing a soiled blue uniform peered out with annoyance.

"You cannot come in until you're called, ma'am," he admonished.

"Excuse me. My name is Elizabeth Darmon. I've come upriver from New Brunswick. May I see the person in charge?"

The official gave her a moment's look and disappeared inside.

He returned a few minutes later with an older gentleman dressed in a tattered black suit and a soiled white shirt, turned up collar and a narrow tie. His baldhead contrasted with a bushy gray mustache giving his stern expression a comical appearance.

"Madam Darmon," he spoke in a hushed voice, "don't you know where you are?"

He stared expectantly.

Elizabeth's shoulders squared at the implication she was an

ignorant tourist. "Sir, I've been paddling upstream to Quebec, but have run out of food and water. If I might trouble you for some refreshment and the means to complete my journey, I'd be most grateful."

He solemnly shook his head. "Madam, you've landed on *Grosse Ile*. I'm Doctor Panet. This island is a quarantine site for immigrants arriving in Canada."

"My presence here is strictly accidental," she protested.

His brow furrowed in a scowl. "There's cholera epidemic. The disease spread to the British Isles last year, and now immigrants are bringing it to the Colonies."

"Well, yes, I suppose so..." she replied uneasily, "but I'm not an immigrant. My family and I have spent the summer here, visiting my sister in New Brunswick."

The physician held up a cautioning hand. "Nearly fifteen thousand newcomers have been processed since we opened this facility five months ago. Many arrive from Ireland in deplorable condition, some ill prior to boarding, others exposed during the voyage. What you see here are the worst of the lot. Hundreds have succumbed, and more will die within the next few weeks. It's unfortunate that you landed on the Eastern Shore where the severest cases are isolated."

Elizabeth's eyes widened.

"Immigrants are confined to quarters for only a few days on the west end of the island," he continued. "But you have been exposed, and I cannot allow you to leave the Island for at least one month."

"One month! I shall be dead myself if left to this confinement for such a period," Elizabeth exclaimed.

He shook his head. "I repeat, Mrs. Darmon, you have been in contact with the severest cases. You have no choice but to remain here."

"At least, permit me to move to the healthier location."

"I'm sorry. I can let you stay in the compound to the east side of this building, which is reserved for those in slightly better condition. If you show no signs of the disease in a few weeks, I'll see that you're escorted to the next area for a brief stay."

"Please!" Elizabeth exclaimed, nearly in tears. "It's a matter of life an death for my family. I must be allowed to continue."

The doctor shook his head once more. "Lives of many more are at stake if you infect the citizens of Quebec. You must remain here for awhile."

"Is there any way to speed up the process?"

He shrugged. "Try to keep from interacting with the others. I'll see that food is sent over to you."

Doctor Panet turned to the other gentleman who stood nearby. "Frederick, please escort Lady Darmon to the Westside staging area."

With that, he bowed stiffly and was gone.

Chapter Four

Days passed slowly.

Elizabeth sat with her back against the building, head cradled on her knees. She could not help feeling distressed. Each day put her family further away. All her hopes now depended upon deputy Amos. She had to keep her mind occupied. Doctor Panet warned her to keep away from the other tenants, but what was the use? At least, conversation might provide distraction.

She rose and stepped over to three Irish women. "Excuse me, my name is Elizabeth Darmon. Have you all recently come here from the Continent?"

"Aye, cannon at the Laurentian gateway forced our ship ashore at de west end for inspection," one woman lamented.

Another lady grimaced in a staunch hands on hips pose. "We were 'erded like cattle through the disinfecting station, detention building and processing room. Waited 'ours, pressed shoulder to shoulder to learn de location of our confinement."

The third broke into tears. "Me mum and me got separated, she was kept at the other end of the island. By now she's somewhere in Quebec. It's not right, an eighty-year old woman without escort in an unfamiliar city. Don't know if I'll ever find 'er again."

"What are those buildings for over there in the center of the island, between the compounds," Elizabeth asked.

"Dey belong to permanent residents, doctors and maintenance staff. Dat section also 'olds sailor's quarters and food store'ouses. I 'ear a chapel and school'ouse are to be built."

"Is there a hospital on the island?" the newcomer questioned.

"No. Doctors place everyone in open areas for observation. I've 'eard it said, if you're not gone in a month, you'll never get off *Grosse Ile*. Many die, even among dose 'bout to be released to de next station."

An elderly widow took hold of Elizabeth's arm. "Aye, dere's a new Irish cemetery over on de west side, near Cholera Bay. Dey say upwards of t'irty t'ousand immigrants are expected to make port 'ere dis year."

The English woman looked longingly toward the center compound.

A long fence spanned the entire width of the Island, separating 'Easties' from better conditions on the west side. A single gate permitted access between the two areas, and guards stood posted day and night. The passageway appeared busy most of the time. Besides arriving and departing refugees, Elizabeth witnessed medical personnel reporting for work each morning and leaving at night. A bakery cart arrived twice daily, bringing two meals per resident. Occasionally, wagons carrying construction workers passed through the portal, laden with supplies for a number of projects.

Several barracks were under construction to protect East side occupants from winter's cold. Anxious workers kept their distance and received no help from the island's confined visitors. Among the area's three hundred detainees, sanitation was a constant concern. It was difficult to maintain one's health without ready water access.

After two weeks, Elizabeth and six others received clearance for transfer to the island's west end. Doctor Panet wished her well and predicted that she would be off to Quebec City on the next ship.

Unfortunately, it did not happen.

She had no papers to register her presence at the facility. All records of origin and her stay in New Brunswick were lost in the Hudson fire, and none of Constable Thomas' men were close by to vouch for her status. This circumstance forced her to wait for word from Newcastle and another two-week delay.

Once more, Elizabeth watched ships come and go with mounting frustration and worry over the waning prospect of finding her family.

At last, she boarded a small merchant vessel and gratefully watched *Grosse Ile* recede downriver. Her ship sailed by the *Ile d'Orleans* two hours later, and Elizabeth finally caught a first glimpse of Quebec City high on a hill on the north shore, overlooking the confluence of the Saint Lawrence and Saint Charles Rivers.

She spotted several large buildings within the fortified city. A fellow passenger identified them as the *Chateau Saint Louis*, the Archbishop's Palace and further to the west, the recently restored Citadel. The latter fortress nearly kept James Wolfe from victory over the French in the pivotal Battle of Quebec during the Seven Years War. Had it not been for the discovery of a small passageway called *Ause du Foulon*, that allowed British troops to reach a plateau above, France might yet lay claim to the city.

Her ship pulled into the port of lower Quebec City at *Pointe a Carcy*.

Once passengers were allowed to disembark, Elizabeth walked quickly toward hilly streets leading to the Upper City where she would find Government Buildings and Louis Joseph Papineau, leader of the French freedom movement. If her family's abduction was a political ploy, he would be at the heart of it.

Busy workers and countless tourists created chaos near the wharf.

Further inland, warehouses, old storefronts and taverns lined *Rue Saint Andre*. The narrow street was crowded with an uncouth lot, sailors, drunken wastrels and beggars. She could not walk fast enough to escape the rude inhabitants and dearly wished for an escort more than any time during her days in the wilderness.

An hour after leaving the dockyards, she trudged up *Rue Cote du Colonel Dambouges* and reached an entrance to the Upper City.

By the time she reached *Chateau Saint Louis*, it was too late for service at the Government office. Consequently, she sought lodging at the prestigious *Hotel de Ville*, which towered above tree-lined avenues three blocks inside the main gate.

Using her new identification papers and the precious gold coin, she secured a room and a letter of credit.

Moments later, Elizabeth collapsed onto a soft bed expelling a huge sigh of relief. Stress drained from her body.

Two hours of rest, followed by a sumptuous meal in the hotel dining room, lifted her spirits. She decided it was not too late to purchase a much-needed wardrobe and replace the plain cloth dress provided on *Grosse Ile*.

Invigorated, Elizabeth emerged from the hotel lobby to look for millinery shops.

By 8:00 PM, she had ordered four dresses, shoes and accessories to be delivered to her room the next day. Quite satisfied to have managed without servant help, she strolled leisurely down *Rue Sainte Anne.*

Passersby greeted with polite nods. Their apparel was much improved over that worn by Lower City residents.

Lamplighters worked busily at street corners in fading evening light. Air grew chilly, so she decided to return to the Hotel.

Elizabeth crossed the corner of *Rue Sainte Ursule* when three men approached.

Two of the individuals supported a third, all staggering side to side, singing loudly in French. They acted unaware of their surroundings, bumping into objects while trying to keep their companion upright. Tangled hair partially covered bearded faces and unbuttoned plaid shirts hung in disarray outside their pants.

A distinguished looking gentleman, wearing a fur-collared topcoat rounded the corner between Elizabeth and the drunkards. His path lay blocked by the stumbling louts. He jumped into the street, narrowly missing collision with a passing coach. The aristocrat glared at their backs, but thought better of accosting the individuals.

The trio bore down on Elizabeth. She did not care to leap into the avenue like her predecessor, so she held her ground. The burly Frenchmen carried their comrade to within a few feet of her before coming to an abrupt stop.

They straightened, staring through liquid eyes a long moment.

Putrid smells of ale caused Elizabeth to gag on bile rising in her throat.

The lout nearest the street smiled knowingly. He stepped back with an exaggerated sweep of the arm, indicating for her to pass. The middle drunk's head remained bowed with sandy-colored hair covering his face. He chose that moment to lift his chin to see why his colleagues paused. Glassy eyes focused on Elizabeth's sudden look of surprise.

It was Richard Hudson.

His expression changed from annoyance to terror while struggling to free himself from his associates. They watched with puzzled expressions as he backed away.

"No, no!" he protested, raising his hand to push her image away.

"Richard!" Elizabeth croaked. "Richard, what are you doing here? What's the matter?"

Ten feet away, he turned, half-stumbled and ran.

Her shouts echoed off the pavement. "Richard! Stop! Please come back!"

She started after him.

His figure rapidly diminished in size before disappearing around a bend that took him west on *Rue Saint Louis*. Despite his besotted condition and her own frantic pace, she could not close ground on the frightened man.

She reached the corner just in time to see him veer left onto *Cote de la Citadelle,* causing a few surprised pedestrians to turn heads.

In twilight, Elizabeth panted two hundred yards behind when Richard arrived at the fortress gate. The Citadel entrance stood open in the absence of any threat to the city. A surprised guard jumped back as the Englishman flew past. The attendant shouted to halt, and then took off after him.

Elizabeth passed through the entry without noticing anyone else.

A large open area lay beyond the portal. Dark shadows cast by buildings bordering the square stretched across the expanse under gathering moonlight. A large number of lighted windows within the silhouettes suggested most of the garrison had already retired to quarters.

Elizabeth stopped in the middle of the parade ground, gasping for breath.

There was no sign of her brother-in-law or the guard. Minutes passed while she scanned the surrounding two-story barracks. No one sounded alarm. At the far end of the compound, an imposing structure looked like the administration building. She walked quickly toward the stone columned edifice and darted inside.

Dimly lit hallways stretched to the left and right interspersed with office doors. She called Richard's name, but no one stirred. Another door, at the end of a short hallway directly in front of her led to the rear of the building and back outside. Her heart pounded as she rushed toward the exit and plunged out into the night air once more.

The area behind the building also appeared deserted.

Elizabeth chewed nervously on her lower lip. *Where did Richard go?* Did he simply vanish into thin air? She squinted into darkness for a better place to view the complex. A moment later, she spied steps leading to the top of a ten-foot-high perimeter wall.

Elizabeth charged across the open space and climbed the stairs.

A spectacular view of Quebec Harbor and the Saint Lawrence River met her gaze. The sight enthralled her. The fortress stood two hundred feet above the Lower City and a mile west, providing a breathtaking panorama of moonlit countryside and twinkling lights from the distant harbor. She stood and indulged herself while recovering from her winded dash.

A distant voice intruded upon her reverie. She turned to see a sentry rushing to the bottom of the steps.

"Madam, you must get down from there at once!"

"My brother-in-law was just here. Have you seen him?" she shouted back.

The soldier reached the top of the wall and paused for an instant.

He shook his finger at her. "No one's allowed in the Fort at this hour, ma'am. You might have been shot! Please, come down and I'll escort you to the gate."

"But you don't understand—!"

Words froze on Elizabeth's lips when her attention diverted to a light swinging to and fro far below, near the base of the cliff. A bobbing carriage lantern illuminated two persons running from a hansom parked under a street lamp. The figures stopped.

The glow of the lantern flooded a lifeless form sprawled on the rocks directly below.

Elizabeth gasped.

"You there," the sentry yelled. "What have you found?"

"Some bloke's fallen from the fortress," a distant shout reported. "You'd better come down here."

The soldier escorted Elizabeth to a small room in the administration building and told her to wait until he returned. She heard his rapidly receding footsteps echo off a marble floor as he went to wake others in the garrison.

For an hour, she waited seated next to a flickering table lamp. *Must I sit here all this time just to be lectured on the sin of trespassing?* In the stillness she could hear her chest rising and falling with a heavy sigh. By now, Richard was probably back in the City. Would she ever see him again?

The door opened.

Another sentry gestured. "Please, follow me."

They walked in silence across the compound to a squat building. A guard stood by the entrance. She hustled through the anteroom, past three soldiers dousing smoking torches and folding a stretcher.

At the end of a short passageway, she entered a well-lit room lined with white gowns and medical supplies. A body lay on a table in the center of the space.

Elizabeth stopped at the sight. In front of her lay the pale, lifeless face of her brother-in-law. She collapsed in a dead faint.

When the doctor revived her, she was helped to a nearby room and spent a half-hour answering questions. The commandant's response to her story of the kidnapping was sympathetic, but she detected a tone of patronized interest. Apparently, he thought she exaggerated the incident, but agreed to contact the Constable in Newcastle to obtain further details.

They found nothing inside Richard's pockets or any possession near the site of his fall. Elizabeth wrung her hands in despair. Richard was dead. *What had become of Victoria?*

Elizabeth did not sleep that night.

She could not understand his reaction at their encounter. Why had he not recognized her? Did his drunken state cause him to imagine some demon the sight of her triggered or maybe he fled because she brought to mind horrible events he had been through during the kidnapping.

She refused to think about the most likely explanation—Richard was behind the plot. His reaction, brought on by feelings of guilt for betraying the family. If he jumped from the wall, it suggested fear of retribution for his part in the conspiracy, but she could not fathom why he would destroy his own home in the process.

If any good came from the tragedy, it was confirmation she was on the right path. She could be confident the abductors and their victims were here in Quebec City. It gave hope that the rest of her family still lived. She remembered conversation with Deputy Amos, who predicted no one would go to the trouble of such a journey, risking apprehension with unwilling hostages, if their intent were simply to kill their captives.

Richard's discovery brought a second path of inquiry. The three men probably came from a tavern on *Rue Sainte Ursule*. A proprietor might remember them. Richard's companions might even be fellow gang members. She decided to pursue this lead before attempting to see Monsieur Papineau.

Elizabeth eagerly awaited first light to begin searching for the tavern, but as she prepared to leave the hotel, new clothes arrived. The distraction kept her inside for another hour. She donned apparel with tears of pleasure, enjoying the appearance of a more formidable lady, one with which to be reckoned.

A doorman furnished her with a carriage and by 10:00 am, she was back on *Rue Sainte Ursule*.

Cool morning air portended autumn's end, but bright, clear skies over the sun-washed stone buildings promised a fruitful day. Numerous shops already welcomed a brisk business inside the narrow storefronts. Per instructions to the driver, the hansom moved slowly southward from the corner of *Sainte Anne*. Many grey stone exteriors all looked alike, and not one advertised serving drinks to their patrons.

A block from where Richard bumped into her, she spotted a small sign over a doorway boasting the name *Le Taureau Rouge*. The door stood open, so she bid the driver to stop.

Inside, a large, unlit room showed no sign of a customer.

Elizabeth felt relief. An unescorted woman of her station would not be proper in such an establishment. To her left, a polished counter extended to the rear of the room where a barkeep diligently washed dishes, setting rows of glasses on the bar for future patronage.

The portly fellow squinted at the doorway's bright light surrounding her silhouette. He came across to her. His annoyed expression changed to surprise.

"*Oui, Madam, qu'est-ce que vous voulez?*"

"Excuse me, sir," she spoke in English to make sure he would do the same and she would not misunderstand his responses. A Quebec businessman would undoubtedly be comfortable with either language.

"I'm looking for a gentleman by the name of Richard Hudson. I believe he was in your tavern last night with two friends. Are you acquainted with him?"

The bartender paused, mentally reviewing the previous day's customers, then shrugged. "Richard Hudson? No, the name's not familiar. There weren't many in last night, it being a weekday and I don't recall any newcomers. The only threesome was Jacques, Frances and William. They've been coming in nearly every night this past month."

Intrigued, Elizabeth took a seat on the barstool. "Those three gentlemen, was one of them tall, in his mid-thirties with long, sandy-colored hair, a narrow face and a sharply pointed chin?"

The innkeeper thought for a moment.

Perhaps he expects a reward for the information, she mused.

"The description could fit William," he replied, seemingly trying to help her.

"That gentleman comes in with his wife on occasion. I believe her name is Elizabeth. That's it. William and Elizabeth Darmon. A fine English couple if I do say so. They sat over there two nights ago with a third gentleman they called Charles."

Elizabeth blinked.

"Would you please describe the woman for me?" she posed, trying to keep her voice steady despite disbelief.

The barkeep stared for a moment. "Well, I believe she looks a lot like you, ma'am, short dark, curly hair, about your height, weight and age. If I may say so, she could be your twin, if you have one."

"No, I do not, thank you."

The description did not match either of her sisters. Despite some family resemblance, neither sibling could be mistaken for her. Emily stood taller, older with light brown hair. Victoria was also taller, but ten years younger. Someone must have impersonated her in the company of Richard Hudson and her brother-in-law, Charles Bagwell.

She recovered her composure. "Those companions of William, Jacques and Frances, do you know where they live or work?"

The man shrugged. "No, I don't pry into my customers' affairs. They come and go. This place is a refuge from the outside world. I can't afford to be nosy."

Elizabeth rose from her seat and was about to leave when the barkeep raised an index finger on his right hand.

"I can tell you this. Their coats carried the insignia of Laval University. It was a bit strange, come to think of it. I mean, two Quebecois with an Englishman."

Elizabeth thanked the man, and decided she must go to a bank with her letter of credit and get coins for occasions such as these. She stepped outside, wincing at his last remark that sounded a bit sarcastic.

"Glad to be of service, Madam."

Elizabeth climbed into the carriage and bid the driver to stop at the nearest Bank of England.

She settled back to consider her options. She might be able to trace Richard's two friends from the Catholic University. Richard had ties to the Catholic Church, and she had requested the Citadel Commandant arrange a funeral mass. Perhaps when word got out of his death, her impostor and Richard's accomplices would make an appearance. The service was to be held at *Notre Dame e Quebec basilica* in one week.

Her carriage picked up speed. She looked out the window to discover open fields had replaced city buildings. In the distance, she could make out ramparts of the Citadel. Where were they headed?

The horse's fast trot became a full gallop. A bumpy dirt road tossed the vehicle up and down, shaking violently.

"Driver, where are you taking me? Driver stop!" she shouted.

No response came.

The careening carriage hit a bump and threw her against the opposite side of the compartment.

She grabbed the window frame and stretched out as far as possible. Her head extended far enough to discover an empty driver's seat. The transport raced toward the distant blue of the Saint Lawrence and cliffs of the Plains of Abraham lay straight ahead.

Frantically, her mind raced. *What can I do?*

It would mean certain death if the carriage stayed on its path, but she might also die if she jumped from the vehicle. Maybe the horse would turn before reaching the cliff Could she take the chance?

Whoever set the carriage in motion was either trying to scare or kill her!

Time was running out.

Jump or be killed?

Jump!

Pushing the door open and grasping the edge of the doorframe, she faced a blur of scenery whizzing by. Summoning courage, she flung her body out through the opening.

For an instant, she soared clear of the vehicle, suspended over the roadside.

Ground rushed up to meet her, and she smashed into rocky earth.

Chapter Five

Elizabeth opened her eyes in total darkness.

She touched her eyelids, making certain it was not an hallucination and winced at sharp pain stabbing through her arm to the wrist. Her elbow was either broken or severely bruised. She forced herself to lie still without panic. *How did she come to this world without light or vision?*

Impact of her head against the ground could have caused blindness—and possibly deafness. Her ears did not detect the minutest of sounds. Tentatively, she dragged fingers across the surface and exhaled a sigh of relief when soft scraping noises met her ears. The floor under her was rough, cold and damp, but not dirt, rather coarse stone or cement. She was not lying in a ditch on the Plains of Abraham. So where was she and who moved her?

She rolled to a sitting position. Extending her good arm, she groped for anything that might give a clue to her whereabouts. Touching nothing, she pushed herself up on shaky limbs and gingerly pressed fingers against tender ribs. The bones felt unbroken.

A sudden thought widened her eyes. She stuffed her good hand into first one pocket and then another, and moaned in anguish. Her new identification papers were missing.

Still, no sound or light penetrated the blackness. Elizabeth edged forward, arms outstretched. She took six paces before hands felt a wall. A smooth vertical surface spanned upward five feet, and then slanted toward her, sloping to a ceiling somewhere out of reach.

She turned left and immediately collided with a large object. Her fingers probed a gradual curvature comprised of wooden slats. A large barrel of some sort lay on its side, six feet long and three or four feet in diameter. She discovered a small hole at one end and stuck a finger inside. It came out dry. A second barrel sat three feet behind the first one, and another next to that.

A few minutes exploration revealed two rows of five empty caskets situated along opposite walls inside a twenty by thirty-foot room.

She concluded it must be a wine cellar.

Exploring fingers also discovered a sturdy door, towering more than seven feet tall constructed of boards held in place by three long metal fasteners leading to massive hinges on the frame's right side. She crouched closer to the floor and detected a dimly lit gap under the door. She dropped to hands and knees to press her face against the crack. She smelled fresh air. An eye next to the opening could not see more than six inches beyond because a tall step just outside blocked her view.

"Help!" she called. "Please, someone help me!"

Will I be fed, or have I been left to die in this horrible place? Elizabeth swallowed a sudden dread lodging in her throat. Her mind recoiled at the image of a skeleton trapped under a deserted building with no chance of escape.

Using fingers to search each corner of the room, she found a flat metal object laying beside one of the barrels, one-half inch thick, four inches wide and four-feet long.

She dragged it over to the door. Grooves along the sides of the frame were too small to wedge the implement into and pry the door open. It did, however, slide under the bottom gap.

That gave her an idea.

Elizabeth backed up against a barrel, rocking the cask back and forth until it fell off its mounting blocks. The rolling container crackled noisily across the concrete floor. She slid one of the mounting blocks over to the locked entrance, and lifted one end of the rod onto the block with the other end stuck in the gap under the left edge of the frame, directly below a board where the outside hasp would be mounted.

Next, she lay on her back and used her feet to wedge the block as far as she could under the extending metal bar. The free end was now nearly a foot off the floor.

She stepped on the lever and heard a loud creak.

She jumped on it, causing the rod to flex an inch and the door's wood to complain more loudly, but further attempts only produced sounds of strain.

Elizabeth walked over to the freed barrel and pushed it to the wall opposite the entrance.

She began rolling it as fast as she could toward the metal rod. The cask rumbled forward. When it reached the extended metal bar, the barrel slowed, rose slightly and then reversed its course, returning back to her. She leapt free as it splintered its way to the wall and came to rest.

Undaunted, she tried again.

This time, pressed against the wall, she started pushing farther from the protruding lever, trying to give the container more speed.

The rolling object smashed into the metal piece with a sudden snap and made Elizabeth jump back.

It rode up, and the drum slammed into the door before bouncing off sideways. When the noise died away, she picked herself off the floor and gazed at the portal.

Light spilled inside through a two-foot hole at the bottom of the doorway.

Elizabeth stepped gingerly over the rubble to the six-inch wide opening where a section of planking had snapped off. She reached upwards through the gap. A metal rod and hasp lay only a foot above where the board broke.

She wiggled it free.

Her heart beat rapidly while she tugged the door. It squeaked open, and she silently congratulated herself for such ingenuity to escape from her dark prison.

A short stairway led to another door, which opened into a poorly lit hallway.

She held her breath, stepping into the passage and tiptoed toward another doorway on her right. Her heart slammed against her breastbone as she peeked around a corner into a chamber void of furniture or decoration. Narrow rays of sunlight streamed through cracks in boards barring the windows.

She sensed stillness about the place.

She continued down the hall to a front door. Rooms on either side of the entrance also stood empty. With a sharp intake of breath, she realized she had been locked in the deserted building and left to die.

Without further hesitation, Elizabeth flung open the front door, and shaded her eyes against the brightness. Her vision found a path leading from the front of the house to a road fifty-feet in the distance. Further to the east were the unmistakable outlines of tall buildings.

She limped outside up to the avenue. She paused to look back at the two-story stone structure. It was a formidable residence, probably belonging to a wealthy merchant or city official. She could not help wonder if the owner was aware of her confinement as she began a long walk back to her hotel.

Elizabeth opened the door to her room and froze. The space was in complete disarray. Furniture tipped over and disheveled linens spread everywhere. Clothes she purchased on the previous day were gone. She battled back tears to stand at the window. *Had it really been only one day?*

She charged out the door, downstairs to the lobby. The hotel clerk's mouth dropped as the woman lunged to a stop at the front desk. "Mrs. Darmon, what happened to you?"

"Never mind about that. My room has been broken into. All my things have been taken."

"But, your appearance, madam…"

"Please, we don't have time to waste. Notify the police at once and send someone to straighten my room," she demanded, turning back to the stairs.

Twenty minutes later, a concierge reviewed the disorder and a cleaning lady set things straight. Elizabeth sat at a table absently surveying the space while she waited for the police to arrive. Not one item of her former possessions remained.

Why me? She mused, knowing she had nothing of great value here in Quebec. Perhaps it was the work of a thief who took note of lodgers receiving sizable deliveries. Yet, her clothes would not be of much worth to a robber. She was not even a common size…

She shot up in her chair. Someone might have needed the clothes to impersonate her—someone like the phony Elizabeth Darmon.

Elizabeth's breath caught in her throat at the implication the kidnappers now knew she was in Quebec. It could mean the runaway carriage was no accident. Her imprisonment was meant to silence her.

She intended to tell everything to the police, but hesitated remembering she again lacked papers. She might not be able to convince a magistrate who was the *real* Mrs. Darmon if they caught the imposter. The kidnappers would then know police were involved and might leave town. It was better to avoid legal entanglements for now, but she had to get out of there. The police could arrive at any moment.

The hallway stood empty. Her heart began racing as she walked quickly to the stairway. Halfway down the steps, she spotted a man dressed in uniform talking to the hotel clerk across the lobby. She paused.

"Madam, will you be returning soon?" a voice startled her from the bottom of the stairs. A cleaning woman gazed up, her arm draped with towels.

A nervous smile trembled Elizabeth's lips. She shook her head and gestured for the woman to come on up while casting a furtive glance toward the desk. The gentlemen continued to converse.

Holding her breath, she boldly crossed the room without looking in their direction. She reached the door and stepped outside.

With a sigh of relief, Elizabeth leaned against the building, expecting to hear her name called. Her hand grasped a railing to steady her shaking body.

Thirty feet down the walkway, a doorman helped a guest from his hansom. He was not the same person who summoned a carriage for her the day before—the carriage doomed for destruction on the Plains of Abraham. Was it possible the other doorman was an imposter too? Could *this* man be watching her?

Elizabeth decided not to take chances. There would be no one to track her movements this time. She set off on foot.

Elizabeth headed down *Rue des Jardins,* looking over her shoulder to see if someone followed. The street was crowded; some pedestrians paid her too much attention, others looked quickly away at her merest glance. She knew there was little she could do if a gentleman across the street or someone in a passing carriage was part of a surveillance team. The safest strategy was to get off the street as soon as possible.

The Englishwoman rounded a corner at the end of the next block and darted inside the Union Hotel at 12 Rue Sainte-Anne. The clerk expressed sympathy for her situation and agreed to send a message to Lady Carlisle in Kent and initiate a transfer of credit. Although the procedure could take up to two months, she was sufficiently convincing as a lady of means that the hotel manager agreed to take the risk of future repayment for a small fee.

Elizabeth found her room without assistance. A sparse interior of the second floor accommodation lacked the luxury of the Hotel De Ville, but she gratefully collapsed onto its bed. Within moments, she fell asleep.

The next morning, Elizabeth rose with a backache, several bothersome twinges in her limbs and numerous annoying scratches. She crossed to the window and gazed out at a gray and windy day. Trees nearly bereft of brown leaves lined the boulevard. Carriages moved quickly back and forth along *Rue Sainte-Anne* while gentlemen on walkways held hats tightly as they bent into gusts. Pedestrians seemed to sense winter's coming fury, hurrying to perform tasks before weather forced them indoors.

Down the street, she glimpsed a large park.

Swirling leaves blew in every direction across an open area. Drab apartment buildings crowded its perimeter, offering more affluent residents an attractive view. Near their doorways, however, another class of individuals huddled—a class accosting passersby for charity. These human beings braved the elements dressed in tattered rags that gave scant protection from cold and sickness. Elizabeth shook her head, certain many would fall victim to the cholera epidemic despite efforts of *Grosse Ile*. She was grateful for a day indoors to heal her aches and pains.

She padded across the room to a small table holding a water pitcher and washbasin. Over it, hung a chipped, two-foot high mirror.

She jumped back from the refection. "My God, who's that?"

The image staring back was a complete stranger. Her skin, formerly satiny smooth, had become creased and withered in past weeks. Most alarming, however, was her hair. Short black curls were now stiff blonde straggles. Someone had tried to change the color of her hair! Her relief at escaping confinement in the house on *Grande Allee Ouest* had been so great she had paid no attention to her appearance until now.

It must have been done while she was unconscious. Why would anyone go to such trouble, especially if she had been left to die in a cellar? *Maybe,* she mused, *the abductors tried to change my appearance so if my body were found, I would not be identified as Elizabeth Darmon, and my imposter could continue to live my life!*

Elizabeth sent for an attendant to redo her hair. After several washings and application of cocoa mixture, her tresses resembled their original color, but she feared the damage would not be completely repaired until new hair grew out.

While drying the limp brown mess with a coarse towel, Elizabeth drifted back to the window. The afternoon looked even colder. A storm was likely on the way. Watching the changing scene, she spied an elderly woman in dark clothing holding an arm full of flowers. The old lady appeared to be in dire straits, trying to eke out a living at the mercy of distracted businessmen. What drew Elizabeth's attention, however, was the lady's fixed gaze up at her window, paying no heed to passersby.

Elizabeth's brow furrowed. *Why is that forsaken beggar gaping at me?* There were two possibilities, she decided. The woman was either envious or keeping track of her movements.

She suddenly felt the need for a breath of fresh air, and the purchase of a few roses might brighten the rest of her day. Earlier, she had left a request at the front desk for delivery of several pieces of warm clothing, but since they had not arrived, it would be a short trip across the street.

Air felt colder than she expected. With frosty breath, she dashed between carriages to the opposite side of the road. The old woman stood a short distance down the avenue, her pale, withered face wrapped in a frayed black shawl still pointed at her window. Wisps of thin gray hair waved in the wind. The tiny creature stood a foot shorter than Elizabeth's five feet, four inches. She clutched flowers to her chest, allowing only paying customers to touch her wares. The meager blooms were hardly attractive, but Elizabeth approached her, determined to understand the crone's fascination with her room.

She opened her mouth to speak, but the woman interrupted with a thick French accent.

"So, *vous* come at last."

Elizabeth hesitated, goose bumps rising on her flesh. Perhaps she should not reveal herself. "Yes."

The old woman's smile showed few remaining teeth. "I watch *femme avec* light-hair, but she not come out *tout de jour*. I expect a day's wage for standing in the cold."

Glancing up at the empty window, then back at Elizabeth, the withered crone paused and went silent. Suddenly, she spun on a weathered heel and sprinted off, down the street.

Elizabeth charged after. "Wait!"

She dodged an approaching gentleman, came up behind the fleeing figure and grabbed the woman's bony shoulder. The wheezing creature slowed, trying to shake off the hand with a weak struggle to free herself. All at once, she slumped onto the pavement.

Elizabeth gathered the limp torso in her arms and lowered it against a doorway. She reached out a shivering hand and placed it on the woman's chest. The heart was racing. "C'mon, get up. I won't hurt you."

She lifted the peasant woman's head and lightly tapped her cheek, but the eyes remained shut.

Elizabeth's darting gaze searched for help, but no one paid attention in the howling wind. With resignation, she reached down and half-carried, half dragged the hag's small frame across the street.

She paused at the hotel entrance to awkwardly sling the bundle over her shoulder and painfully climb stairs to her room.

Panting, Elizabeth dropped the burden onto her bed, watching closely for a telltale rise and fall of the old woman's chest. Her shoulders relaxed in relief. The woman still breathed and, hopefully would recover without a need for medical attention.

"Only time will tell," she muttered.

She pulled up a chair next to the bed and regarded the immobile form. A mental list of questions began to form. This tiny creature was the key to finding the miscreants who threatened her safety—the same brigands who kidnapped and robbed her family.

She damn well better not die.

Chapter Six

A stranger awakened at the edge of a stream.

He lay on his stomach with tan breeches buried in mud up to the top of brown riding boots. A crumpled olive-green waistcoat spread over his back and long chestnut hair covered a face immersed in the grassy slope. The body shuddered. His back heaved a convulsive breath. Slowly, the head turned toward a nearby patch of ground.

After a moment, arms came forward and placed hands under his shoulders. Slowly, the chest drew upward.

A loud moan came through clenched teeth. The form abruptly collapsed.

For a time, he lay motionless.

An arm thrust out. He rolled onto his back. Veins in his head throbbed mercilessly as he tried to focus on shapes spinning above. His vision sharpened on massive, dark gray clouds and overhanging branches swaying fiercely to gusts of wind.

He brought a pale, freckled hand to his face and tenderly touched his right temple, wincing in agony. Crusty clumps of caked blood came away on his fingertips from a depression in the side of his head.

Carefully, he succeeded in working the frail torso up to a sitting position and stared at the gurgling stream near his feet. Glassy water flowed in rhythm to swarms of blowing leaves darting fervently, fleeing a forthcoming menace. His gaze fell on mud-covered pants. An expression of bewilderment spread over his face.

He looked out at the surrounding area, shaking his head at the stream meandering among sprouts of straw-colored grass and occasional birch trees to interrupt a dirt path in the distance. Beyond, thunder echoed across a panorama of lead-tinged mountain ridges lit by flashes of lightning—flashes that caused eyelids to close tightly.

His mouth fell open. "Where on God's earth am I?"

Sounds of brook and wind gave way to the rising pounding of approaching hoof beats.

He strained to make out the face of a single rider. A woman leaned forward on a gray horse, urging it onward over the path traversed below.

When it reached the stream, she reined her mount to a stop.

Casting a worried glance up and down river, she urged the animal to pick its way through the steady flow. On the other side, it resumed pace and disappeared behind a copse of trees.

The man's jaw parted with a feeble call lost among rustling leaves. Thumping hooves faded away.

Light rain began to fall.

The stranger winced when cold drops splashed against his head. Searching eyes found a clump of cedars ten feet away. He hauled himself to hands and knees and painstakingly crawled to the base of a tall conifer, where he managed to twist his back against its sturdy trunk.

For hours, he drifted in and out of consciousness.

When he finally awoke, wetness permeated everywhere.

Despite overhanging branches, matted hair and saturated clothes clung to his body in soggy bunches. Rain came in a steady downpour, dimming light of day behind a curtain of cascading water. He turned his head, but could no longer see the path below. With a sigh, he flexed fingers numbed by coldness and massaged his temple to ease his dull headache. Still, he made no effort to get up.

The sharp crack of brush resounded over the storm's din.

A dark form on horseback materialized within the gloom. It sloshed directly at him.

"Who..who are you?"

The rider halted five feet from his tree. A heavy coat concealed his body and a broad-brimmed hat covered his face as he dismounted.

"Get away from me, stand back, I mean it."

The visitor bent over to inspect the stranger's head wound.

"Are you all right, sir?"

A maroon neckerchief slipped from the rider's mouth to reveal a young man in his twenties. Behind him, his horse snorted and shook itself fiercely to shed water from its back.

The stranger gazed up through fearful eyes.

Trembling lips issued a few words. "Can you get me to a doctor?"

"What happened to you? Looks like you've been shot."

"I don't know…"

"You've been out in this rain for sometime," the horseman observed.

"A while ago, a woman rode by on the road over there," he rasped, raising an arm downstream. "I can't remember anything before that. Where am I?"

"We're not far from Humphrey's Valley," the rider replied, intently watching the victim's face less than a foot away.

"Where?"

"You're in New Brunswick Colony. I'm headed to Petit Sault on the Saint John River. If I can get you up on this horse, we can share a ride upstream, but I don't have much time to waste."

The injured man nodded. "Didn't catch your name."

"Name's Peter. Peter McDougall."

Peter put his arms around the stranger's waist and slid him up the tree trunk to a standing position. He turned to retrieve a small flask from his saddlebag and handed it to the beleaguered person.

Several swallows of burning liquid brought a small smile. "How far is it to town?"

"Two day's ride, but it may take longer in this weather. Best we get started before it gets any worse. C'mon."

Peter gripped his arm and guided the injured individual stepping unsteadily toward the horse. With a grunt, the young man helped the other onto its back. "So, you've no memory of how you came by this injury?"

"None."

Peter climbed up behind him and urged the horse to a gentle gait.

At first, the victim grimaced with every jolting movement.

Soon, he drifted into a dull malaise while the horse picked its way over muddy ground under persistent rain.

~

Two days brought better weather and arrival in the puddled streets of Petit Sault.

The riders found an aging hotel on the main road.

Peter went inside to secure a room.

He reappeared and took the injured man around back to help him up a shorter stairway.

Once inside, the stranger stripped down to long underwear and sagged onto a coarse bed, where dry warmth put him into deep sleep.

Sometime later, loud voices disturbed his slumber. He stared blankly at an unfamiliar room, unable to retrace his path to present surroundings.

Suddenly, he remembered Peter McDougall and sat up. His attention drew to voices in the next room. He pushed himself up to his knees next to the wall and pressed an ear above the headboard.

Muffled voices became clearer.

"Why didn't you just leave Bagwell there if you couldn't kill him?" a woman's voice demanded.

"You said to make sure I left no traces. Wouldn't the discovery of a body alert the authorities? Besides, he claims to have no memory," Peter answered.

"You fool! His presence here is just as revealing," the female shrieked. "Ian warned me you might botch the job. And, by the way, just how did Elizabeth Darmon manage to escape? She'll tell the authorities. There are too many loose ends, and now you've given them the trail to Quebec!"

Another male voice protested. "Keep your voice down. Charles Bagwell knows nothing, and Elizabeth Darmon doesn't have a clue to what's behind the setup. Let the boy alone."

The woman's response came in measured tones. "She'll report the crime to the sheriff of Newcastle. They'll send trackers. Did anyone see you bring Bagwell into town?"

"I brought him 'round back and checked into the hotel by myself.

Even the clerk doesn't know he's in my room."

Her tone rose once more. "He must be killed and his body disposed of in the woods."

"No, there's been enough killing," the male voice objected. "You've gone too far. I've had enough of your highhanded dealings. I'm giving Ian a full report."

"Listen, you idiot. When Elizabeth Darmon shows up at Quebec City, all hell's going to break loose with the *Patriotes*. Our operation will be set back years."

Silence followed.

Drops of perspiration formed on the wounded man's forehead. They were talking about him. He rubbed his stubbled cheek nervously. He had to get out of there. He rolled off the bed and landed on his feet. Instantly, he gripped the bedside table for support and waited for the world to stop spinning.

He staggered to trousers hanging at the foot of the bed.

A loud explosion thundered from the next room.

He froze. "Gunshot!"

He yanked on his pants as a door latch sounded in the adjacent room.

Footsteps echoed in the hallway, coming closer.

His window was the only way out. Forgetting the rest of his clothes, he stumbled to the sill and tugged desperately at its stubborn sash. The casement released with a groan.

He tumbled though onto a slanted roof and slid down to the eave before dropping feet-first ten feet into soft mud. A jarring thud made his head pound, but he dove into an alley just as light spilled from his room.

Charles trudged down a passageway to the rear of the hotel and stumbled two blocks along a narrow lane before spotting a darkened house. Panting, he lumbered through a yard and clamored around back where he slumped to the ground in exhaustion.

Minutes passed while he lay watching the azure sky swirl overhead, listening for the sound of pursuers.

Will the woman track me down? Apparently, her companion shot Peter. She was not about to tolerate more loose ends. He squeezed handfuls of dirt, attempting to settle down. Maybe they would leave town and join the others in Quebec. That would be a safer than risking the possibility he had already alerted the local constable.

His racing heart began to slow. At least he had a name. *Charles Bagwell*. He smiled at the oddly comfortable epithet. A tiny clue to his past sharpened the urge to find this Elizabeth Darmon.

Charles pushed himself to his feet and knocked tentatively at the house's back door.

No answer.

Quietly, pushed his way inside.

In the bedroom, he lit a candle and found clothes close to his own size.

After pulling on boots and a jacket, he stopped. The break-in prevented any chance he could report the shooting, and he had neither identification nor memory to vouch for his veracity. He sagged onto the edge of a bed, realizing he could not consult a doctor. If his wound was inflicted by a gunshot, as Peter suggested, the physician would report it and that could make him a likely suspect in the hotel shooting. He rose abruptly, determined to leave town before his presence led to embarrassing questions like where he got these clothes.

On his way out, flickering candlelight illuminated a large map hanging on the bedroom wall. The ragged parchment indicated it was more of a decoration than a recent chart, yet Quebec City and Petit Sault were clearly labeled near the Saint Lawrence River. What was unsettling, however, was their separation of ninety miles and the necessity of a water crossing to reach the other location.

A sudden uneasiness grabbed him. His knees weakened. He held onto the edge of an oak bureau and began to wonder if he was too fragile and ill-equipped to make such a trip on his own.

He had no choice. Voices in the hotel room said Elizabeth Darmon was on her way there to rescue others who knew his identity.

He stepped into the kitchen and began looking for food.

Charles covered fifteen miles before nightfall. Bread and apples taken from the vacant house improved his strength, but progress toward the Saint Lawrence evolved at a tottering pace. Without more food, his feeble body would never make it to the river's edge.

The next morning, Charles spied a man and woman on the path, coming toward him.

They were headed toward Petit Sault, so he felt confident they would not be aware of his recent exploits. The man carried a large backpack and moved with the assurance of an adept woodsman. Behind him, the woman also toted a backpack along with a walking stick. A goat followed tended by a young boy, which kept him well behind the other two.

They stopped in front of Charles.

"*Mon Dieu, Monsieur. Allez-vous malade?*"

Somewhere in the back of a confused brain, Charles understood. "*Ne pas concernez. Mais, J'ai faim. J'ai besoin nourriture a manger. Si vous plait...*".

Drops of sweat trickled down his face. Trembling legs forced him to sit.

The woman looked anxiously at her husband. She took off her dusty pack and unwrapped a large piece of goat cheese. He accepted a portion, trying not to appear ill-mannered. His fingers fumbled with the slippery white chunks before he plunged morsels between salivating lips.

After a moment, he smiled weakly and regained his stance.

The man pointed toward a nearby wooded area. "*La baie de cet buisson est bon. Il y a ces pommes aussi.*"

Charles' eyebrows shot up, realizing that edible fruit grew all around. He nodded appreciation, and the family bid farewell.

While the threesome walked away, he crossed to bordering trees and eagerly began filling pockets with green apples.

Two weeks of foraging along the riverbank and searching for the means to cross the Saint Lawrence brought Charles to the settlement of Beaumont.

Cold morning air awarded him the sight of smoke rising behind distant pines. The thought of a campfire excited his hunger. A diet of berries and nuts had him aching for meat of any kind. He plunged through dense underbrush and stumbled into a clearing, where startled individuals sat around a smoldering campfire.

One of the hide-covered males jumped to his feet and raised a rifle.

The frightened visitor quickly put up his hands and halted without flinching a muscle.

"Excuse my intrusion! I've been without food for days. Have you any to spare?"

"And who might you be?" growled a dirty-faced person behind the gun. Mangy black hair covered shoulders of his fur jacket. Behind the curly beard, a squinting eye sighted along the musket's barrel. He outweighed Charles by fifty pounds.

"Name's Charles Bagwell. I'm on my way to Quebec to..." Charles gulped at a dour expression overtaking the grizzled face.

"Quebec?" the woodsman spat at the ground. "Why would any right-minded person want to go to Quebec?"

Charles swallowed, wondering how to answer. If an appeal to their charity would not work, there was no point in continuing conversation. "I've some friends there. I had an accident and need their help."

A seated man laughed. "Looks as if someone tried to shoot you."

The rifleman spat again. "We don't take to Frenchies."

"Please. All I need is a little food..."

A loud bang tore a whistling sound past Charles' right ear. He instinctively fell to the ground and lay face down for a moment.

The others watched him struggle to his feet.

His face contorted with rage, Charles rose and leaped on top of the startled gunman. The pair tumbled backward, rolling over on the long grass. Charles flailed wildly without landing a blow until strong hands pulled him off the squirming woodsman.

"This one's got some piss in him," a hunter with a coonskin cap observed, pushing Charles away while holding his arms.

Another bystander grinned as the rifleman regained his footing. "Might be we can use his spunk to get back our packages."

"He's not worth much if you ask me. I jest got caught by surprise," the marksman snarled, angrily tossing his musket toward the campfire.

The hunter jerked his thumb. "Martin, go see to the canoes."

He relaxed his grip on Charles' wrists. "Name's Anderson. That fellow with the rifle is Martin. These others are Lesnick, Halldorson, Jolly and Espitallier. We're all trappers from down in New York. We finished our season and came up the *Richelieu River* to shipping lanes before winter closes down the passage."

Charles calmed down a bit and took the man's outstretched hand. "You say you've lost some packages?"

"Uh-huh, after we passed the rapids, a boat manned by soldiers from Fort Chambly blocked our way. They claimed we'd trapped illegally in this territory and confiscated our pelts. They told us to go back to the States. We were trying to figure out how to get back what's ours when you barged in."

Charles was sympathetic, but had his own problems. "I wish you luck, but I must be on my way."

He started off, resigned to more nut and berry picking.

Anderson raised a hand. "Hold on, now. We might be willing to share some grub, if you'd do us a favor."

Charles paused. "And what would that be?"

"I've been thinking. If you went to the Fort, claiming to be lost like you are and not being an American, maybe they'd let you spend the night inside. Then, while they're all asleep, you could sneak out and unlock the gate. We'd be waiting to slip inside and take back our pelts before anyone knew what happened. You could leave with us or stay 'til morning and claim you knew nothing, then be on your way."

Others muttered among themselves, hearing a workable plan for the first time.

Lesnick stepped over to the fire and retrieved a cup of stew. He offered the cup of brown steaming liquid under Charles' chin. "What do you say?"

Smell of the brew was overpowering. Charles licked his lips. "Well, perhaps I could help you."

Anderson grinned. "Good. If we break camp within the hour, we can be back at the Fort in three days ready for a raid on Saturday night."

Charles stopped chewing on a piece of meat and frowned. "So

long? Why did you come so far if you were planning to recover the pelts?"

"We were to meet a ship down river tomorrow," Anderson uttered in a low voice. "The Frenchies don't take kindly to Americans on their waterway. We've friends onboard who we hoped would come back with us for a fast strike at the Fort. It'd be risky, but it's all we could think of 'til now. This way's better. We'll leave the canoes here and make our way overland. It's only 'bout ninety miles."

Charles looked anxiously at the forest. He had not fully recovered from lingering headaches and lack of food. Now, he had to make a forced trek through unknown territory with men who had little concern for his condition. But, wandering through the wilderness by himself was dangerous, too.

He clenched his teeth. One way or another, he had to secure a canoe from these trappers and get across that blasted Saint Lawrence. Despite his ineptness, he had learned one thing. They thought him to be an Englishman. If Canadians were more friendly to Englishmen than Americans, he might be able to use that advantage once inside the fort.

Charles could barely keep up with the trappers as they tramped through woods and fields of the *Chaudiere Appalaches*. Lack of stamina had him frequently bent over, trying to catch his breath, then desperately exerting himself trying to catch up with disappearing woodsmen. Nevertheless, they made good time until the morning of the third day, when rain returned. An overcast sky dumped enough water to slow pace to a sloshing trudge on treacherous ground.

After an arduous march along the banks of the *Richelieu River*, the small party huddled in a grove two hundred yards from the entrance to the old stone fort.

The huge somber structure towered ominously at water's edge in a late afternoon mist, reminiscent of a medieval castle guarding passage to the North. Sentries and cannon barrels dotted battlements at the corner parapets. Most soldiers, however, directed their attention toward the river, south of the nearby town of Chambly, where a threat from Americans was most likely.

Charles shivered with foreboding, certain his role in the plan would come to naught. Summoning courage, he stepped into the clearing and waved goodbye to his comrades. He walked steadily through light rain to the ramparts, rehearsing his story.

When he reached huge gates on the Fort's eastern façade, a voice from a small opening in slate-colored blocks bellowed.

"Stop! State your name and business."

"Charles Bagwell. English citizen on my way to Quebec City. May I please speak to the Commandant?"

He waited patiently in front of ten-foot high wooden framework becoming wetter with each passing moment. He gazed upward, surprised by the size of the doors. *Would he have the strength to open them?* A small smile curved his lips at a thought that once inside, he could seek asylum and inform the regiment about this band of ruthless trappers lurking outside.

He sighed. It would only lead to his undoing. If any of his comrades escaped, the survivors would track him down when he tried to make his way north.

Finally, massive gates creaked open, and a stern-faced sentry motioned him to follow. He scrambled after the soldier, crossing a soggy central square, and ducking into a low-roofed barrack at the rear of the fort.

Inside, a Commandant rose behind his small desk with an outstretched hand and a friendly smile. A tall, square-jawed officer, he looked to be in his thirties with dark flowing hair and a neatly trimmed mustache. Following a perfunctory handshake, he directed Charles to a plain comb-backed chair.

"Mr. Bagwell, what brings you here to Chambly, so far from the Isles?"

Charles hoarsely voiced his monologue. "Thank you for seeing me. I came to the American colonies on holiday. A week ago, while riding north from Boston to visit my aunt in Quebec, a gang of ruffians attacked me a day out of Montpelier. They took my papers, money and my horse. I was left to wander in the wilderness for days."

He pointed at his head wound for emphasis. Anderson advised him not to mention New Brunswick, just in case he was wanted for questioning in Peter's shooting.

The Commandant glanced at the bruise. "I see you've had an unfortunate incident, Mr. Bagwell, but activities outside Quebec territory are beyond our jurisdiction. From time to time, Americans come up here and, on occasion, trappers have threatened our townspeople and tried to steal our game. When such trespassing occurs, we take immediate action. Can you describe your attackers? Do you know where they were headed?"

Charles scowled indignantly. "Some sort of woodsmen, I guess, five of them dressed in fur coats. They set out east after taking my horse. It serves me right for venturing into the wilds without escort. I'd heard tales of danger on the American frontier, but I thought some civility existed in this part of the world. Hopefully, visitors are treated better in British North America in spite of rumors about uncouth French Canadians."

"They prefer to be called *Quebecois* here in Lower Canada," the Commandant admonished. "French Canadians are fiercely proud of their heritage. They have done remarkably well for themselves under British subjugation over the past eighty years.

"Tell you what, I'll send a patrol to the American border at Lake Champlain. You may rest here tonight and stay in the town of Chambly until they return in a few days. If we catch those brigands and recover your things, I'll send for you. We'll need a statement confirming their identity. Afterwards, one of my men will see that you get passage on a riverboat to Quebec City."

"Thank you," Charles breathed relief.

"Sergeant Woolcott, please take this gentleman to the kitchen. Give him some food and show him to a bed in the second quarter room. Good day to you, sir."

Charles rose from his chair feeling slightly guilty the plan was proceeding so well, but the Fort did have the trapper's bounty.

At night, Charles lay on his cot listening to falling rain. He worried about the gate. A weighty beam lay across locking channels eighteen inches thick and fifteen feet long. He doubted he could lift it out of its groove by himself. He had not seen guards maneuver the bar, but it might require two persons just to slide it out. He was also fearful a sentry might be manning the entrance. He might walk up to the gate without seeing sentries on such a dark, rainy night until it was too late.

Time slowly passed.

He had no timepiece to tell him the hour. He was supposed to unlatch the entrance shortly after midnight. Then it would be up to the trappers to find their pelts. He would return to his bed and remain with the soldiers until they sent him north on a riverboat. Why should the Commandant suspect him of helping the trappers? He had already alerted them to the danger of a marauding band.

The cot was a welcome relief after sleeping on cold ground. Despite his anxiety, he drifted into light sleep.

Charles awoke with a start. At first, he did not remember his location. Officers snored loudly on nearby cots. Through a window across the room, he could see changing moonlight as leftover storm clouds parted. *What time is it? Did I sleep too long?*

Quickly, he pulled on his boots, trying not to make a disturbance. He tiptoed to the door and squeezed out into frigid night air. Lingering on the wooden porch for a moment, he looked across the courtyard at dark outlines of the far wall. Rapid expulsion of his cloudy breath was the only sound in a frosty stillness. Overhead, silver rimmed clouds drifted past a glowing moon, and icy stars dotted a black sky.

There was no time to waste.

Keeping close to shadows at the periphery of the square, Charles crossed muddy earth to the front gate. He remembered sentries positioned at corners of the Fort and prayed the gate lacked a guard at this hour.

Footfalls softly squished under each step as he pressed toward the front gate.

When he reached the entrance, he held his breath waiting for someone to come out from ink-black shadows to stop him. No one appeared. He let out a small sigh. His hands touched the damp rough-cut beam held by two channel locks, one at each side of the gate.

He stepped to one end. Crouching under the massive spar, he nestled a shoulder against it and heaved upward with all his strength. The bar creaked and rose a foot to the top of the channel brace. With great effort, he stepped sideways and gently lowered it by kneeling to the ground. He slid out, and it fell the remaining distance, striking the ground with a dull thud.

The other end was different story. No matter how hard he tried, it would not come out of its cradle. It had become wedged in place by the severe angle. He rushed back to the freed end, but he could neither lift it nor budge it closer to the gate. One side was partially unlocked, but the gate opened inward and swung only eight inches before hitting the beam.

At the open end, he was able to wedge his body between the frame and the bar tip resting in mud. With his back against the gate, he used his legs to push the embedded log further away. A cracking sound came from the other secured end. Charles strained, and the cradle's rung creaked again.. Suddenly, the channel guide broke, releasing the beam. The remaining portion fell to the earth with a loud thump.

Charles froze, waiting for sentries above to sound an alarm. His gaze swung back to the barracks, searching for a light that would signal arousal. His attention fell on footprints extending all the way back to his quarters. How could he deny his involvement with the break-in with this glaring evidence to the contrary? It would be impossible to erase the tracks without making new ones.

He made a fist and slammed it into his other hand, exasperated for getting involved. For the sake of a little food, he had become an outlaw, and he was the only one known to the commandant. Hopefully, absence of the pelts might not be sufficient cause for the soldiers to track him down.

Shuffling sounds interrupted his thoughts. Trappers were already edging inside the gate. A dark figure moved toward him.

"Good job," Anderson said softly. "We were waiting against the wall for a sign, it wasn't hard to recognize the sound of the gate unlatching."

Charles sensed the man's patronizing grin in the darkness.

Well, the job was done. He was about to say he would be joining them, but Anderson had run off to join the others. There was nothing more to do but wait at the entrance for their return.

A shot rang out. Another followed.

Charles jumped with alarm. *Gunfire!* That was not part of the plan.

Shouts echoed overhead. Lights flickered on inside barracks' windows. A figure leapt out of the shadows to Charles' left and aimed his rifle at a soldier on the parapet above. A loud report preceded the sentry's scream. He pitched to the ground twenty feet below. More flashes and thunderous explosions erupted. *Why they were they shooting; killing each other over animal pelts?*

A trapper emerged from the direction of the Commandant's office and scrambled toward the gate. Behind him, a soldier charged out from the barracks. His gun discharged, and the trapper stumbled awkwardly before plummeting face down at Charles' feet. Another soldier followed, pointing a musket in Charles' direction. The frightened accomplice dove for the gate just as a bullet splintered wood where his head had been.

He crawled outside, leapt to his feet and launched himself toward the trees along the river's embankment. Shots rang out behind.

After a headlong dash across the field, he made it to safety within a cluster of poplars. He leaned against a trunk, gasping for breath, looking over his shoulder to see if others had escaped.

Shouts faded into the moonlit background, but no one appeared at the entrance.

Why am I waiting? His mind screamed. These men were not his friends. Now, he was part of an even bigger crime—a crime that involved the slaughter of soldiers. How could he explain his presence as anything other than a premeditated plan for murder? There was no doubt he would be followed and, if caught, hanged for the deed.

Despair settled over Charles as he fled into the night.

Chapter Seven

Two weeks later, Charles Bagwell sat in a tavern on *Rue Saint Anne* in Upper Quebec City. He managed to elude his pursuers by keeping to wooded areas away from the Richelieu River.

At Saint Pierre Lake, he boarded a flat-bottomed boat that ferried passengers down river to the Saint Lawrence. Once in the City, he found a job at the docks off-loading cargo from ships recently arrived from Spain and Italy. A day's pay earned him a week's lodging in a dingy room three blocks from the harbor. After-work hours were spent walking the streets, inquiring if anyone knew Elizabeth Darmon.

When the last crate had been unloaded and the job ended, he moved his search to the Upper City. Before leaving the small apartment, Charles cut his long red hair, dyed the remaining growth black and removed a shaggy mustache. Donning new clothes, he nodded with satisfaction at the appearance staring back from the room's cracked mirror.

Authorities were looking for a backwoodsman. He felt comfortable assuming the role of an urban merchant. Gazing at the pale, freckled skin and fine bone structure, Charles was convinced he did not belong in such a harsh environment. He had no survival skills and little understanding of the people. At first, it was easy to blame his memory, but a feeling of being an outsider would not go away. He shook his head at the reflection. *Where did I come from?*

The following day, with very few shillings remaining in his pocket, Charles entered an Upper City tavern. The owner confirmed that a female customer with the last name of Darmon visited his establishment several times over the past two weeks. Charles' pulse raced.

Patrons began to fill the premises, celebrating an end to the day's labor. *Le Taureau Rouge* was popular with English speaking customers who often directed their loudest sentiments at illiterate *Quebecois*.

In gathering darkness, an English couple entered. The tall gentleman removed a sable-colored top hat and a gray tweed redingote with doeskin collar. His light-brown hair contrasted with dark, close-cut locks of the lady he escorted. Her gold, gauze dress, adorned with sewn flowers of blue silk under a short, brown, postilion-back jacket hugged a trim figure. The woman stood barely five feet tall, but as she surveyed the room her haughty expression suggested a person used to the accommodation of others.

They nodded to several occupants while making their way to a table in the far corner.

The lady removed her bonnet and suede gloves. The gentleman rose to place an order at the bar.

The bartender caught Charles eye, tipping his head toward the woman with a meaningful dip of the eyebrows. Charles took a deep breath, blood throbbing wildly in his ears. *Was she the woman he sought? Could he be that lucky?*

He began angling through the crowded room toward her table. An uncertain feeling washed over him. His palms grew moist. He wiped hair from his forehead with a shaky hand. *Am I about to make an utter fool of myself?*

The woman glanced up with a trace of annoyance. Charles spoke softly for her ears alone.

"Madam, please excuse my boldness, but is your name Elizabeth Darmon?"

"Yes it is. And who might you be?"

His face grimaced with disappointment at her lack of recognition. "Apparently I've made a mistake. Forgive me for intruding upon your privacy. My name is Charles Bagwell..."

Her eyes widened in surprise. She came to her feet. "Charles? Charles, is it really you?" She hugged him fiercely. "I didn't recognize you without your red hair, and you've lost so much weight. I can't believe you're alive!"

Charles stepped back and heaved a sigh of relief. "Yes, I was shot and left for dead in a place called New Brunswick. When I came to, I had no memory of who I was or where I belonged."

"Oh, Charles, I'm so sorry."

"A passerby rescued me," he continued. "Later, I overheard him talking in the next room of a hotel. They said a woman named Elizabeth Darmon was pursuing the rest of my family here in Quebec."

He glanced surreptitiously at her companion standing at the bar, his back to them. "Are you with this gentleman under duress?"

"Duress?" She smiled. "No, Charles. That gentleman is my husband, William. Don't you remember your brother-in-law? We were staying at Victoria's lodge when you, William and the Hudson's were ambushed on a carriage ride. William said one of the villains shot you before they were kidnapped. I followed him here and discovered he'd already been released. We presumed you were dead."

Charles' brain had trouble keeping up. For an instant, he saw the image of a gun pointed through the window of a carriage; a flash, then nothing.

"You mentioned the Hudson's. Who are they? What became of them?"

An almost imperceptible frown touched Elizabeth's forehead. Her voice became shaky and a tear dropped from her eye. "Victoria and Richard Hudson, my sister and her husband. Alas, William said the ruffians killed them, as they were of little use to their cause."

"Their *cause*?" Charles muttered absently as he tried to remember the unfortunate couple.

Her gaze narrowed, and she waved him closer. "Charles, there's great unrest here. People are upset with English authorities for permitting so many poor and sickly immigrants into the port. French Canadian farmers are suffering because of a fall in wheat prices, and local fur traders face new competition from the Hudson's Bay Company. There's a band of reformers who want an independent province. They call themselves the *Patriotes,* and their leader is a man named Joseph Papineau. Those men responsible for your ambush are part of a fanatic fringe group who advocate violence."

He frowned. "You seem well informed about community politics."

Lady Darmon reclaimed her chair and motioned for Charles to sit opposite her. "I'm sympathetic to their complaints, yes, but not their methods.

"It's rumored this fringe group, which goes under the name *Sons of Liberty,* is procuring ammunition for an insurrection. They've offered Jean-Baptiste Cazeau, a member of the City Legislature, one thousand pounds to provide guns. I fear these radicals will bring the wrath of Parliament down upon us all."

Mister Darmon returned to the table, holding two dripping glasses. Carefully placing one drink in front of Lady Darmon, his wary eyes regarded the stranger. Suddenly, he stopped cold. His mouth dropped. "Charles! Is it you? I must be seeing a ghost!"

His wife reached out and pulled him down onto a third chair. "You must excuse my husband. It's such a surprise to see you alive."

"Charles, forgive us..." Mister Darmon began.

"For leaving you behind," Lady Darmon finished quickly. "Until William's release, I did not think to return and conduct a search for you." She turned to her husband. "He's lost all memory of the events leading up to the abduction."

The other man lifted an eyebrow and fell silent.

Charles studied the couple. *Can I trust these two?* They acted sincere, and the gentleman did recognize him. He had no choice if he wanted to fill in his missing past.

Mister Darmon returned his gaze, his own clouded with concern. "Charles, you look terrible. Have you been in the wilds all this time?"

"I tramped along the Saint Lawrence for weeks, hoping to find Elizabeth. I stumbled across some trappers who coerced me into joining them in a raid on Fort Chambly. Several soldiers were shot. I fear I'm a wanted criminal, hence the disguise."

Lady Darmon glanced around the room. "You need a place to recover, Charles. We'll find you accommodations nearby." She reached out to lay a hand over his. "You've been a dear friend of our family for many years. Unfortunately, we can't spend more time with you tonight, but we shall be at your disposal tomorrow to provide more details about your background."

Charles' shoulders slumped with a sudden fatigue. "I'd be most grateful. The ordeal of the past weeks weighs on me like a heavy burden. I just hope we can straighten out this mess."

They rose and escorted Charles from the tavern.

At a small hotel two blocks down the street, the Darmons paid one week's advance for his room. Before departing, they agreed to meet at *Le Taureau Rouge* the following night.

Charles returned to the tavern the following evening with a much lighter step. When he entered the establishment, however, he discovered that Lady Darmon was absent. Mister Darmon sat at a corner table, talking with two rugged-looking individuals on the opposite side of a surface cluttered with empty tankards.

Charles moved hesitantly in their direction, overhearing a few words spoken in French.

Mister Darmon looked up through glassy eyes. "Charles, my man, 'ow good of you to join us. Come 'ave a pint. Barkeep, more ale! Allow me ta introduce my friends, Jacques and Frances."

Both of his companions were impressive in size. Jacques' shoulder length brown hair framed a pudgy face with a large, bulbous nose. He measured over six feet tall and easily three hundred pounds with immense hands encasing one of the steins. Frances could have been even taller, but possessed a slimmer frame. Bare arms, visible beneath rolled up sleeves of a red and black plaid shirt displayed sinewy muscles that could snap a man's neck with just the twist of a wrist. Dark, disheveled hair tumbled over his forehead to meet sinister looking eyebrows.

Charles scowled. "Where is Lady Darmon?"

Mister Darmon smiled, but the gesture did not quite reach his eyes. "Ah yes, Lady Elizabeth. She could not be with us tonight and sends her apologies. Perhaps tomorrow...."

Charles shifted impatiently. Mister Darmon's patronizing grin seemed to mock his attempts to recover his memory, and his two comrades reinforced a suspicion the Darmon's were involved with the French radicals.

He glared at the other men contemptuously. "Listen William, I don't care if you're involved in this *Patriote* cause. It's none of my business. What I don't understand is why you aren't doing everything possible to bring those kidnappers to justice. My God, those Frenchmen murdered your sister and brother-in-law!"

Mister Darmon looked perplexed. The Frenchman to his left rose abruptly, knocking over several glassed.

Glaring fiercely, he advanced on Charles. "*Monsieur,* if I were you, I'd keep such accusations to myself."

He placed a large hand on Charles' chest and shoved him backward. The Englishman stumbled, regained his balance, but the ruffian kept coming. Outdone by a hundred pounds and at least six inches, Charles gulped with alarm. *Is this roughneck going to trample me?*

Jacques snarled with another threatening push. "You'd better leave and keep your nose out of our business, eh?"

Over the brigand's shoulder, Charles glimpsed the other Canadian helping Mister Darmon to his feet and dragging him toward the door. The remaining patrons displayed little interest, apparently convinced the Englishman was just another disorderly customer.

Charles recovered his balance once more, determined to face the browbeating Frenchman. "See here, you blackguard…"

A massive fist slammed Charles into the back wall. His already tender head met the wooden structure with a crunch. His body crumpled to the floor.

Jacques turned and rejoined his friend as the threesome staggered out into the street.

In dizzying pain, Charles groped for a chair to rise up. He struggled to his feet, stumbled to the bar and asked for a pint of ale. The Innkeeper regarded him with sympathy, but most of the customers refused to look in his direction.

He returned to an empty table. After taking a long swallow, he stared at the half empty glass, failing to notice Mister Darmon run by the door, chased by a short, dark-haired woman.

Charles awakened from a drunken stupor to the sound of urgent pounding on his hotel door. He stumbled out of bed, squinted into the mid-morning light and yanked open the portal. Lady Darmon stood outside, tears running down her checks. "Charles, something terrible has happened! William has had an accident! They found his body at the bottom of a cliff below the Citadel."

He took her arm and showed her to the one chair within the room.

Sitting on the bed next to her, he tried to recall the past night's events. "I saw him last night at *Le Taureau Rouge*. He was drunk in the company of two Frenchmen. They left the tavern together."

His eyes widened. "Maybe they did him in."

Lady Darmon shook her head. "No, no! Jacques and Frances are helping us track the *Patriote* movements. There's going to be a meeting at the *Chapelle des Jesuites* next month. Reformers from all the major cities are coming to consolidate their forces. William was trying to learn their intentions, so we could alert the authorities. It's been difficult to convince the English magistrate that a threat really exists. We were hoping to get proof at their meeting."

"Do you think someone killed him?" Charles interrupted.

Lady Darmon took a deep breath. "I didn't tell you, but the leader of the kidnappers is a woman. She looks just like me, but is ruthless. She directed the killing of Victoria and Richard, and forced William to accompany her to a bank for a transfer of funds to their organization. They extorted twenty-five thousand pounds from us!"

"My God, so that's what happened," Charles exclaimed.

"But she let him go once they got their money," she observed carefully. "On condition he immediately return to England. She must have found out we're spying on her band of conspirators."

His brow was creased with alarm. "What can we do?"

"She must know that William was at *Le Taureau Rouge* and will probably return to see if the barkeep remembers my presence. I have Jacques watching the place. Once she's inside, he'll waylay her carriage driver."

Charles shifted nervously. "But won't the radicals be alerted to her arrest and call off their meeting?"

Lady Darmon hesitated. "You have a point there. It will be difficult to have her detained without proof of guilt, and now, the only remaining witness to the kidnapping is dead."

She pulled a lace handkerchief from her sleeve and dabbed at her eyes. "It might be better if we just confine her someplace until after the meeting. I know of an abandoned house not far from here. You could keep an eye on her in case she tries to escape."

"Escape?" Charles paled to a sickly pallor. "You want me to guard the place because there's a chance this she-devil might escape?"

She laid a reassuring hand on his shoulder. "Don't worry, Charles. The basement is secure, and you'll have the run of the house, but someone has to feed her."

He shook his head vehemently. "Maybe Jacques or Frances would be better at that..."

Another series of knocks sounded. Charles opened the door to find Frances standing in the hallway, gasping for breath. He spied Lady Darmon and pushed the Englishman to one side as he charged into the room.

"Madam, *cette* woman 'as arrived at the Inn. Jacques disposed of the driver and awaits 'er return."

Lady Darmon glanced at Charles. The three raced downstairs to the street.

Two blocks away, the imposter was returning to her carriage. Frances ran into the road and waved frantically at an approaching hansom.

The driver hauled back on the reins and Charles and Lady Darmon climbed inside. Charles overheard a muffled discussion between Frances and the driver, but could not make out the words. A moment later, the driver jumped to the ground, and their vehicle leaped forward with Frances at the reins.

Charles turned to his companion. "Where's Jacques taking her?"

"To the Plains of Abraham," she shouted over the noisy clatter of the vehicle. "We can transfer to her carriage there without attracting attention."

Charles leaned out the window to see the other carrier five hundred yards ahead. Hoof beats from their vehicle echoed loudly off retreating buildings as the pace quickened.

Soon, the road turned to dirt, and structures disappeared, revealing an empty plain stretching to the St. Lawrence's blue waterway near the horizon. Ahead, the carriage sped recklessly, swaying back and forth behind a cloud of pebbles.

Charles felt their horse leap into a full gallop.

They were closing fast.

Suddenly, Jacques jumped from his perch, rolled and landed in a ditch. The driverless carriage continued on barreling toward cliffs in the distance.

"My God, Jacques fell off her carriage!" Charles exclaimed settling back in his seat.

Their own conveyance slowed and pulled up alongside the Frenchman. Frances yelled down at the figure hobbling toward them. *"Est-ce vous allez bien?"*

The carriage door opened. Jacques landed with a thud on the facing seat.

Charles stared in disbelief.

The other man looked back with a smirk. "I was fighting a swarm of bees. They stung the horse. The reins slipped out of my hand."

Just then, Frances' voice rang out from the driver's seat. "She's jumped!"

They lurched forward again. Seconds later, the horse came to a prancing halt alongside the woman's body.

Charles climbed out and squinted into the distance. Her runaway horse now galloped parallel to the cliff. His gaze dropped to the figure lying in the brush. Frances turned her over. Blood trickled from her forehead. Lady Darmon bent down and put her cheek next to the woman's mouth. "She's still alive. Let's get her into the carriage."

The hansom moved off again. Charles gazed at the unconscious woman whose head bobbed on the seat next to Jacques. Her resemblance to Lady Darmon was amazing. She appeared softer, more serene, which might be attributed to her comatose state. It was hard to believe such a comely woman engineered this mayhem and directed ruthless acts of terrorism.

At the safe house, Lady Darmon mixed a concoction of bleach and dye, and the two Frenchmen helped saturate the unconscious woman's head with the mixture.

"Why are you coloring her hair?" Charles asked, confusion marring his brow.

"I've had enough of her charade," Lady Darmon retorted. There will be no more confusion about who is the real Mrs. Darmon while I'm in Quebec."

Francis and Jacques carried the dripping body to the basement, leaving Charles with instructions to provide food for the prisoner twice each day for the next two weeks, while the others prepared to infiltrate the *Patriote* convention. He stood at the front entrance watching their carriage head back toward the city, feeling alone once more.

After several hours, Charles grew restless of his role as house sitter. Stillness inside the house was disquieting. He explored both cobweb-laden floors, finding nearly empty rooms occupied by a few pieces of sheet-covered furniture. He found a cot upstairs and table and chairs in the kitchen, together with a well-stocked larder.

Twice, he crept down to the basement and cautiously listened at the basement door, but heard no sound. He lacked the courage to open the portal and face the evil mastermind, not knowing when she might regain consciousness. But how was he to feed the captive? It might come down to what could be slipped under the door, unless he could make a small opening by removing part of a board at the bottom. He continued to marvel that this single Englishwoman could have such power and use it for the cause of French Canadian independence.

At sunset, Charles took a walk in the garden. The house stood by itself, with no neighboring structures for at least half a mile. Overgrown shrubbery prevented visibility of the first floor unless one was directly in front of the residence, looking up the pathway. An unkempt yard of tall weeds encroached all the way up to domicile's ivy covered stones. Charles shuddered at an eerie thought of being swallowed up by undergrowth.

If he jumped, he could catch a glimpse of Upper City's rooftops, municipal buildings already darkened by twilight. Cold air swirled around, and overhead, the first stars appeared in a deep blue sky.

Clip-clops drew his attention to two horsemen on *Grand Allee* hurrying by toward the city where street lamps were being lit.

Charles felt very alone. His chest rose and fell in a heavy sigh. He went inside to eat a meal before retiring upstairs. The vixen below would have to wait until light of day before he attempted to serve her breakfast. For now, he looked forward to resting on the musty cot. It was a luxury he appreciated after days spent in the wild.

~

A loud crash jarred Charles awake the following morning.

He lay still for a moment, trying to get his bearings. He crept to the window just in time to see his prisoner charge out of the house. She cast a furtive glance right and left, then headed off down the path to the road.

Charles raced downstairs and burst out the front entrance. By the time he arrived at the street, his charge was a tiny speck, half way to the city. He decided not to recapture her, but follow the imposter and determine her location for Lady Darmon.

It was early afternoon by the time Charles reached Lady Darmon's room. Jacques answered the door.

"So, the little rabbit returns already. Outsmarted by the lady, eh?"

Charles cast him a grudging look.

"Never mind," the Frenchman sneered. "Lady Darmon is here. I've business to attend to elsewhere."

The door shut behind him.

"She escaped," Charles confessed. "I followed her to the *Hotel De Ville*. She came out again ten minutes later and went to the Union Hotel at 12 *Rue Sainte-Anne*. I waited there for two hours, but she didn't reappear."

Lady Darmon smiled. "Come sit down, Charles. May I offer you a drink?"

Charles collapsed into a chair. "I'm sorry I let you down."

"You did your best."

He took the glass. "Do you think she'll rejoin her gang and come after you?"

"We'll keep an eye on her now that we know where she's hiding."

He looked out the window. "I wish I could have been of more help. Maybe if I knew more of what went on before you came to Quebec... Can we discuss my past?"

The congenial atmosphere was disturbed by a commotion in the hallway. Scuffling and muffled voices grew louder. A loud bang pierced the door.

"Open up! Open the door!"

Charles stood in alarm when Lady Darmon started toward the portal.

"Wait!" he cried. The door flew open.

Three uniformed men barged into the room. A captain walked over to Charles with a look of vehemence. "Mr. Bagwell, you're under arrest for murders committed at Fort Chambly."

The other two lawmen took hold of his arms and clamped handcuffs around his wrists. Charles shot a glance at Lady Darmon who seemed as surprised as he. The captain directed them out, and the officers marched their captive into the hallway where two more officers fell into step as they made their way to the stairs.

Just as they turned to go down, Charles spotted an onlooker at the other end of the hallway. Jacques leaned against a window showing his condescending smirk.

Charles existed in a dream world during the next four weeks. He was taken to prison at *Trois Rivieres*, thirty miles upriver, and thrust into a small cell to await trial. It took only two weeks to assemble a tribunal before a British magistrate.

The prosecutor was merciless.

"You admit going to Fort Chambly with the express intention of committing a crime?"

"I was only trying to help the trappers get their pelts back," Charles implored.

"And did you not lie to the Commandant? A lie, incidentally, that prompted him to send a patrol to Lake Champlain, where five innocent woodsmen were shot because of your story!"

"I cannot be blamed for such consequences!" he protested.

The prosecutor's eyes bore into him. "On the night of October 1, Mr. Bagwell, did you not sneak out to open the Fort's gates, a crime in itself, and let thieves inside for the purpose of robbery?"

"I was trying to help them recover their goods."

"Is it not reasonable to expect that disreputable men—men who possess guns and are about to commit a crime—would more than likely be willing to harm or kill their victims?"

Charles floundered. "I suppose…"

"When gunfire erupted all around you, did you try to stop it? Witnesses have testified that you watched from the gate, waiting for your friends. And, after they fell, you deserted them too, running away as a coward would, unwilling to face up to your deed."

"You don't understand! They weren't my friends. I was on my way to Quebec and just happened to meet them. They offered me some stew in return for a favor."

"So, because you were hungry, six trappers died and four militiamen at Fort Chambly," the court official exclaimed triumphantly.

Charles never felt so abandoned. "I was hungry, but thought I was doing a good deed by helping them."

"It never occurred to you that the soldiers at the Fort might have had good reason to confiscate their bounty?"

"No, it didn't. I'd been wandering in the wilderness for weeks. I was shot by unknown assailants in New Brunswick and left for dead. My memory is gone. I can't recall how I got there."

"Oh yes, your missing memory. Would it surprise you to learn that we've made inquires in all the major settlements of the Colony, and no one has ever heard of you?"

Charles thought of Peter in Petit Sault, but decided it was better not to reveal his involvement or he might be accused of his death as well.

"I was with some friends, Elizabeth Darmon and her husband, William. She can testify to my past and the reason for my injury."

"And where is this witness? Why haven't you produced this lady?"

Lady Darmon and her friends failed to appear at the trial. Their whereabouts were unknown. He had no clue as to who else could be called to testify on his behalf. In the end, it did not matter.

The officer of the court turned to the magistrate.

"As prosecutor, I submit that this man's *condition* is irrelevant. Whether or not he was hungry, whether or not he could remember his past and whether or not he had good intentions have no bearing on this case.

"He knew he was committing a crime. The law within the

Provinces is clear on this point; deaths that occur during the commission of a crime are the responsibility of the perpetrators. Such persons are guilty of murder, regardless of how death happens."

The black robed attorney pointed an accusing finger at Charles.

"Therefore, I ask the magistrate to deliver justice on behalf of innocent soldiers whose lives were sacrificed for a few, measly pelts."

The verdict was swift and unsympathetic—death by hanging six weeks hence.

Chapter Eight

William Darmon hated snow. As a child on a trip to Edinburgh, a record snowfall kept him indoors for long days, feeling suffocated inside crowded, overheated rooms. Throughout his life, first sight of winter's white brought back a feeling of oppressive warmth.

He gazed at snow cloaking dark spruce trees surrounding the clearing. Wind's steady low whistle through trees penetrated a cold, gray stillness in their forest shelter. Thousands of white particles blew randomly like a giant swarm of gnats. Huddled together with his sisters-in-law in the back of an open wagon, he reflected on the past two months of captivity.

Their ride to Grand Falls ended abruptly when six men on horseback waylaid their carriage. Poor Charles tried to escape before falling to the blast of gunfire.

A mile north of the ambush, he, Emily, Victoria and Richard were forced into the back of a feed wagon with hands tied and bodies covered by a stiff canvas. Their next vision came at night on the shore of the Saint Lawrence, where guards directed them at gunpoint onto a small sailing ship. A quiet arrival in Quebec City was met by another wagon, which carried them to a house west of town, where they were locked in a dark basement.

The next day, each prisoner was blindfolded and taken one by one upstairs for an interview. Their captors requested details of lives back home, relations and business affiliations. William recoiled at the experience, and no one offered an explanation for the treatment.

During Richard's inquisition, shouts burst forth beyond the basement door.

"...I will not abide by these lies!"

If they were Richard's words, he could not tell. Scuffling sounds followed, and a door slammed shut. A gunshot rang out behind the house—then nothing. From that time forward, they never saw Richard again.

Later that night, they were removed from the house. A ride in a bumpy wagon ended at the river where they were shoved into the hold of a fishing scow.

Twenty-four hours passed before it docked up river and another wagon took them further into the wilds of Rupert's land. William estimated they had traveled two hundred miles since the ambush and wondered if they would ever again find their way out of the wilderness. He could get no answers from the brawny outdoorsmen who kept watch and seldom spoke.

Emily looked at the lone hunter tending campfire fifty paces away.

"At least they no longer keep watch during these stops."

The fire crackled.

Distant musket reports echoed from the five Frenchmen off in the woods, scouring for game.

William nodded. "Yes, but I have no doubt if we tried to escape, they would easily track us down before help was found."

"I've lived in the Colony three years now," Victoria remarked pulling her coarse woolen jacket close to her neck. "You learn to respect the wilderness and above all, keep warm in the winter."

Emily shivered in the frosty air. "There's truth in that. Charles and I never experienced such cold nights. Charles... Alas, he came so far from home never to return. Now, I must persevere without him. Sometimes I feel so lost. Will we ever get out of this place?"

William bit his lip in sympathy. "I can't accept Charles' loss. Elizabeth must have sent for help. A search party should have found him within hours of the attack."

The smell of coffee teased from a steaming metal pot next to the flames. William slid down and strolled over to the sentry.

"Fire feels good on a day like this."

The bulky fellow wore a faded woolen jacket with sleeves that rode up as he poked at embers with a stiff branch. He tossed it into the fire.

William persisted. "Do you think this snow will let up today?"

The caretaker bent over and retrieved two dented metal cups from a backpack.

"Are we far from our destination?"

"Not far," the woodsman replied without looking up. He poured the enticing liquid into a second cup and handed it to William. The welcome brew reminded him of Richard's remark regarding how popular the drink was becoming in the Provinces.

William squared his shoulders. "May I ask where you're taking us?"

The man glanced at his captive's manacled hands. "There's a cabin on an island out on Lake Champlain with food enough to last through winter. A boat will come for you next spring. By then, you'll not see us again."

William clenched his teeth, resisting an impulse to lunge at the man.

Instead, he grimly sipped the cup of hot drink and walked back to the two sisters who spoke quietly in puffs of frosty breath.

Offering the cup, he sat down. "Victoria, do you remember when you decided to extend an invitation for our visit?"

She's looked up remorsefully. "I know what you're thinking. Why did you ever come to our lodge? It's the Hudson's fault. Well, you're right of course, but how could we have foreseen such a tragedy?"

"No, it's not to cast blame that I ask," he reassured. "Our abduction was clearly no accident. Someone chose us and carefully planned this remote captivity. Does Richard have any enemies who might have done this?"

"Richard is not a person of great wealth," she responded defensively. "There are some in Halifax who think we are intruders, competing for timber and milling work on the Saint John."

"What about his politics? Does he support popular causes?"

Victoria tightened her grip on the wagon frame. "Richard is sympathetic to the plight of the Acadians. A few have been invited to the house for meals, but their presence didn't sit well with the townspeople of Newcastle. Acadians are regarded as second-class citizens."

William frowned. "Were there any visitors at the lodge just

before our arrival?"

Victoria furled a brow.

"We did have a problem a few months back. An Acadian named Joseph came to the lodge one evening. We'd just sat down for dinner, when a woman was announced at the front door. After being shown to our table, she flew into a rage upon seeing Joseph and demanded he be removed. Can you imagine? A stranger comes to your home and tells you to evict a guest. Richard slammed the door on her. When we finished dinner, I saw her outside talking to our stable hand, Peter, but later he said that she was just asking directions to Halifax."

"Do remember her name?"

"Yes, I believe the servant announced her as Miss Canerci."

William paused. "And the invitation for our visit, was it a sudden impulse?"

Her eyes narrowed. "Oh no, Richard had wanted you to come for months, as did I. But we agreed to get settled so we'd have freedom to spend the summer with you. It took two years for his business to permit time to enjoy this holiday."

She blinked back tears. "Now, it's all come to heartbreak."

"William, what did the guard say?" Emily interrupted.

"He says we're to be marooned on an island 'til spring. They must want us out of the way without intending a permanent disposition. I suspect it may be a plan to get ransom for our release."

The women gasped.

"My God, won't this create an international incident?" Emily objected. "Parliament will never tolerate such outrageous behavior within the colonies!"

Victoria scratched her head. "What about your aunt, Lady Carlisle? Can she raise the money?"

"Hah!" William laughed. "She'll tell the kidnappers to take a flying leap, and expect us to get out of this mess ourselves."

Victoria frowned. "But wait, there would be no fuss if William withdrew his own money from the bank."

"Fat chance," William said with a scowl.

"Those questions the kidnappers asked," she persisted. "They could have been posed to establish a false identity."

He swallowed slowly, gazing off at the trees.

"Between Charles and myself, I suppose fifty thousand pounds might be extracted from our accounts at the Bank of England. Sir Cosgrove would never permit such a withdrawal unless he was absolutely certain of its legitimacy. It's unthinkable they could pull it off without the family."

Emily's expression changed to worry. "It's difficult to imagine strangers could carry out such a deed unless there were a person with intimate knowledge of our background. Who here, so far from home, possesses such knowledge?"

Silence fell over them.

"So, you think Richard's escape was a ruse?" Victoria woodenly voiced. "His invitation was a ploy to steal your money?"

The next morning, the small caravan broke camp in darkness.

Days were never very bright this time of year, especially on forested pathways. A Cree Indian of the *Chisasibi* tribe joined them as they made their way south. He brought news of a disturbance at Fort Chambly. A patrol of ten soldiers was observed riding in their direction, and the tribesman advised to keep well east of the river until they reached Lake Champlain.

On the following day, they sighted the northeast shore. A vast expanse of calm water mirrored an irregular coast of pine trees giving way to a distant featureless horizon to the south. William reached down to touch icy cold water lapping softly over coarse black pebbles on the embankment. In dismay, he turned his head away from the women to hide his anguish at their fate.

Their escorts retrieved three birch canoes within a nearby cluster of bushes. A pile of heavy clothing was also cached in the brush, and the hostages gratefully wrapped themselves in beaver lined coats before settling into the boats. Within minutes, the craft headed out into the water, with one prisoner in each canoe.

William peered out of his beaver hood. Emily and Victoria resembled furry animals sitting in two boats slicing through the water ahead of him. There was little opportunity to overpower his two oarsmen, and escape was impossible with the women separated from each other and himself. He leaned back, searching the heavens for an answer. Overhead, formations of geese glided southward. Not even wildlife looked forward to the approaching winter.

After two hours of paddling, a small group of islands came into view. Closer inspection revealed three landmasses, nothing more than windswept rock.

William stared in shock. "Where's the cabin? How can we last on such exposed terrain?"

The man in front of him snickered. "You might get lucky. Some years the lake freezes almost to the islands."

The canoes beached on the largest outcrop. William climbed out to join the others already surveying the isle. No trees or bushes grew on a barren surface that stretched one hundred yards long by thirty yards wide. He could see no material for building a fire or constructing a raft. The only shelter was a shallow cave within an outcropping of irregular boulders at one end of the landform. Three bundles of food were stacked inside. William bit his lip; the supplies might last a week, maybe two. *They had to get off this rock, but how?* Swimming in the frigid lake was unthinkable—even if the ladies were not terrified of the water. A boat was the only way, but the captors returned to their canoes without so much as a wave goodbye.

William and the two women gazed forlornly at the disappearing craft. He could still hear the men laughing at his complaint the supplies would not last until spring. He kicked the rigid ground and sadly looked at his charges. They knew there was little hope. Drawing a deep breath, he set his teeth. He would not give up.

When night fell, the three castaways crouched together within the tiny cave measuring four feet deep below an overhang. Gusts of wind blew with increasing intensity, scattering tiny ice particles at their backs.

"How could Richard do this to us!" Victoria lamented.

"Maybe he intended better accommodations on another island," William offered. "For all we know, those blackguards decided on their own to make sure we'd never survive to testify against them."

"I never thought, I'd long for the comfort of those wagons," Emily remarked. "We've got to find a way out of here before we freeze to death."

Victoria turned to her brother-in-law. "I'm so sorry for all this, William. At least we can take some comfort that Elizabeth avoided this misery. She's safe at the Lodge."

William smiled appreciatively. "It's not your fault. I imagine this will be one Christmas we will want to forget. Do you remember the year our tree fell over in the great room…"

Conversation ran to stories of more pleasant times. They did not hear sounds of gunfire from a distant shore, nor the woodsmen's cries as Fort Chambly's cavalry shot their abductors.

Three days ensued fraught with wind and sleet. The hostages made only brief excursions away from their meager shelter. Biting gales stung their faces, even beaver fur could not keep out bone-chilling cold. Half the food supply was already gone. William found a fishing line within the packages, but after a few fruitless attempts, he gave up. Without fodder to produce a fire, they could not cook the fish and, more importantly, it appeared they would freeze to death before starving.

"I have to try and swim to shore. There's no other way," he announced. "Once on land, I can build a raft and come back for the two of you."

Emily's brow furrowed. "I know you're an excellent swimmer, William, but five minutes in that icy water would kill you."

Victoria brightened. "Maybe we can fashion lightweight boots and mittens from the arms of our beaver coats and tie them with the fishing line. Only your face would be exposed to the water, but you can turn over now and then."

On the first clear morning, William trundled down a steep rocky incline to the water's edge with a promise to return the following day. The costume resembled a sea lion out of its element. He hugged his sisters-in-law. They smiled reassuringly, trying to hide their apprehension; failure to reach the mainland would mean certain death for them as well.

William paddled into the water, setting his sight towards a rising sun.

Cold water felt like a slap in the face.

He thrashed at the surface, which kept his body warm inside the bulky clothes, but it was difficult to get into a smooth rhythm. He fought to stay afloat—and tried not to think of the miles ahead.

For awhile, exertion was manageable, He barely paid attention to the icy liquid. Gradually, clammy dampness penetrated the fabric and his body succumbed to a growing chill.

An hour's effort reduced the islands to tiny specks, but did not enlarge the shoreline trees. He was tiring. The watery quest separated him from all land. Numbness overtook his body, and more effort was required to complete each stroke.

He turned over to float on his back. The icy chill permeated his muscles to the bone. With strength sapped, he decided to spend ten minutes resting in a motionless position.

Loss of feeling in both arms and legs was a dangerous sign that his body temperature had dropped to a critical level. Mittened hands trembled in an uncontrollable shiver. His breathing rasped shallower with rising panic.

"What was I thinking? Those bastards knew there was no way off the island!" he shouted at a pale blue sky.

Rage built within him. He steeled himself against the chill.

Resolutely, he turned over and began pulling his arms once more, determined to fight to the end. In his hasty effort, the crude hand covers tore away from the fishing line ties and bared his hands. He felt nothing. He was going to beat those villains—or die in the process.

Another hour crept past. Irregular spikes of distant trees edged closer on the horizon. He wasted no time celebrating.

All at once, numbed hands scraped mud. Murky water masked the lake bottom only three feet below. William dragged his frigid body to a standing position.

Shore was still three hundred feet away. He opened his mouth to cry elation, but his vocal chords refused to produce sound.

Moments later, the Englishman collapsed onto a rocky beach, drained of will and the strength to move further. He lay face down, trembling violently. Frosty breath came in hoarse gasps, drawing air into frozen lungs.

Suddenly, a hand tangled itself in his hair and jerked his head upward.

His frightened gaze met the dark glaring eyes of four Indians.

They yanked him to his feet. Long, black hair framed their chiseled faces—faces painted with yellow markings. The savages pointed their knives. A shove from behind sent William sprawling to the ground again. The tribesmen kicked dirt in his face before they grabbed and tied his lifeless hands. A second rope was attached to his wrists and they pulled him to his feet. A sharp tug on the leash led him off into the woods.

Hours of forced marching ended in a clearing.

A long, bark-covered hut stood in the middle. The crude structure measured forty feet long and twenty feet wide. Inside, two rows of straw mats extended to its far end, where a middle-aged native sat cross-legged. He wore a dark suit and top hat, presenting a curious picture of an Indian pretending to be a white man. Long gray hair draped his shoulders, and a wrinkled left hand gripped a smoking pipe while staring at an open book held in the other.

He looked up as the braves entered with their captive. They all spoke rapidly in grunts and cackles.

Finally, the old Indian's attention fell on William. "To whom am I addressing?"

The white man could not control his rage.

"Look here, I'm William Darmon, an English citizen with ties to His Majesty's government. I've urgent business to attend to and cannot tolerate any delay!"

The brave puffed away, unperturbed.

"Perhaps you should have chosen not to trespass on land belonging to the Six Nations of the Iroquois. Your predicament is unfortunate; my braves would kill you if not for my leadership. I try to avoid unnecessary bloodshed that might bring soldiers after our little band."

"Well then, release me, and we shall have no further need for discussion."

The old man puffed again on his pipe. "In time we may do so, but I require a service. Have you heard of the Indian Removal Act?"

William shook his head.

"It is the white man's law to displace my people whenever he decides more land is required to satisfy your greedy population. My brother, Joseph, has been taken from his birthplace and placed under custody in a town you call Rochester. In seven sunsets, he will be carried west by boat and I shall never see him again."

He drew on the pipe once more. "As Indians, we are powerless to stop this process. But you, as a white man of some influence, may be able to help."

William regarded the other man warily for a moment. "Just how far away is this town of Rochester?"

The old Indian smiled. "I will send three of my braves to guide you to the edge of town. You should return with Joseph before ten sunrises."

William's mouth dropped in disbelief. "Ten days! I've a life and death matter to attend to by tomorrow!"

"This too, is a life or death matter," the Indian replied coldly. "If you do not return with my brother, my braves will kill you. The only way to ensure your life is to accomplish the undertaking as quickly as possible."

Four days' scrambling through woods and fields brought William to the town of Rochester. He gave a silent prayer of thanks to once more be among familiar elements of civilization. Streets crowded with pedestrians, horsemen and wagons made the frontier a distant memory, but hardly a moment passed when William did not think of Emily and Victoria, waiting for his return.

After some inquiry, he learned that a group of Indians were being held in a courtyard behind the Hotel Genessee awaiting transport on the Great Lakes aboard the *Exodus*. A local militia set up camp to ensure these particular 'troublemakers' were safely transferred to the packet-boat the following morning. They would then be transported to a military outpost at the western edge of Lake Superior. Icing and bad weather made this voyage the last for several months.

William passed through the marble entrance of a three-story, brick courthouse and crossed the foyer to present himself to a clerk seated behind a long counter.

He informed the Englishman that a local judge sentenced the Indians for removal, and therefore it would be up to William to obtain a court order for the transfer of Joseph into his custody.

William sighed. "Can you direct me to the judge responsible for objectionable Indian transports?"

The attendant's eyes gave him in a brief inspection before returning to his work. "That would be Judge Mallory in Room 2E. Upstairs, three doors down the hallway."

William found a door on the second floor with *2E* painted on an inset window made of translucent beaded glass. He knocked softly and entered the chamber.

A large desk occupied most of the room, with only a narrow space for visitors. Behind the workbench, a balding man of fifty sat writing in a leather-bound volume. He glanced up through thick glasses to view the visitor's entrance.

"Judge Mallory, I'm William Darmon, recently of Kent. I have an unusual request on behalf of an acquaintance at Oxford; a professor of Indian cultures. He wishes to interview an Indian of the Mohawk tribe, preferably an elderly man with some history. I've learned that the Indian Removal Act permits one to take custody of such an individual. I've also heard that some are in captivity here in Rochester awaiting transport."

The judge leaned back from his paperwork and scrutinized William closely.

"Yes, it's true there's a small group of indigents awaiting relocation, but their crimes would hardly make them suitable for custody by a gentleman such as yourself."

He opened a drawer and retrieved several loose pages that he plopped on the desk in front of him. Licking a thumb, he leafed through the pile until the last sheet was scanned.

"None of these men fit your description," the judge announced. "The only elderly brave died of dysentery three days ago. His name was Joseph."

Color drained from William's face. *How will the old Indian react to this news?*

He was suddenly fearful of the braves awaiting his return outside of town. Now, he had to think of a way to avoid being taken back to their chief. His only chance was to secure a fast horse and outdistance the savages, who were on foot.

William left the building. His attention was drawn to a crowd shouting bids to an auctioneer down the street. Farm implements, wagons, and livestock were assembled in front of a livery stable. Unfortunately, the kidnappers had taken his papers and money, so there was no point in trying to buy a mount. He circled around to an alleyway located in back, next to a fenced area stocked with animals.

Walking quietly to the gate, the Englishman went inside and untied a rope attached to the bridle of the first horse he came across. He boldly led the steed out into the alleyway, pulled himself up onto its bare back, and trotted off to the next corner without looking back.

In ten minutes, he was at the outskirts of town and galloping well south of the spot where he was to rejoin his escorts.

William completed a two hundred-mile journey to Burlington three days later. His only difficulty came in crossing the Hudson River south of Lake Champlain. The fast moving body of water required considerable detour as well as trust in his horse's prowess to step over a rocky bottom within rapid current.

In Burlington, William used the horse as collateral to borrow a boat and by mid-afternoon, he had paddled out onto the lake. The trick was to find the right island. Fortunately, early December frosts had not yet frozen much of the lake, and two hour's plying oar had him well on his way to his abandoned sisters.

At last, dark outlines of three islands rose ahead of his craft. With only an hour of daylight remaining, William eagerly pulled the oars to his destination. The hour was not of concern since he planned to make the return trip under cover of darkness to avoid detection by the Indians.

Nine days after his fateful swim, William ran the boat up onto a small rocky beach. He jumped to the ground.

"Emily! Victoria!"

William ran to the cave.

He stopped dead. It was empty. Bundles of food remained just as they were when he left—enough for another week's survival.

He turned on booted heel, left the cave and climbed the boulders to survey the other islands. They, too, appeared deserted. His anxious gaze examined the ground for tracks, but the rock was too firm to show any markings.

Chest heaving with exertion, he ran back to inspect the cave's walls for any sign; perhaps some hastily scratched message the women left to tell him what happened.

He found nothing. Not a trace of their existence. *Did they try to swim on their own?*

A chilling thought flitted about the edges of his mind; the Indians may have come to the island while he was in Rochester. His shoulders sank in dread as he gazed at the distant shore.

William shook his fist with futile anger at the land around him, and slumped to the earth inside the cave.

They had vanished, perhaps to become victims of a hideous fate devised by the aborigines. In gathering darkness, he was suddenly overcome by a feeling of loss. He had to return to Burlington and organize a search party, yet he could not make himself leave the place where they were last together.

Chapter Nine

The old woman stirred. She moaned softly without opening her eyes.

Elizabeth dozed in a chair she had pulled up to one side of the bed. Instantly, she awoke. She leaned over and grabbed the woman's bony shoulders.

"Wake up! Wake up, you!"

Aged eyes opened without comprehension. They began to focus on Elizabeth. Pupils expanded, then darted back and forth searching the room.

Elizabeth brought her face to six inches from the woman and spoke deliberately. "Who are you? Who's paying to have me watched?"

The crinkled face etched with fright. Her fingers twitched, but the hands remained stationary. Lips parted slightly, but no sound came out. Her mouth widened to form a single word, barely above a whisper. "Darmon"

Watching the ashen features, Elizabeth grew certain the poor lady had suffered a stroke, leaving her nearly paralyzed. Regardless, she needed more information.

"Where's Madam Darmon? Where were you to meet for payment?"

Again, eyes bounced from side to side. Beads of perspiration dotted the old woman's upper lip and forehead. Each breath produced a rasping echo deep within her chest.

Elizabeth reached into her pocket and held out a gold coin. The woman's eyes stopped. Her lips quivered once more, whispering an inaudible message. Elizabeth bent closer. Her ear touched the crone's mouth.

"*Hotel de Palais.*"

Elizabeth straightened. She paused momentarily at the edge of the bed, regarding the pathetic form.

Pallid limbs poked out of rumpled rags streaked with brown and black soot. Aged hollow cheeks and flaccid skin made it appear as if she were starving to death. *How long since she had a hot meal?*

Elizabeth tucked the coin inside the lady's pocket and stepped out the door. Before leaving the hotel, she informed the clerk on the *rez de chaussee* that a visitor in her room required medical attention.

"I'm sorry," the uniformed *Hotel de Palais* attendant reported. "Madam Darmon checked out of the hotel yesterday. I guess all the fuss the day before caused her to seek less eventful accommodations."

"What do you mean?" Elizabeth asked.

The clerk shrugged. "A fugitive was arrested on the premises."

"A fugitive?" Elizabeth asked.

"Yes. The police caught a trapper who'd broken into Fort Chambly and killed some soldiers. You never know what's going to come out of the woods these days."

She absently agreed. "Did Madam Darmon leave a forwarding address?"

The silver-haired employee brushed a speck of lint from his lavender sleeve. "I did overhear one of her companions mention entertaining visitors at an abandoned house on *Rue Grand Allee.*"

Elizabeth flinched at the memory of her captivity. She thanked the man with a sigh of resignation and turned to begin the long traverse once more.

An hour's stroll during a cold, blustery afternoon brought her to the path in front of the familiar residence.

She rubbed her arms with apprehension surveying the darkened dwelling. Above boarded lower windows, she spotted an uncovered casement over the doorway. An eyebrow shot up. She had not noticed the second floor when she made her hasty escape. A steep pitched slate roof with three gabled openings indicated still another level further up. There was more to this house than she thought.

The door stood ajar.

Has no one returned since my escape?

Cautiously, she stepped to the entrance, wary of making a sound that might alert any occupants.

Inside, the dimly-lit hall appeared as she remembered. With trepidation, she eased through the doorway and tip-toed over to the parlor archway. Peering around the edge, her eyes fell on an empty, dusty interior. Stillness brought goose bumps to her flesh, but it should mean that she was alone.

After the parlor, quiet footsteps took her down the hall.

Sudden scurrying noises made her heart stop. Clatter disappeared. Too small a sound to be human, an animal must have found its way into the house.

In the kitchen, the sight of two rats gnawing on rotting food pieces confirmed her fear. She backed out, fraught with a new anxiety.

Elizabeth climbed exceptionally creaky stairs and found herself within another musty hallway—one that extended to the room with the open window she saw from outside. Inside, a small canvas cot, free of dust stood in the middle of the chamber, but no other sign of habitation was present.

As she left the room, she remembered the gables and began looking for a hatchway overhead.

At the far end of the corridor, near the stairway, a small metal loop hung unobtrusively from the ceiling. She retrieved a pole with a hook from an adjacent linen closet and, with a tug on the ring, caused folded steps to drop from the opening.

Carefully, Elizabeth mounted the passageway up into the attic.

Three gabled windows on both sides of the roofline provided light within a dusty, sloping enclosure. A small writing desk stood next to one of the windows. She walked softly over to it and sat on the bare wooden chair. The desktop held an oil lamp and flint. She lit the former and began exploring its compartments.

Under the writing board, several hand-written papers lay, all in French. She spent a few minutes translating a portion of the top document, which turned out to be an essay on the right of humanity to the freedoms enjoyed by French and American citizens.

Underneath it was a paper with a list of fifty names.

Several other scraps of paper occupied the enclosed space,

including a receipt scrawled on pink paper for fifty pounds of gunpowder, signed by one Charles Cazeau. The dusty documents made her palms itch. She sneezed, scattering a cloud of dust motes that twinkled in light streaming from the window.

At the bottom of the pile, lay a tightly folded four-inch square of thin parchment. A single word was written on the outside: '*Hudson*'.

She carefully unfolded the sheet, which grew into a twenty-inch square map of the region south of Montreal. In the middle of the page, she discerned an outline of Lake Champlain with a small cross, midway between its shores.

Elizabeth frowned. Richard never mentioned owning property in the middle of the Lake. It might be a clue to where her family was being held.

A loud crash below interrupted her thoughts.

She identified it a split-second later as a slamming of the front door.

Men's voices filtered up. Several sets of booted feet began rapidly ascending the stairs. She gasped. Her panicky eyes settled on the oil lamp. Its glow must have alerted them to her presence. Her carelessness had trapped her.

A deep voice bellowed beneath the opening. "*Qui est ici?* Who's there?"

Elizabeth snatched up the lamp and ran to the hatchway.

A bulky individual brandishing an evil grin on his upturned face stepped onto the unfolded ladder.

She hurled the flaming lamp down at him.

Glass shattered, splattering oil over his body, engulfing him in flash of fire. He screamed and tumbled backward onto his companion.

Elizabeth yanked the rope and pulled the attached steps up into the opening at her feet. She ran to the nearest window, released the latch, but it refused to budge. No matter how hard she tried, it would not budge more than two inches above the sill.

"Lady, come down here, now!" a harsh voice penetrated from below.

It would be only a matter of seconds before they found the pole and reopened the door. She rushed to the next window, but it refused to open at all.

Elizabeth charged over to the desk. Grasping the chair, she lugged it over to the first window and rammed its two legs into the small opening under the casement. She then threw herself on top of the projecting chair back. The frame lifted a little more than a foot above the sill before her chair clattered to the floor.

Attic steps crashed down behind her.

Elizabeth squeezed through the small opening.

Three feet below, at the base of slanting shingles, a narrow ledge bordered the roofline. She reached down and took hold of the shelf, pulling her legs through the window as thuds echoed inside the room. She tumbled downward, her fingers gripping the ridge in a frantic hold as her legs fell over the edge.

Precariously, she hung twenty feet above the ground underneath.

Smoke began to fill the stone house. Heat from the ever-increasing flames reached out through the second floor window sending hot air blasting at her arms.

One of the men stuck his head out the attic opening. *"Ici! Elle est ici!"*

He lunged toward her, but she managed to edge away from the window. He tried to squeeze through the portal. Another shout came from behind him. *"Le feu! Le feu! Venez! Venez!"*

The man disappeared inside.

Elizabeth clung desperately to the ledge.

Suddenly, the second story window exploded, showering her with shards of glass.

Her grip let go. She plummeted feet first and hit dirt with jarring abruptness before falling forward onto her palms.

She pushed herself to her feet. In terror, she felt no pain from her limbs as she plunged down the path, racing toward *Rue Grand Allee*.

Elizabeth ran down the causeway.

A half-mile down the road, two men on horseback approached.

She waved frantically, but they galloped past taking no notice, their attention drawn to rising smoke behind her. Elizabeth hurried on.

She reached city streets and slowed, ignoring increasing stabs of pain from her legs. Limping to her hotel, she desperately focused thought on securing passage to Montreal and on to Lake Champlain.

Two days later, Elizabeth gingerly made her way down to the waterfront.

She hired a local boatman named Marcque, and soon the pair was paddling on the Saint Lawrence in a birch bark canoe. They passed the prison at *Trois Rivieres*, where she observed construction of a gallows underway. They pushed on, further west to the Richelieu River outflow at William-Henry, a settlement named for the Duke of Gloucester who visited the area in 1787.

Once on the Richelieu, the canoe turned south, passing ten miles east of Montreal heading towards the American states. Rapids forced them to carry their craft overland for a mile, but once past the town of Chambly, the remaining twenty miles to Lake Champlain was negotiated on water.

At last, the boat made its way out onto the Lake's placid surface. Behind, shoreline receded from view and with it, the last vestiges of British North America. They now straddled the border between the states of New York and Vermont.

"Marcque, can you get us to the location of this cross on the map?" Elizabeth asked.

He nodded. "*Oui,* it's a large lake, but I know the islands."

"I think my family may be stranded there."

"*Mon Dieu*! Why would they go to such a place?"

She frowned. "I don't know. Someone may have wanted them out of the way."

"It's unthinkable. Even with food and drink, there is no protection from wind and snow. Most of the smaller isles are completely barren," he observed.

Elizabeth's brow creased with worry. "I just hope William is looking after my sisters."

In late afternoon, three islands expanded into view.

Cold air turned every spoken word to a foggy mist. The boat closed in on the middle rock. Elizabeth spotted two figures waving frantically.

She could not restrain herself. "Emily! Victoria!"

She jumped to her feet. Marcque immediately stopped paddling and lunged to steady their vessel.

A few minutes later, three women embraced in a bevy of tears. It was a long time before anyone could manage coherent speech. Finally, they sat on the rocks and began to share their experiences, which made their time apart melt away.

Elizabeth was relieved to hear of William's escape, but horrified that Charles might be dead. Her news, however, hit them hard.

Victoria wiped tears rolling down her cheeks. "Richard is dead and the lodge burnt down?" she repeated in disbelief.

Emily hugged her sister. "No matter what happens, we'll always be a family."

Victoria stood with new resolve. "We must go back and try to make some sense out of this. William said Richard might have been behind the whole thing."

Emily turned to her other sister. "Elizabeth, how did you ever find us?"

"Believe it or not, some woman has been impersonating me. I managed to track her to a house near Quebec City. I found this map with Richard's name on it. You can see the cross mark indicates this island."

Emily's mouth dropped. "It confirms he planned the abduction!"

Elizabeth nodded. "It would seem so."

She looked at her sister with sympathy. "Victoria, was Richard in the habit of going to Quebec?"

Victoria turned her stained face to her older sister. "He made two trips earlier this year. The last one, a month before your arrival."

She burst into tears once more. "It doesn't make sense! Why would he destroy everything we worked for and bring tragedy down on everyone?"

Emily gazed out at the glassy water.

"Perhaps he only intended we be detained here for a short while. Shooting Charles would not have been part of his plan. There are other forces at work here. William said he heard Richard arguing with our captors before he escaped,"

She looked at Elizabeth. "This woman impersonating you may be behind it. Richard probably got caught up in the scheme and it cost him his life."

Emily hugged Victoria. "And we've both lost our husbands."

Elizabeth frowned. "One of the notes with the map was an essay on the right of French Canadians to be free of British rule. The Constable of Newcastle said many *Quebecois* support a group calling themselves the *Patriote Party,* which advocates revolution."

Her gaze, too, strayed to the water. Suddenly, several tiny, dark specks appeared on the southern horizon.

She called to the boatman in the canoe. "Marcque, what are those objects over there?"

He lifted his arms above his head in a leisurely stretch, and then he squinted in the direction she pointed. The dots quickly became five separate craft, heading directly at their island.

"Indians!" he shouted. "They must have seen our crossing. Get in the boat! Maybe we can lose them behind these rocks."

Three women clamored to the water, while Marcque steadied the canoe as they crowded on board causing the boat to sink lower as he strained to get underway.

Elizabeth raised herself up at the bow holding the second oar to paddle in step with his efforts at the stern. Emily and Victoria splashed with their hands at mid-ship. They managed to maneuver the vessel around the island behind a cluster of boulders.

A moment later, a distant report was followed by pieces of outcropping splattering alongside the boat. The women screamed. Elizabeth glanced over her sisters crouching low and clinging to one each other.

A canoe had arrived at their land mass. The craft held three Indians and another individual wearing a tall hat, reloading a musket.

The savages beached their canoe and began searching the island on foot.

Elizabeth glanced at Marcque, who gestured to paddle *away* from the island.

They rowed furiously, paying no attention to their pursuit. A stiff breeze blew in their faces and the water became increasingly choppy. The boat pitched forward and back, splashing its' occupants with icy water, making it nearly impossible to get up speed.

After ten minutes fighting the onslaught, Victoria shouted. "Here they come!"

Elizabeth glanced over her shoulder. A canoe rode the waves not more than thirty feet behind them. Four oarsman paddled furiously, gaining on their prey every second. As the boat closed toward her right side, she saw two of the tribesmen slip knives between their teeth, preparing to jump.

The Indian's craft splashed to within three feet when a sudden swell lifted their bow completely out of the water. Marcque reacted quickly, back-paddling to turn their canoe over onto the other.

The impact capsized the savage's boat, and four braves spilled into the icy lake.

One of the Indians lunged at the side of their canoe as he fell overboard, but Elizabeth hit his arm with the paddle until he fell back.

Marcque steadied their craft, and the two boats drifted apart. The braves swam to their overturned craft and attempted to right it, but the churning water made the task difficult. Within moments, two more boats arrived to perform a rescue.

Elizabeth watched with a satisfaction as their canoe gained a lead of several hundred feet. The pursuing boats were lower in the water with the weight of extra bodies and the separation continued to grow.

"With luck, we'll reach the Richelieu before they can catch up!" Elizabeth yelled back to her sisters.

"Once we're in sight of Fort Chambly, they'll have no chance," Marcque shouted.

Elizabeth could see relief on her siblings' faces.

The Indians dropped further and further behind and, by the time they reached the river, their pursuers had disappeared from sight.

Emily trembled with exhaustion. "Will we ever get out of this God-forsaken territory? Savages, kidnappers, desolation, I can no longer endure the torment. Will we ever find our way home?"

"Well, answers aren't going to fall from the sky," Elizabeth rejoined.

Victoria scowled. "Emily is entitled to her fears, Lizzy. We narrowly missed being killed by those renegades. We're hundreds of miles from Humphrey's Valley, which, according to you, no longer holds a refuge and the first snows of winter aren't far off."

Elizabeth's chest heaved in a sigh.

"At least we're safe. Emily, it's hard for all of us. I guess I take some satisfaction that I came all this way and found you. I also know there's an evil woman back in Quebec who is bent on taking away my birthright. She may think she's won, but I'm not ready to give up."

She slammed the oar on the side of the canoe with such force that Marcque jerked around. "Good Lord, woman! I thought someone shot us!"

The Englishwoman smiled sheepishly. He nodded and returned to paddling.

Elizabeth leaned toward her sisters. "I want to return to the Lake with men from the fort and find out what happened to William. There has to be a reason why he never came back for you."

Emily looked horrified. "You can't mean that! We just barely got away. Let the soldiers conduct a search, but we don't belong out there. It's too dangerous. You've gone daft!"

Victoria frowned. "Maybe we shouldn't all go…."

Emily's jaw set. "You'll never get me on that lake again! If you feel you must, I'll remain at the fort. I'm not taking any more chances."

Their reception at Fort Chambly was less than amiable.

Marcque remained outside the Commandant's quarters while the ladies reported their abduction and abandonment on the Island. Elizabeth's pleas to track down the tribesmen and search for William were met with little enthusiasm.

The officer wrung his hands.

"Madam, you English people have no business running around the countryside, demanding we exterminate your enemies. Less than a month ago, one of your countrymen insisted we bring justice to some bullies who attacked him. It turned out his friends were waiting outside and during the night, he let them into the Fort. They killed four of my men. "Meanwhile, our patrol shot five *innocent* suspects, thinking this man told the truth. Your countryman later insisted he was simply bamboozled, taken in by some misguided trappers…"

"An Englishman?" Emily interrupted. "Who was he?"

"Ha!" he laughed. "I'm surprised there's anyone in the Province who hasn't heard his name. He calls himself Charles Bagwell. A more sinister scoundrel you'd never want to meet. A magistrate sentenced him to hang at *Trois Rivieres*."

Emily shrieked and slipped from her chair in a dead faint.

The Commandant sent a soldier for water, while Elizabeth and Victoria dropped to their knees, waving hands above her face in an attempt to revive her.

"She's not been well," Victoria observed. "The ordeal we've just been through must be taking its toll. When will this man be executed?"

"On the 16th, six days from now," the Commandant replied slowly, his puzzled expression quickly gave way to sympathy. "See here. I'll send a patrol back to the lake for you, but if they don't find your man within three days they'll have to return."

"Victoria, I intend to accompany the patrol," Elizabeth whispered as the two women settled Emily's limp body into a chair.

"I must be there if they find William. It's been three months since I've seen him. You and Emily go back to *Trois Rivieres* with Marcque. He may know a way into the prison. If you can find some means to get Charles out, return to Newcastle; all of Quebec will be alerted to an escape."

Emily opened her eyes and took a sip of water.

After a few minutes, a shaky nod indicated she was well. The sisters helped her to her feet. They thanked the Commandant for his assistance, and a guard was summoned to escort them to their quarters.

During the night, it rained and freezing temperatures turned the downpour into sleet, which confined them to the fort another two days. Emily was beside herself with worry and threatened to go on to the prison by herself if the weather did not let up.

On the third day, Emily, Victoria and Marcque left the compound, ostensibly to visit the town of Chambly. Elizabeth rode out with the patrol, making its way on horseback back to Lake Champlain.

Once they were back on the Richelieu, Emily and Victoria broke the news to Marcque. Their guide was horrified at the suggestion of facing a garrison at *Trois Rivieres.*

"*Mais, c'est impossible de la faire!*" He shook his head. "We cannot simply walk into the prison and take this man. I don't care how quickly we act. Guards will shoot us if we do anything the least bit suspicious."

Emily could not hide her frustration. "What are we to do, just let him die?"

"I'll put you ashore outside the compound and wait down river," the Frenchman offered. "They'll be less concerned with two women visitors."

Emily smiled, setting her teeth with determination to somehow stop Charles' execution—whatever the cost.

Despite new frozen hazards within the river, the trio reached the Saint Lawrence on the morning of the hanging.

Their boat glided to a settlement a mile up river from the prison.

As they neared land, Emily noticed a large number of soldiers milling about the shoreline conversing with clusters of townspeople, while others boarded boats anchored in the harbor. Still other militia marched in regimental fashion through the streets.

Marcque steered the canoe onto a narrow beach, instructed the sisters to wait, and quickly walked off toward the village. Within a few minutes, he disappeared into the melee.

"I pray we're not too late," Emily uttered softly, her brow creased with worry, while she wrung hands in her lap.

Victoria reached over and patted her sister's hand. "Me, too."

Emily's gaze returned to hundreds of uniformed men who wandered within the crowd. "I wonder if they assemble these soldiers as a precaution."

Marcque barreled back to the boat ten minutes later.

He held his sides, speaking breathlessly. "You won't believe what's happened! Your husband has escaped!"

Emily sprung to her feet nearly tipping over the canoe. "What? I don't believe it!"

He grinned. "It's true. Two prison guards are also missing, including the one who had keys to his cell. Sentries were found in a drugged sleep when the hangman's escort arrived to take Charles to the gallows. The Commandant is outraged. He faces great humiliation if the prisoner isn't found quickly."

Victoria frowned. "But, who…?"

Marcque's expression turned grim. "The missing guards are English. It's rumored the act may be a loyalist plot in service to the British Parliament. It's unthinkable."

Emily could not contain her elation. "My countrymen have come to his rescue! Charles is safe at last!"

"Why do you say it's unthinkable?" Victoria asked.

"It's more reason for antagonism between French Canadians and the English. This is a slap in the face for our justice system. It says Englishmen are above the law in Lower Canada. People like Papineau will insist on retribution for an outrageous intrusion."

Emily's elated expression turned to disdain. "I care not about politics. My husband is free."

Victoria looked askance at her sister. "Is there any hope of finding Charles before the authorities hunt him down?"

The man scratched his chin thoughtfully.

"Well, if the loyalists have him, they'll leave the Province as soon as possible. They could leave Canada altogether and head out to sea. But, if there's another purpose behind his rescue, they might be moving in any direction, possibly further inland, even to Upper Canada. That would give us more chance to catch up."

"What shall we do?" Victoria asked.

Their guide shrugged. "I suggest we make for Quebec Harbor to see what ships are about to depart."

Chapter Ten

William could hardly restrain his emotion when he entered Humphrey's Valley. His broad Germanic face expanded into an uncontrollable smile. It seemed like a lifetime since his family enjoyed their reunion at Hudson's Lodge.

Upon leaving the island in Lake Champlain, he spent a day of futility searching for Emily and Victoria along shore. Wary of tribesmen, he dared not venture inland, but saw no sign of them from his canoe. He decided to return to Elizabeth at the Lodge. They could come back to the lake together and bring help.

In Burlington, he reclaimed his spotted mare and secured supplies for the two hundred mile journey to Humphrey's Valley. The following morning, he left town on a muddy road heading northeast.

He picked his way through the countryside beneath gray skies of winter-shortened days and freezing rain, which forced him under a tree-covered shelter the day before his arrival at Hudson's Lodge.

With his mission nearly complete, the anticipated meeting with his wife created impatient fervor as the weather began to clear.

Billowing clouds scattered through a powder blue sky above the valley, now sparsely dotted with tawny colored grass. Withered trees held dark, barren branches, dripping yesterday's moisture onto puddles scattered over the soggy ground.

The weary Englishman urged his mount up a final rise leading to the rim surrounding the basin. His climb was painfully slow. Every now and then, the animal slipped attempting to cross ruts in the muddy path, and William frantically clutched the reins.

Near the top of the ridge, tiny black particles blew among tall, bending reeds. His horse cleared the final turn and William pulled back on the halter. His eyes widened in disbelief. A mass of charred spikes stood in place of the once secure country home.

"Elizabeth!" he cried out. "Elizabeth!"

William leaped from the horse and ran to the pile of blackened timbers. *What happened?* He gulped at a thought that the fiends behind the kidnapping had made certain the annihilation of his family was complete. He flung soot-covered boards in all directions and, only after tiring, reason returned. *There are other explanations*, his mind insisted. *An accident or a lightening strike...*

William's distraught gaze scanned the terrain. Even the stable had been razed. The destruction left pieces of charred pottery and twisted metal melted from the intense heat wedged within wooden fragments.

He stepped over ash-laden logs to where the kitchen once stood. A fallen beam rested on top of the large cook stove, sitting against what was left of the chimney. The upper floor had collapsed onto the main living area before fire consumed it.

A few hours of poking around blackened William's hands and pants, but he found no trace of Elizabeth nor the servants. Dusk was approaching. He counted on finding shelter at the lodge. It was doubtful he could find any place else to sleep before dark, so he set out to create a temporary refuge amid the cinders. He cleared a space in the kitchen under a cluster of fallen girders and searched the wreckage for clean pieces to make a crude door.

In Richard's former study, he picked up a few boards less damaged. An end of one piece caught on some fabric beneath, and William yanked it free. A tattered rug pulled away, revealing the corner of a trap door. Intrigued, he set down the boards and cleared remaining debris before returning to the kitchen in search of something to pry open the hatch. He found a bent serving knife and, returning to the study. After working a few moments, he pulled the door upright, revealing a wooden ladder that descended into darkness below.

The cellar was pitch black.

Ten steps down the makeshift stairway, his head bumped a hanging lamp. It swung back and forth emitting eerie squeaks in the darkness. He reached bottom and took two paces before stumbling against a table. Its contents clattered onto the stone floor. Slowly, he dropped to his knees and blindly felt for the objects until his hand closed around a flint. A moment later, dim, but steady lamp light lit the musty interior.

The room extended thirty feet by ten feet with walls constructed of rough-hewn logs. Besides the table and two small chairs, the basement held wooden boxes lining both sides of enclosure. Each container measured one-foot across and five feet long. Using his sturdy knife, he pried one open and whistled surprise. The crate held six brand new muskets, neatly stacked three across and two deep. He opened other boxes and discovered similar contents. Given the number of containers, he estimated that one hundred-eighty rifles were stored below.

His eyes swept the room once more. This time they settled on small black barrels of gunpowder and sacks of musket balls piled to the ceiling at the rear of the space. Adjacent, three long, gray rolls of paper, stood on end, each tied with a thin cord.

He brought the coiled scrolls back to the table and unrolled large maps under light from the flickering lamp. The first one presented the entire eastern half of the Canadian Territory, all the way south into American territory. Peering closely, William spotted tiny 'x' marks just south of the Saint Lawrence. They stretched from a settlement named Cleveland, south of Lake Erie; past Lake Ontario and up to the state of Maine. Under the marks, he found numbers. In New Brunswick, Hudson's Lodge was labeled *#1*. The last was designated *#27*.

An owl screeched in the distance, reminding him of fast-approaching night. He needed to shelter his horse before darkness. With a grunt, the Englishman climbed out of the cellar and proceeded to lead the animal inside enclosure he built in the kitchen.

As he walked back toward his new haven beneath the floor, he paused to gaze over the valley into cold, foreboding darkness. No sign of life showed below. Once again, a feeling of loneliness overwhelmed him. The multitude of stars between parting clouds emphasized how small he felt on this part of the planet, a wilderness nearly barren of civilization.

A heavy sigh lifted William's shoulders.

He froze. A glimmer of light flickered among the trees miles across the valley floor. The flame blinked out, came on again, and sputtered back and forth as if someone carried a lamp through the woods passing behind tree trunks that interrupted the flow of light. A cold shiver raced down his spine. *Who is out there?*

The light abruptly went out. After several minutes of impatience, William steadied himself and returned to the cellar.

Inside, he securely closed the trap door.

Spine-tingling cold permeated the underground fortress, but, because of the gunpowder, he dared not start a fire. His fur-lined pelisse and leather, beaver pelt insulated boots kept the discomfort tolerable, yet William slept fitfully while the wind howled outside.

Disturbing dreams taunted him. He was back in Kent, returning home from a long journey. His manor lay deserted. Elizabeth and the servants had disappeared. He rushed to the nearby town of Langdon, but streets there were also empty. His desperate eyes searched storefronts, but none of the townspeople were to be seen. The entire community was abandoned.

William awakened in a cold sweat. It was pitch black in the cellar. He lay motionless not wanting to move a muscle. In the silence, he could hear blood pulsing inside his ears. The frigid air felt completely still except for long breaths heaving into the quiet.

A thump on the trap door caused him to jump. His heart pounded wildly in his chest.

Another bang resonated.

"Who's there?" he croaked, praying it was just the wind blowing something on top of the lid.

Another thud echoed overhead.

He bounded to his feet and paused. *Surely a friend would answer my call.*

The banging stopped.

William waited for an eternity. *Do I dare look outside? At least I'm safe locked in here until morning.*

He returned to his bed atop a musket case, but sleep would not come. He lit the lamp and loaded a musket. Propping himself against the wall he aimed his rifle at the hatch and extinguished the lamp. He waited.

Thoughts turned to the guns. *Had Richard stored them here for hunting parties?* The map suggested this cellar was one of a series of outposts. Twenty-seven lodges, times one hundred eighty guns meant over 4000 weapons stockpiled along the American border. Were they leftovers from the war, armaments strategically deposited by the Americans to protect themselves against a British invasion from the north?

William shook his head. Hudson's Lodge was only two years old.

The next morning, William pushed open the trap door to an opaque world of white. Snow blanketed everything, and an overcast sky warned more could be on the way. His horse survived the night and William gratefully fed it the last of his rations, despite a gnawing ache within his stomach.

He retrieved gunpowder, musket balls and his rifle from the stockpile below.

Eagerly, he mounted the steed and began a descent into the valley confident that breakfast would not be hard to find. Besides a passion for hunting, he was glad to be free of Hudson's lodge--a place that had caused him both heartache and confusion.

Three hours roaming the valley floor netted two pheasants. He started a small fire under the gentle shower of snowflakes. The task of plucking and dressing game with a pocketknife might have been distasteful under more prodigious circumstances, but he was grateful to have the means to satisfy his hunger.

He settled onto a nearby rock, watching the birds sizzle on a crude skewer held over the fire. Flames crackled and the meat steamed making his stomach growl with anticipation. Suddenly, the ground shook beneath him, followed by a distant crack of thunder.

His horse whinnied nervously twenty feet away.

William scanned the cloud formations, thinking another storm was might be bearing down on him. An eye caught movement on the horizon. Just above the valley rim, debris roiled within a rising dark cloud. It came from the direction of the lodge. Smoke billowed upward as the pieces thinned and dispersed.

An explosion at Hudson's Lodge.

It did not take a military genius to realize that Richard's stockpile of guns and gunpowder had just blown up. A shiver coursed through William's back. He could have been inside. But what set it off? He had not left the lamp burning in the cellar. Did the kidnappers follow him there during the night? Was someone was trying to kill him?

Charles awoke to his last day on earth. Glazed eyes moved to two uniformed men standing solemnly outside his cell, then slipped to the tiny barred window where he watched the hangman's preparations over the past few days. A faint light of pre-dawn cast weak shadows into his sparse surroundings.

He jumped when one of the guards rattled a key in door and gestured for him to begin his final walk to the scaffold.

Fear roiled in his stomach, and yet he was strangely resigned to the fact his life would soon be over. He rose from the small cot, took a final glance of farewell at the room that caused him so much despair over the past weeks and left the cell. The first guard abruptly turned away while the other fell in behind Charles. They began a slow death march down the empty hallway in eerie solitude.

At the far end above the stairway, another soldier sat on a wooden chair propped against the wall, his head tipped forward in sleep.

The trio descended two flights of stairs in silence before entering a large room cluttered with tables and chairs. Each of its four walls held a door leading outside. The area was deserted save for a single guard at the far door.

The procession moved toward him. He saluted and opened the door.

The three stepped out into cold, damp morning air. They paused for a moment, facing a fifty-foot walkway leading to a gate at the East end of the compound. The scaffolding was nowhere in sight. Charles turned to question one of the guards, but words never left his mouth. Instead, the officers pushed him down the path. As he stumbled up to the fence, a fourth sentry unlocked the gate and opened it just wide enough for a man to pass through. Needing no further encouragement, Charles quickly slid outside. He stopped. Before him, two individuals stood dressed in black cloaks and top hats. Behind them, a carriage waited.

The taller of the two pointed to the vehicle. "Inside, quickly!"

Charles did as instructed. Within seconds, the hansom charged off along a narrow road paralleling the prison wall. The condemned prisoner held his breath. Surely, he would awake any moment and the dream would end.

The carriage wound its way inland between grassy knolls, farther and farther from the river and the village was left behind. Charles' hands shook uncontrollably, his body trembled with relief and words would not come. He stared at the two individuals who saved his life, but they paid him no attention, each staring out opposite windows.

An hour passed. Charles' curiosity grew by leaps and bounds. Finally, he could not hold his tongue. "See here, I'm forever in your debt, but I must know to whom my gratitude is owed for this rescue."

The man next to him, elegantly dressed in a gray vest under a heavy woolen coat with matching gloves and leather boots, turned with a smile. "All in good time, Mr. Bagwell. All in good time."

The narrow-faced stranger looked to be in his twenties with long hair combed neatly behind the top hat and a thin mustache giving a dapper appearance. This well-met appearance combined with posh, red velvet upholstery of the carriage, suggested an expensive operation, not a spur of the moment act by defiant townspeople.

The other gentleman sitting across from him appeared considerably older, portly with receding hairline and sagging jowls. He coughed frequently into a crumpled handkerchief. A rumpled shirt and creased waistcoat visible through the parted cloak, gave a less formidable impression. In his right hand, he held a pistol, resting on his lap.

The older man regarded Charles, swaying with impacts of the fast, bumpy ride. His lined features and confident eyes emanated a quiet command. "Speak only when spoken to. No unnecessary conversation."

Their carriage raced on for four hours before finally stopping at a small cabin in heavily wooded hills. The three individuals had barely stepped out to the ground when an elderly man came from the dwelling with a bundle of clothing and a sack of food. Charles was directed to change his clothes. By the time he complied, a different carriage emerged from behind the cabin. They quickly scrambled inside.

Night was spent in another cabin on an isolated hilltop. A damp, fireless room and threadbare blanket made sleep difficult. Just when slumber finally came, Charles was shaken awake, and another eight hours of travel ensued.

In mid-afternoon, the carriage entered a small village and stopped in front of an ivy-covered, grey stone cottage. A smartly dressed woman warmly greeted Charles' two escorts and gave the escaped convict a nod with sympathy-filled eyes. She showed them to a well-furnished parlor. Charles was permitted to take a bath and put on fresh clothing before rejoining the others.

His two guards peered out the two dormer windows, looking anxiously up and down the avenue. Charles eased his tired, aching body into a leather winged-back chair and surveyed the room. Three tawny overstuffed chairs faced a small fireplace under an ornate mirror, and several still-life paintings hung on cornflower blue walls. A large oval rug with a blue and yellow flower pattern covered the dark floorboards.

Charles' revere disappeared at the sounds of a carriage drawing up in front of the house. The two men hunched as one toward the window. Over their shoulders, Charles discerned forms of two men exiting the hansom. Moments later, their hostess escorted the arrivals into the parlor.

The first gentleman presented an imposing figure at least six feet four inches tall, large in both height and girth. Charles observed thick forearms carelessly discarding a brown cloak, hat and gloves. Long, curly blond hair tumbled down to his shoulders, a bushy mustache punctuated his ruddy complexion and pale blue eyes looked at him intensely over a jutting chin. He moved with casual athleticism, ready to counter any challenge.

The second individual sharply contrasted with his companion. A foot shorter, displaying fine bone structure and wire-rimmed glasses, he carefully removed his own outer garments and laid them atop their hostess' already heavy burden.

The taller of the two men turned to Charles with a deep resonant voice. "Mr. Bagwell, I'm happy to see that you've safely left confinement at Trois Rivieres. Allow me to introduce myself. I'm Lord Ian Stewart, Aide to Lord Howich, Minister of War and Member of the Executive Council to Lieutenant Governor Aylmer. This is my secretary, Hume Reynolds."

Charles stood and bowed, though his brow furrowed in bewilderment.

"These two gentlemen are in my employ," Lord Steward continued, nodding to the guards. "I trust the escape went without incident?"

Charles responded shakily. "I'd given up hope. I am grateful to you, sir, but do not understand why you chose to help me. Am I now to be a hunted man who may yet perish in this God-forsaken place?"

Stewart waved for all to sit and did the same. "Yes, it seems you've gotten yourself into a nasty situation, but I believe we may yet rectify matters, if you're worthy of our trust."

Charles' eyes narrowed with suspicion. "What must I do?"

"There's a woman—I believe you know her as Elizabeth Darmon —who leads a faction of French separatists belonging to the newly formed *Patriote Party.*"

Charles shifted uncomfortably. "I'm not a political reformist! What makes you think I'd have anything to do with such a group?"

"Come now, Mr. Bagwell. You were with her when you were arrested, and testified at your trial that you visited with her prior to your accident," the aide admonished.

He shook his head adamantly. "She said she intended to infiltrate the radical group. I helped her track down the woman who is really in charge, and we altered her appearance. You're mistaken on one other point. Elizabeth Darmon is not the leader."

Lord Stewart stared at Charles for a long moment. "I fear that you've been misled, Mr. Bagwell. This person who calls herself Elizabeth Darmon is in truth, Catherine Cazeau, daughter of Jean Cazeau. She is attempting to organize a demonstration in Lower Canada. Her followers advocate violence, and they are enlisting the aide of Americans to bolster their insurrection. The Executive Council has been most vocal in opposing these Reformers. I fear they will be their next target."

The large man leaned forward to emphasize his concern. "Our

foreign office has requested we thwart her plan without offending the French populace. Most local citizens are farmers and merchants who have little or no political interest and many in government are happy with the status quo. However, these young activists continually send lists of grievances to Parliament, and now, they control the Assembly. Support grows each day. This *Patriote* faction may cause enough dissatisfaction to create a full-fledged rebellion. We cannot permit that to happen."

"So, why don't you just have her arrested or send men to subdue her?" Charles asked.

Stewart's gaze moved to the window as he considered his answer. "We have no proof of her crimes and she has powerful friends, such as Cuvillier. We must fully understand her intention before we act. If she is removed now, it would foil our plan to instigate another means of stopping these fanatics."

A cold tingle raced down Charles spine. "Another means?"

Ian settled back. "Yes. We have an idea—an idea that concerns you, Mr. Bagwell. Since you're now a fugitive, your sympathy for the rebel's cause would not be questioned. There is to be a meeting of the *Patriotes* and other reformers within the week. Whether this Elizabeth Darmon is an infiltrator or a leader no longer matters. Either way, we'd like you to be in attendance at that meeting as a trusted aide. If the demonstration is imminent, you must inform us at once."

"But how will I find her? She's been missing since my arrest!" Charles objected with a frown.

Lord Stewart smiled slightly. "The woman whom you know as Elizabeth Darmon has returned to her residence at the Palace Hotel. One of my men will accompany you to a street nearby."

"And what if she considers my presence a danger to their operation?"

The aide shook his head. "You must do what you can to make yourself useful. If you are successful in this endeavor, the governor's gratitude could earn you a pardon. If you do not prevail, it will be up to you to decide whether Parliament or the French Canadians present the greater peril."

Chapter Eleven

The words of a young Frenchman echoed off marble walls. "How much longer shall *Canadiens* chafe under the yoke of British tyranny?"

The speaker paused as if expecting an answer and scanned upturned faces of fifty agitated listeners. A predominantly French Canadian audience comprised of legislators, clergymen and merchants did not have to be reminded of their status as 'second class' citizens. Already, muffled discussions spread as if a wildfire had been started.

"Quiet! Let's hear the man out," someone yelled.

The orator's voice grew louder. "Yet another list of resolutions is being prepared for the English Parliament, repeating the 1827 denouncement of abuses. Year after year, they send us new governors and Executive Councils deaf to the pleas of the *Quebecois*, insisting on outrageous subsidies for a Civil List while governing without consent of the Assembly. What good does it do to prepare lists of protest?"

"Qui! C'est vrai!" resonated on his left.

"Down with the *vaurien*!" came another voice from the back of the sanctuary.

He waited behind the raised dais for outcries to subside.

"Everywhere, we face threats to our way of life. There isn't enough arable land in the seigneuries, yet thousands of new immigrants make their way into the Colony every year. They take our land, disrespect our religion, and bring cholera to our doorstep."

A chorus of affirmations sprouted within the audience.

The leader mopped his brow with a white handkerchief. "Upper Canada turns its back on us, seeking instead free American imports and leave our *habitants* unprotected. They receive tariffs from Quebec Port, while behind our back, they implore London to create a single

Canada with English control of its legislature. English merchants create banks for their own commerce, but ignore the needs of the *Canadien."*

Applause broke out. Sounds of approval increased with every phrase.

His voice rose in pitch. "The Council blocks our proposals. We cannot create new laws. Are we to remain powerless under the Englishman's boot?"

Charles sat at the back of the room. Lady Darmon confided that the speaker, Assemblyman Louis Hiolyte intended to arouse the conspirators beyond their usual discontent. Ultimately, his goal was to persuade the gathering to demand a new course of action. At that point, the *Patriotes* would be ready to present their plan. Timing would be critical if they were to gain unanimous support for their intrepid suggestion.

Charles glanced at the woman next to him out of the corner of his eye, wondering if her name was really Elizabeth. Maybe the truth lay in the fact that Mrs. Darmon had been so successful at infiltrating the group that she actually became their leader. Her speech in the tavern clearly expressed sympathy for the *Quebecois*, but support for the cause of French Canadian autonomy proved nothing.

When he arrived at her doorstep, he had no trouble gaining her favor. In fact, she seemed overjoyed to see him, remorsefully admitting it was Jacques who alerted the authorities without her consent. Charles felt at ease in her presence despite Ian's warning of her other identity. English or French, it was obvious she was not an outsider to the assembly. Several onlookers addressed her as *notre dirigeante*—our leader.

They arrived at the *Chapelle des Jesuites* at *20 rue Dauphine* at 8:00 PM. The chapel provided a natural forum for Reformers to address their religious constituency, and it was certain to be free of English interlopers. Charles marveled at the hundred year old architecture. Flickering light from numerous candles cast shadows dancing above a delicately carved altar and numerous statues of French and Canadian Martyrs interspersed between arched stained glass windows.

Bundled participants huddled together on fifteen rows of bare pews in an effort to warm themselves against near freezing temperature inside the hall. Hiolyte spoke with clouded breath to a forest of opaque puffs rising over the onlookers. He talked entirely in French, but Charles understood most of the message—and the rising number of spectator comments.

"…Therefore, I demand, for the benefit of future generations, that we make a statement for the sanctity of a French Canada, self-governed with equitable rights and a good living for all its citizens. We must act on behalf of our downtrodden brothers to reclaim our birthright and give Quebec a proper place of influence in today's world!"

Applause reverberated loudly and shouts of support echoed above the din.

Hiolyte smiled; his speech produced the desired fervor. He waited for the noise to die down. "Now, permit me to introduce Medard Gery. He will describe a proposal for action."

A slender individual with graying hair rose stiffly from the first pew and marched up to the podium. He nodded briefly to the speaker and took his position behind the dais.

"My friends, we have the choice of doing nothing or making our protests known in a way that Parliament cannot ignore. Presuming you are in favor of the latter, I submit to you a bold strategy for demonstration against our oppressors."

All eyes riveted on the speaker. The aging gentleman's eyes glowed with passion for the cause that would challenge the participants.

"Two months hence, Governor Aylmer is to make a symbolic speech at Montmagny Manor in Fort Saint Louis on the two-hundredth anniversary of the death of Champlain. As you may recall, the manor once served as the residence for governors of New France during the early sixteen hundreds. On the day of his speech, *Patriotes* will march on both Quebec and Montreal. Our objective will be to raze the governor's building, seek out members of his Executive Council and put them to death."

A collective gasp rose from the audience. Heads quickly turned to fellow members with looks of disbelief.

Gery hurried on to reassure the more conservative participants.

"Let me assure you, this action will not be regarded as the work of a few fanatics. Through the efforts of *notre dirigeante* and her people, thousands of sympathizers across the border stand ready to join our march to freedom. At the scheduled time, word will be sent to American outposts to assemble their supporters. *Patriotes* from Maine to Lake Erie will make their way to the cities and merge with our people to liberate the province once and for all!"

A voice from the third row objected. "But won't there be reprisals from His Majesty? Surely the Americans do not want to risk another war with Great Britain."

"Our brothers to the south are dedicated to the principles of freedom," Gery spoke evenly. "These men have been carefully chosen, and they will act whether or not President Jackson supports our intentions."

"What about Parliament? This is an act of treason. They will send troops and take away what little freedom we have left."

Murmurs reinforced the concern, but the speaker smiled, prepared for the reaction. "England is in the throes of an economic recession. King George IV has lost control of foreign policy. The last thing the monarchy can afford is another war; the army is nearly bankrupt. Clearly, the easiest course is for the legislators to sit down with us and accede to our demands."

Shouts of encouragement gave voice to mounting enthusiasm and grumbling was put aside. Excitement grew for a show of power. They were going to make history for the Colony. When all was said and done, English Parliament would never again ignore their pleas.

"I would like to invite our Madam Leader to come forward and give a timetable for the coming events," Gery concluded.

Several members looked over their shoulders at Lady Darmon seated in the last pew. She acknowledged their glances, lips pursed with determination. Before standing, she turned to Charles.

"Charles, I'd like you to go to America and alert proprietors of our outposts. They, in turn, will inform locals who've agreed to organize assembly of their forces. Frances will give you a map and arrange supplies for the journey."

Charles mouth dropped. "I thought you were working undercover to stop this radical organization," he hissed.

She hesitated, looking into his eyes with fierce resolve. "We'll talk later. You know I believe in this cause. You are a fugitive of an arrogant justice system that is intent upon your hanging. Our only hope is to stop the English from further exploitation of the Provinces."

"But what about William and Richard's kidnapping and this other woman we apprehended?" he whispered.

"I told you, she is Madam Cazeau. She convinced the *Patriotes* the kidnapping was a way to raise money for weapons. In the process, she killed Richard Hudson, one of our trusted contacts. Now she's disappeared and, I hope, left Quebec for good."

Charles scratched his head, uncertainly.

"So, are you with us?" she asked.

He could not back out. Both sides wanted him to play along. "I'm with you."

"Good. At each outpost, identify yourself as Richard Hudson, delivering a message for freedom. It's a name they know and it will confirm the truth of the information. Begin the process in New Brunswick. Go to the town of Petit Sault and find a man called Samuel Jesterman who lives on Main Street. Deliver the call to assemble and tell him of the destruction of Hudson's Lodge. He will know what to do."

Charles rubbed his chin, thinking of all the days of travel lying ahead. "I hope I'm not arrested along the way."

She raised an eyebrow. "This could be the most important mission of your life. The future of New Canada depends on it. Just think of the gratitude our new government will bestow upon you. Your past crimes would certainly be forgiven."

There it was: both sides offering exoneration for his crime. As tempting as it was to rectify Canadian injustice, Charles could not hold with wanton murder of the governor and his cabinet. Despite his death sentence handed down by a British tribunal, he felt more disposed toward helping foil the plan. He would inform Lord Stewart of these developments at their appointed rendezvous two day's hence.

Their meeting took place in a small tavern on *Rue Saint Pierre* near the docks. Charles was due to depart for Petit Sault within the hour by *bateaux*, a flat-bottomed riverboat with a crew of five servicing ports along the Saint Lawrence. A horse with supplies would be waiting ashore thirty miles from where he was to make his first contact for the *Patriotes*.

Charles had no trouble recognizing Stewart's man seated at a corner table. They spoke softly of the planned insurrection and Charles' role as bell weather.

"It sounds like an army of sympathizers is already out there intent on storming Quebec City and bringing down the Provincial government," Charles confided.

The agent drew closer, talking barely above a whisper. "Yes, we must do everything we can to delay this demonstration. We have informants at a few of the sites, but there's only one way to slow down their preparations. You must take action at every opportunity."

"What? How?"

"Our agents tell us each outpost contains a storeroom with enough gunpowder to blow them to kingdom come. Once they think you're on their side, find an excuse to sneak into their stockpiles, set a fuse, and be off to the next location," Stewart's man suggested with a satisfied smile.

Charles cast a worried glance toward the window. "I don't know..."

The agent reached across the table and gripped Charles' arm. "Don't be concerned. Once you pick up our spies, they'll help you with the detonations."

"But how will they know me? They'll think I'm Richard Hudson," the Englishman objected.

The agent leaned even closer and spoke directly into Charles' ear. "We have a code phrase known only to Lord Stewart's men. Use it to identify yourself when others cannot hear your words." He glanced quickly to both sides then muttered softly. *"Keep to the green."*

He settled back in his seat. His eyes suddenly darted to the window. The agent abruptly stood up. "Good luck to you. There's more at stake here than you can imagine."

Charles watched him walk to the entrance and step outside. Through windows on each side of the door, two figures appeared from opposite directions. Jacques and Frances drew up next to the agent and escorted him out of view.

Charles leaped to his feet and ran to the door just in time to see the trio turn into an alley. He stood in the doorway for precious seconds, hesitant to expose himself to the Frenchmen, since he had just met with the agent. Anxiously, he waited for them to return, but no one emerged from the alley.

Cautiously, he started down the walk. At the end of an adjacent storefront, he peered around the rough brick edge. The lane appeared deserted. Only discarded crates and barrels of refuse stood behind the buildings for five blocks. He stiffened when his eye caught sight of a boot sticking out from under some cartons fifty feet into the passageway.

Charles crept to the boxes. Warily, he lifted wooden containers atop the prone form and uncovered a lifeless stare of Stewart's agent. A bloody knife protruded from his chest. Charles staggered backward, choking bile that rose in his throat. The shaken man leaned against the opposite wall, gaping at the corpse through unbelieving eyes. *What am I going to do?*

He squinted once more down the alley. The two Frenchmen were nowhere in sight.

A shiver ran up his spine after realizing he might have been followed to the rendezvous. If Jacques and Frances suspected his duplicity, they might be at the dock to waylay his departure. And, if they related their suspicions to Lady Darmon, he would be better off going to America to proceed with the plan. Running away would only prove his allegiance to the British with no one left to stop the uprising since Stewart had not yet received his report. At least, if Charles could find one of the informants, he could send word back.

One thing remained certain; now, he was on his own.

Elizabeth looked at her surroundings in dismay. Snow covered all trace of the road and a mantled countryside offered no clue to the direction of Newcastle. Dreary skies sent flurries of snow particles that clouded her vision. Under better circumstance, the gentle settling of snowflakes might be admired as a peaceful cloaking of nature's terrain, but the air stung her face and bones ached from rawness. Her horse's constant snorting broke the stillness. The animal's hooves disappeared under two feet of white powder while it stepped laboriously on the commanded courses. She could not go much further.

Three weeks earlier, soldiers at Fort Chambly escorted her to Burlington, the only settlement of any size on Lake Champlain. It seemed reasonable to conclude William had passed through the town seeking supplies.

After a day of questioning a population of Irish immigrants, she found a liveryman who remembered loaning a boat to a tall Englishman. Upon his return the next day, he requested a horse for a trip to Humphrey's Valley.

Elizabeth faced the choice of who to follow. Emily and Victoria would not be easy to catch, especially if they were fleeing authorities. The alternative to pursue William, meant a long journey over soggy winter roads back to the lodge—and who knew where he would go once he found only ashes at the site.

At the livery, Elizabeth hired a wagon and the services of a young man who would accompany her on the two-week trip. The livery owner cautioned that weather was bound to turn bad within a few weeks. He also warned of highwaymen, Indians and impassable roads.

The trip began well enough. Robert, her guide, proved knowledgeable and pleasant. At eighteen, he expressed aspirations of attending the University of Montreal to become a doctor. He also demonstrated invaluable knowledge of the countryside, having made the trip from Burlington to Newcastle many times to visit an aunt. "We should take the north road and pick up the trunk route to Quebec City. Once south of the Saint Lawrence, we'll head east and follow the shore to Montmagny."

Their buckboard moved swiftly, passing farmers in rickety wagons and single riders who plodded along the wide dirt thoroughfare. The twice-weekly Montreal-Quebec coach passed them in full gallop, forcing their vehicle into a deep ditch.

"I'm surprised at all this traffic," Elizabeth remarked while Robert worked to free the conveyance.

A short time later, having left the trunk line behind, the causeway narrowed. A rutted, rocky path slowed their progress even more and it began to rain. They forged on, twenty miles short of the settlement at Montmagny. Elizabeth would not seek shelter, determined to complete the journey before winter storms prevented reaching their destination.

Before long, the wagon wheels sank into mud nearly a foot deep. Robert was forced to steer into grassy areas, where they could move under cover of tree limbs out of the rain. Unfortunately, a rear wheel caught the root of a spruce tree and broke into pieces. The collision sent them both tumbling to the ground.

After Robert struggled to his feet and helped Elizabeth up, he unhitched the horse from the useless conveyance and they climbed onto the animal's back. In freezing rain, they doggedly continued over flooded earth between tall, dripping trees. Rain torrents became so violent the horse could move no faster than a walking pace. Elizabeth clung to the boy with her face buried in his sopping shirt. It was hard to imagine a more miserable place.

Twenty miles North of Petit Sault, their horse stepped awkwardly over a branch and slid across the surface of a flat rock, coming up lame. They walked the remaining distance in six hours under the cloak of the drenching cloudburst, leading the injured horse.

At last, two bedraggled travelers staggered into the lobby of a Petit Sault hotel. Warming fire from the ground floor fireplace welcomed them, but Robert could not stop shaking, his lips purple and face ashen. A woman at the front desk called her husband to help carry the lad upstairs and she sent for a doctor.

By midnight, Robert's icy cold became a devastating fever.

In early morning, he died.

During the trip, Elizabeth learned the young man had a history of pneumonia as a child and continued to be susceptible to its recurrence. A mortician promised to send word to his family in Burlington when weather permitted.

Rain subsided the next day. Elizabeth joined the hotel manager and his wife for dinner at a small cafe across the street.

"Sad business that," the hotel proprietor lamented. "It is always a shame when a young man dies before he can fulfill his dreams. It's just a waste of a good life.'

Elizabeth nodded, looking at a muddy thoroughfare outside. "Do you think the weather will stay clear for a while?"

"A few days, perhaps, I give it three or four until the first snow hits."

She turned to him with a raised eyebrow. "That soon? How can you be so certain?"

He smiled. "It's time for a change. Once freezing rain starts, ground stays wet and cold. Mark my words, the next storm will make heavy snow."

"Do you think I can make it to Newcastle by then?"

His wife frowned. "You're not thinking of going on by yourself. A woman in this country can easily become lost or fall prey to all sorts of harm."

Elizabeth sighed, undeterred. "I spent the past summer in Humphrey's Valley and made the trip to Petit Sault several times. I know the way. It's not even one hundred miles."

The proprietor looked at her disapprovingly. "More like one-fifty. Suit yourself. I'm sure Brewster over at the livery can find you a better horse than the nag you led into town."

Convinced she could make it to the Lodge within two days, Elizabeth decided it was best to press on as fast as she could through Humphrey's Valley. If she found no sign of William, she would continue on another day's ride to the coast. Perhaps the Constable of Newcastle would know his location and have news of the kidnappers.

The following morning, Elizabeth said good-bye to Petit Sault. The path to the south was pleasant enough, but the soft ground made it difficult to hurry her horse along. Despite urgings, the animal leisurely sloshed its way between puddles and ruts. The first day passed quickly under a high overcast sky. At nightfall a tired Elizabeth tied her mount to a tree in a small clearing. She shook her head disappointingly, having covered only twenty miles.

After spreading out her bedroll on damp ground, she made a small fire. Cheered by its warmth, she settled in for the night. Air felt uncomfortably cold, however, and wind sailing through the trees reminded her of the hotel owner's prediction of impending snowfall. She drifted into restless sleep.

Morning found her damp and stiff in the cold. She felt worse realizing the sun was well up and she had wasted good travel time. Her horse stood patiently a short distance away, expelling fine mists from its nostrils. Elizabeth repacked her bedroll and munched on an apple. Once more, she started off on a day spent maneuvering through brush on foothills of the Appalachian Mountains.

An hour after sunset on the third day, Elizabeth spotted the familiar rim of Humphrey's Valley in fading light. Unfortunately, her horse stood on the far side of the valley, a considerable distance away from the Lodge. A feeling came over her making it impossible to resist the temptation to complete the remaining distance despite approaching darkness.

Swatting branches that frequently assaulted her within gloomy woods, she stopped and tied twigs together to fashion a crude torch. The makeshift lantern did not last long, but it did see her safely to grasslands beyond the forest and into natural light under a starry sky.

In the dark, Elizabeth found no evidence of William's presence on the lodge property. She called to no avail. Blackened spikes of wreckage stood silently in the chilly night, much as they did when she first searched the area with the constable. Above, clouds moved in, wind was picking up, and the temperature rapidly dropped. She had to seek shelter in the protection of the valley below.

By the time she reached a cove of trees on the valley floor, snow particles drifted around her. The storm she feared bore down on Humphrey's Valley. Huddled against the base of a tree, she wrapped herself in her bedroll to wait out the night.

Turning back toward Newcastle, Elizabeth was dismayed at how quickly fresh powder covered the horse's tracks. Swirls of endless white dots settled on her clothes, and the damp scarf wrapped tightly over her mouth felt like an encrusted frozen mass of ice. Panic rose within her. She could not shake the feeling of being buried inside a frigid, white grave. *Why was it so hard to find the way back to Newcastle?*

True, she had made the trip during a rainy night, but there had been a trail for the horse to follow. Now, it vanished under a blanket of white and the surroundings all looked the same. She was lost. At this point, she doubted if she could find the way back to Humphrey's Valley.

Her only recourse was to find shelter and wait out the storm. Hopelessness washed over her as she attempted another direction through a growing wall of white that closed in around her.

Chapter Twelve

It had been a very good year for Carleton St. Clair.

As owner of the *Wild Stag* Inn, he benefited from burgeoning use of the Quebec City to Boston Road. The busy thoroughfare wound its way along the Chaudiere River and came within five hundred yards of his tavern. Not much further away, the Montreal to Halifax route was a favorite of mail carriers who frequently diverted a half-mile to seek a good meal at his widely known place of business. Despite mid-winter, two coaches a week found their way to his doorstep, thanks to engineering efforts of the Canadian military who kept roads passable all the way to the Vermont border.

Despite his good fortune, Carleton was aware construction had begun on a new form of transportation, the railway, which might ultimately cost him his livelihood. Many of his customers predicted that within two years, the *St. Lawrence and Atlantic Company* would carry most travelers between Montreal and Portland on tracks many miles from his establishment.

For now, however, he smiled contently at a profitable year and winter's respite from demands on his staff.

The Inn was built in 1801 to house a wealthy fur trader no longer interested in foraging the wilds of western America. During the war of 1812, British troops spent time at the residence and the business of serving passersby became a flourishing enterprise. A 'Wild Stag' theme arose from the many trophies provided by patrons as well as the owner's talents. Hunting proved bountiful in the territory and remained a key to surviving the severe winters. Durable goods could be secured from the nearest town, *Sherbrooke*, twenty miles to the north.

Carleton leaned against his long counter, surveying the communal room with its large windows facing the distant snow-covered road. Outside, a gray day's howling wind buffeted glass panes, but within the chamber, an energetic fire crackled at the hearth of a massive stone fireplace. Six tables stood unoccupied now that winter kept all but the bravest adventurers from his door in stark contrast to summer time, when fifteen employees furnished room and board to a steady flow of tourists. By November, the workforce dwindled to five. He would not let the staff size drop below this level in case the day arrived when a call came from allies to the North.

Carleton was not a politician, yet he maintained a strong conviction for personal freedom. The loss of an uncle during the war reinforced a dislike for what he perceived as British exploitation of the provinces. Sympathy for the French Canadian increased with each letter from his sister in Montreal, describing worsening economic conditions and lack of an effective government. Consequently, when Richard Hudson visited his tavern with an offer of payment for gun storage, he smiled warmly at the proposal. Within a few weeks, his basement transformed itself into an armory and monthly meetings began taking place at the Inn among discontents on both sides of the border. Rousing sessions often ran into late hours with *Quebecois* remaining the night upstairs in his twelve rooms.

Popularity of the French separatist cause ebbed and flowed with opinions expressed in Parliament. At present, a lack of activity came from several factors: a new governor offered potential for change, Assemblies of city governments were now dominated by Reformers, and new resolutions crossed the Atlantic in hope of attention. Despite mounting frustration, meetings of malcontents had not been held at the Inn for nearly a year. Nevertheless, Carleton kept vigilant for another visit that would alert his community of sympathizers to begin a march to Quebec.

Suddenly, the door flew open, interrupting the proprietor's revere.

A tall individual bundled in heavy clothes tumbled inside amid a cold blast of air which ruffled red-checkered tablecloths and shrank the cheery fire. For a moment, the mummified figure stood brushing snow from his long woolen coat that cascaded into a pile of white clumps below. At last, he unwrapped a chocolate colored scarf from his grizzled face.

"Pardon me, is this a hunting lodge?"

Carleton frowned at the English accent. "Welcome to the Wild Stag Inn, sir. We serve all manner of traveler's needs. However, hunting parties are usually a summer activity."

The ruddy-cheeked visitor relaxed a bit and hung his hat and coat on a carved wooden clothes rack near the fireplace. "I apologize for bursting in like this. I've just ridden in from Humphrey's Valley."

The bartender slowly nodded, not about to turn away business. "What brings you all this way in the snow?"

"Name's Richard Hudson. I run a lodge over there. We had a fire not long ago and lost most everything. I'm looking to move on for better prospects," he responded without turning from the coat tree.

Once unburdened, he strolled over to the counter and slumped onto a barstool. "May I have a pint?"

Carleton stiffened at the name. "I just sent my man, Peter to retrieve a new keg. If you'll wait a moment, I'll check on his progress."

Carleton looked thoughtful when he returned. "He'll be here momentarily. So, Mr. Hudson, you say you're out in this frigid weather trying to find a new place?"

"Yes, I've visited several lodges. I'm prepared to make a handsome offer if the property feels right," the gentleman replied with a wink.

The proprietor rubbed his chin. "Well, I've been thinking the time might be right to retire. What sort of offer would you be willing to make?"

His patron stood up and drifted over to a window, glancing out at the grounds. "If you don't mind, I'd like to take a look at your rooms and inspect your stock of hunting equipment."

Carleton bent over behind the counter. "Let me get my keys. So, what happened at the lodge? Is Victoria alright?"

The visitor's head snapped around.

A kitchen door burst open. Four men rushed at the startled guest, grabbing his shoulders and pulling him to the counter.

"I'm acquainted with Mr. Hudson," Carleton snarled, pointing a pistol at the man's chest. "Who are you?"

The struggling captive glared back. "William Darmon, Richard Hudson is my brother-in-law. My family shared accommodations at his lodge until a gang of ruffians kidnapped us. When I returned, the house lay in ruins. I discovered your tavern on a map in the basement."

"So, why did you pretend to be Hudson?" the bartender sneered.

William shifted uncomfortably. "The map indicated a series of outposts along the border. It appeared that Richard was tied in with some kind of fortification against our Provinces. I thought I could bluff my way in here and get some answers."

Carleton scowled at his captive. "Well, Mr. Darmon, you're on American soil now. I don't think it's any business of an English tourist what goes on in our country. We're no longer your colony and we have laws against trespassing."

"See here, I'm only trying to find a reason for my family's loss," William protested.

"I think you're a British spy!" the owner retorted. "When this weather lets up, I'm going to send a man over to the Hudson place and check out your story."

"Wait a minute, I've broken no law," William shot back. "You can't hold me. I'm a citizen of the Crown."

"Take him to the cellar and lock him up. Unless, Mr. Darmon or whoever you are, you prefer to be shot right here and now!"

William struggled to no avail. They shoved him downstairs into a dark storage room. The staff returned to their duties, leaving Carleton to decide what to do with the intruder. Instead, he prepared a small lunch and fell asleep at a table by the window.

Once again, the front door flew open, jarring Carleton from his nap. A gust of wind propelled another individual inside. This one was slighter in build and strained to close the door's handle against the tempest. He lumbered over to the fireplace, removed his gloves and stretched fingers toward the flames before unbuckling the rest of his outdoor wear.

He turned to Carleton with a congenial smile. "Hello. Is the proprietor about?"

Carleton rose with a look of irritation. "I'm the owner, Carleton St. Clair, and who might you be?"

"Richard Hudson. I've come to inform you of a new timetable."

Carleton's mouth dropped. He stared for a moment, then crossed over to the bar and reached for his pistol.

"I know Mr. Hudson, and you aren't him. Why are you people insisting on using his name?" Carleton replied exasperated.

The individual hunched shoulders indignantly. "Sir, you are to assemble your men and join a demonstration for Canadian independence. You must comply with my orders."

"Listen you arrogant Limey, I don't take orders from the likes of you. Peter! Get the others!" Carleton called to the kitchen.

"I've been sent by Elizabeth Darmon…"

"Elizabeth Darmon, eh? Well, you'll be happy to learn you're about to share a room with *another* Richard Hudson, who claims to be a Darmon. Don't you spies know what each other is doing?"

The hotel staff reappeared and, once more, escorted a captive to the cellar and rudely pushed him into the small room.

"You can't do this! I'm Charles Bagwell, envoy of the Assembly of Quebec. You must release me," Charles shouted.

He landed face down on wooden floorboards, hearing the sound of footsteps retreating up the stairs followed by the slam of a distant door. The room was completely dark, with only a small sliver of light at the bottom of the doorframe.

After a moment, a soft voice came from above. "Charles?"

He attempted to sit up. "Who's there?"

"Charles Bagwell! Is it really you? I thought you were dead!"

In the blackness, Charles felt two hands forcefully lift him to his feet and arms wrap tightly around his back. He could smell the man's breath inches from his face, but could not make out its features.

Charles pulled back. "Sir, I'm the envoy of the Quebec Assembly. Who are you?"

"Charles, it's me, William, your brother-in-law!" the voice said impatiently.

"William Darmon?" Charles answered suspiciously. "I've met William Darmon. You have neither his size nor his voice. In any case, the man's dead."

"Charles what's the matter with you? Have you lost your mind? We spent the summer at Richard's Lodge before our carriage was ambushed. You were shot and left behind."

Charles scratched his head. "The proprietor said you claimed to be Richard Hudson, who was killed in the kidnapping. It's more likely you're some other scoundrel."

"What happened to you, Charles? We've known each other since we were children for Gods sake!" the voice declared.

Charles hesitated. *The man sounds sincere...* "My wound from the ambush erased most of my memory. Is there something about me that you and I alone might know?"

After a brief pause, words came back. "You mean like the scar on your arm from when you escaped from a Turkish prison, three large moles on your back or the slight limp inherited from the time we jumped ship off the Island of Saint Helena?"

Charles stammered with confusion. "But Elizabeth said you were dead."

Another pause.

"You've seen Elizabeth?"

Charles rubbed his aching head. "You say you're my brother-in-law? Does this mean that Elizabeth is my sister?"

"No, Charles, she has two sisters, Victoria and Emily. Emily's your wife, for heaven's sake!"

Silence.

"I have a wife?"

"Charles, I've been searching for Elizabeth these past months. If you've talked to her, you have to tell me where she is!"

"In Quebec City. I left her just three weeks ago. She's attempting to help some French Canadians gain a measure of respect, though I fear her methods will cause bloodshed with the English."

"And she told you that I was dead?" William repeated.

"Yes, I found her in a tavern called the *Le Taureau Rouge.* She was with a man she introduced as her husband, William Darmon. They mentioned the ambush and how she'd tracked you to Quebec City only to discover that you'd already been released by the kidnappers."

"Go on."

"Well, she said they were trying to infiltrate a group called the *Patriotes* who they believed were responsible for the abduction. The following day, when I returned to the Inn, this 'William' was seated with two Frenchmen. He had too much to drink and his friends took him away. I never saw him again. Elizabeth said the poor bloke fell two hundred feet from the Citadel."

In the darkness, William breathed heavily. "Describe this man you thought was me."

"Long, sandy colored hair, pointed nose, double chin, in his thirties."

"My God, that sounds like Richard!" William blurted. "While we were held hostage, they said he escaped. I suspected it was a set up. If Elizabeth was with Richard, and he was posing as me, they must have been in it together. No wonder she stayed behind the day of the ambush. She must have set fire to the lodge! It's in ashes. My poor Elizabeth! What has she done?"

"She said she was only helping the downtrodden *Quebecois,*" Charles offered.

"How did you find her?"

"After the carriage incident, a passerby took me to Petit Sault, where I overheard someone say Elizabeth Darmon was following you to Quebec City. When I got there, I asked around and the bartender remembered her."

"Why didn't you stay with her?" William demanded.

"Well, it's kind of a long story. While I was walking along the Saint Lawrence, some trappers forced me to fall in with them to recover pelts at Fort Chambly. I ran away before the shooting started, but four soldiers were killed. The authorities caught up with me, and I was sentenced to hang at Trois Rivieres."

"Good God! You were to be hanged?"

Charles stopped to draw a deep breath. "Yes, it was a close call, but the Governor's men arranged my escape. Lord Ian Stewart, aide to the Minister of War, said they were aware of this *Patriote* group. I was asked to attend one of their meetings and inform him of their plans. Elizabeth was there, claiming to be after a woman by the name of Catherine Cazeau. We actually did catch up with her. Elizabeth said this woman masterminded the kidnapping. She pretended to be your wife, so they could withdraw twenty-five thousand pounds from your bank account. The vixen escaped, however..."

William's voice rose to a high pitch. "Twenty five thousand pounds! I've lost twenty five thousand pounds?"

Charles managed a weak smile in the gloom. "Oh, sorry. Elizabeth said her husband was released after payment and the Hudson's were killed—"

"What? I was marooned with Victoria and Emily on an Island in Lake Champlain," William interrupted.

Silence.

"Listen, Charles, I think you've been misled. Ask yourself—why would Elizabeth keep company with Richard and steal her own money?"

Charles shut his eyes trying to concentrate. "It does seem strange that she'd take up with him behind your back, and then burn down his lodge."

"Charles! This woman fed you lies. The only way this makes any sense is if *she* is actually Catherine Cazeau!"

"Funny, that's what Lord Stewart said. I thought Elizabeth was just sympathetic to the plight of the *Quebecois*," Charles observed sheepishly.

"So, what happened to this woman you caught up with? I'll wager she was really Elizabeth."

. "We dyed her hair, then she escaped," Charles recalled. "I followed her to the Union Hotel and reported back to this Cazeau woman. Then, I was arrested and haven't heard from her since."

William sighed. "What a mess! I only hope she got away."

Charles' voice quivered. "It's this blasted amnesia..."

A strong grip took his shoulder. "Charles, this is no fault of yours. I haven't helped much either."

"You say you were stranded on an island. What happened?"

"I swam to shore only to be captured by some renegade Indians. When I came back for the women, they were gone. It's another mystery we must attend to."

"My wife's missing?" Charles responded weakly.

William nodded.

After a pause, the other man continued his questioning. "Why are you here?"

"I found a cache of rifles in the cellar of what's left of Richard's Lodge. There was a map of lodges, apparently being used to protect against Canadian invaders. I came here hoping the name Richard Hudson would give me some answers."

"You're mistaken," Charles said. "They're all part of a *Patriote* plot for a demonstration of French Canadian power. Governor Aylmer is scheduled to make a speech at Fort Saint Louis on the two-hundredth anniversary of the death of Champlain. On that day, these malcontents with the help of Americans will march on Quebec and Montreal. They plan to assassinate the Governor and his cabinet."

William whistled softly.

"Unfortunately, I was unable to deliver this information to Lord Stewart before leaving Quebec City," Charles went on. "These Reformers have sent me to the lodges to inform the proprietors of the schedule, but I'm secretly working for Stewart to destroy the places. There are twenty-seven sites... excuse me, twenty-six, now that I've blown up a cache of rifles in the New Brunswick cellar."

"You who did that? You could have killed me! I'd taken refuge in Richard's basement and was out hunting when the explosion occurred," William moaned.

Charles gulped. "That was Hudson's Lodge? I had no idea. Why did we all come there in the first place?"

William thought for a moment. "Richard Hudson married Victoria four years ago. We never knew much about him. He must have been in league with the French Canadians for some time. I never suspected he had an ulterior motive for inviting us to the Colony."

Charles shrugged. "So, we're both here at the Wild Stag acting in the interests of the Crown?"

"Yes, if we ever get out of this place, I'll go to Quebec and find Elizabeth," William announced. "I can seek out Lord Stewart and pass on your message. You must finish the job of disabling these storehouses. Let's agree to meet at Quebec harbor, four months from today. I know a ship, the *Oceana*, which will be returning to London from its annual voyage to the Provinces. It's the vessel that brought us here last spring. If we can gather the rest of the family or determine their fate by then, I propose we all leave for home on that ship."

Moments later, their world disintegrated in a tremendous explosion.

The blast threw Charles and William smashing against the wall. Beams, earth and stones crushed down upon them. Dirt piled everywhere burying them under a mass of destruction. Charles screamed, but the crashing sound drowned out his voice.

Their surroundings settled into a black stillness.

Charles' head pounded in familiar fashion. He began to bring his environs into focus. Damp and cold, he lay outside, propped against a tree. It was night. He could not remember how he got there.

Looking around, his eyes cast on an eerie scene. Several hundred yards away, yellow light from hundreds of tiny points spread across the ground, surrounding a large dark mass. He realized they were burning embers flickering on the dark snow. The black mound spewed clouds of glowing red smoke into the sky while dark silhouettes scurried back and forth, throwing buckets of water on the smoldering ruins.

Charles remembered the explosion. *But, how did I get out of the rubble?* Looking down at his feet, he made out grooves in the snow leading to his spot. Someone had dragged him from the wreckage.

He glanced quickly from side to side. Ten feet away, a horse stood watching him with its reigns tied to the limb of a fir tree. He rolled over to stand up, his arm brushed something on his chest. A note was pinned to his soot-covered shirt. Three words were scrawled on it:

God speed! William.

Charles scrambled to his feet. Someone had blown up the place and completed the task for him. *Stewart said there would be help from his men.* Perhaps, a member of the hotel staff crept into the basement. The blast nearly killed them! Most of the force of the explosion must have gone upward. *We're lucky to be alive.*

William was gone. Thinking back in anguish, Charles remembered that he had not gotten a look at the man's face. No Matter. Recalling their agreement, he was determined to carry out the rest of his mission. Gingerly, he climbed to his feet and stepped over to unhitch the horse.

Silence. His boots made no sound in the snow.

All at once, Charles discovered he was stone deaf.

Chapter Thirteen

Charles rode along the causeway from Montreal to Albany. Bordering the Richelieu River, it wound its way through miles of uninhabited forest. It was one of the earliest inland routes between the two cities, and stretches in Lower Canada still held original planks laid in 1811 to insure year round passage.

Next stop on the list of storehouses was the Royal Coach Tavern.

Charles thought about the number of lodges remaining and their distances spread out over four hundred miles. He could not afford to spend more than one day at each stop and must then average fifty miles on days between rendezvous. In less than six weeks, French sympathizers would be on their way to targets in Montreal and Quebec.

After near disaster at the Wild Stag Inn, he wondered if he was capable of rousing recruits, much less sabotaging their weapons. Instead of receiving gratitude for the message, he had been treated with suspicion and his credentials ignored. It may have been the consequence of William's introduction ahead of time or the fact that he was English purportedly on a Frenchman's errand. The experience convinced him to change his demeanor at the next outpost. Also, he must locate Lord Stewart's men. Ultimately, he had to maintain the appearance of serving both French Reformers and British Loyalists to ensure a chance for a pardon, whatever the outcome.

Charles sighed. At least his hearing improved. The explosion might have damaged his eardrums, but the pain disappeared and gradually he was picking up more sounds of nature around him.

Dirty snowdrifts piled on both sides of the trail. His horse trotted between mantled limbs under a bright afternoon sun. Mile after mile went by without encountering another rider or a trace of settlements. Tangled branches and withered trunks showed no signs of life; a frosty woodland laid waste by winter's fury. Charles shivered atop his mount, maneuvering over frozen ground, trying to avoid shadowed patches of ice and slushy puddles in sunlight.

At last, densely forested hills gave way to a sparsely covered valley. Charles spotted three log houses on a path from the main road, which diverted travelers to a circle in front of the sprawling buildings. He had made the seventy-mile journey to New York in three days. The Tavern stood five miles north of the Plattsburgh settlement and served as a stopping point for the Rupert Stage Coach, which arrived three times each week.

Charles urged his mount up the driveway.

An empty wagon stuck out of the first structure, suggesting a livery to house customer's mounts and repair carriages. A large weathered barn stood behind it. Beyond the livery, a two-story residence occupied the remaining portion of the driveway. A large sign above the entrance announced in red letters painted under a carriage outline: *Royal Coach Tavern.*

No one presented himself outside on the grounds. He dismounted in front of the main building and trudged up to the porch. The Tavern's door stood ajar. Peeking inside, he observed a familiar-looking room filled with tables and a corner counter, but the place appeared deserted.

He announced his presence several times. "Hello? Is anyone here?"

Finally, a teenage boy entered the serving room and looked at Charles with surprise. "Yes, sir?"

"I'm looking for the proprietor. Where is everyone?"

"I'm sorry, sir, they're all down at the lake. About an hour ago, Mr. Foster came in saying he'd seen bodies of two women washed ashore near Stony Point. Everybody took off for the lakeshore. S'about three miles East of here."

Charles swallowed hard. William said Emily and Victoria were missing when he returned to the island on Lake Champlain. With a quick 'thank you' he raced out the door.

In a narrow cove, near water's edge, a crowd of fifty people milled about. Farmers, trappers and plainly dressed women congregated on a coarse-stone beach discussing matters among themselves. Most of the onlookers had their backs turned to Charles when he dismounted. They paid him little notice as he pushed his way into the midst of the circle of bystanders.

On the ground, two forms lay ashen white, still as statues. The women were dressed in simple clothing, about thirty years old with dark hair and round faces. They could have been English or Irish immigrants. There were no markings or signs of foul play on the corpses. Talk among the spectators suggested they were unknown in these parts.

Charles wondered if he was staring at his wife and sister-in-law. It was odd they both drowned together, perhaps in a desperate attempt to swim to shore. He felt no pang of instant recognition, but, for all he knew, he gazed at his family. He decided not to identify himself as a possible relative; an English nationality might create suspicion when he revealed his mission.

Charles took a last look at the unfortunate pair and turned to go back to the tavern, hoping to search the premises before the others returned. Near the perimeter of the milieu, he spotted a familiar face. A young man quickly turned away and disappeared behind the throng of people.

Charles took off after him. Slightly built with shoulder length brown hair, the youth darted between bystanders with remarkable agility. By the time he cleared the multitude, Charles glimpsed the lad's white tunic entering a distant grove of trees. He put his head down and ran at full speed until he caught up to the runaway in the woods.

Placing his hand on boy's shoulder, he pulled him to a stop. "Peter, don't you remember me from the Wild Stag?"

"Let go of me! I don't know you."

"You do so. You shoved me into a locker in the basement."

He stared blankly at Charles.

A sudden inspiration came to mind. "Keep to the green!"

The fugitive's eyes widened. "Aren't you a messenger for the Reformers?"

Charles grinned. "Ostensibly, but I'm also working for Lord Stewart to destroy these places. He said there would be help among each proprietor's staff. Was it you who set off the explosion?"

Patriote Peril

Peter nodded. "When you arrived, I knew time was running out. After the blast, I took off and show'd up here yesterday. I've found the gun stash. It's in the barn behind the main building. Meet me there at midnight, otherwise don't go near the Inn."

Charles frowned. "But I must deliver the message."

"Why? So these meddling Americans can marshal their forces?"

"My cover will be blown if word spreads that I didn't show up," Charles protested. "The Reformers will know I used their information to obliterate the caches. I could never return to Quebec."

"Small loss,' Peter replied. "Do what you must, but don't queer tonight's job."

They separated. Neither one noticed a bearded individual sitting against a tree, ten feet away.

This time, his reception went quite well. The proprietor, a forty-some gentleman named Walter John raised an eyebrow at the name Richard Hudson, but did not object to initiating the procedure. There was no celebration, however, not everyone in the community supported the French activists. Messengers were dispatched to the towns of Burlington and Saint Albans.

He was served a meal without much conversation. No one seemed very interested in his mission. Charles learned from a waiter that Walter John was not an avid supporter.

At eight o'clock, Charles retired with an excuse of early departure for the next station. When midnight arrived, he crept outside. Under starlight, the barn's dark silhouette loomed ominously. Peter stepped out of the shadows by the front door and gestured they slip inside.

Peter lit a candle casting a dim light. The large interior showed no evidence of livestock, only piles of bundled straw. At the far end, a ladder led up to a shelf, which held stacks of long wooden crates and small barrels. Quietly, they climbed up. Peter removed a cover from one of the barrels and poured its contents over the boxes. Charles could smell gunpowder while his companion continued a trail of dust over the platform. They climbed down, extending the powder's path onto the floor directly beneath the pile of guns.

145

He set down the barrel and fished in his pocket for a flint.

The barn door creaked. A voice shouted from the doorway. "Hold it! Don't move!"

In one motion, Peter pulled out the flint and set fire to the explosive trail.

A shot rang out.

Peter clutched his chest and dropped to the ground just as the floor next to the ladder burst into flames. The bearded intruder covered his eyes against a blinding glare. Charles saw fire spreading up the rungs, lapping at the shelf. He threw himself toward the gunman. They crashed against the door and somersaulted outside.

Charles rolled, regained his feet and began running as fast as he could.

The back end of the barn exploded. Pieces of roofing and splintering sideboards flew in all directions. He plunged headlong past the tavern and tore on to the stable.

Charging up to his horse, he grabbed the reins and hurried it out to the driveway.

After mounting, he turned one more time toward the raging blaze to see dark forms rushing out of the inn, heaving water at the fire. One of them, Walter John, stopped and shook his fist at Charles. Trembling with fear, the emissary quickly maneuvered his steed down to the main road and galloped off.

Hours of riding in cold night air finally calmed the shaken Englishman. Once again, the violence at the Royal Coach Inn confirmed how ill qualified he was to perform either mission. He was neither a rabblerouser nor a saboteur. How many more episodes would he have to endure before they caught on and finished him off?

Two days following the hasty departure, Charles came upon the village of Watertown near the western New York border. From a small hill, he gazed at the panorama of over a hundred buildings clustered along the Black River and shook his head. *How can I pull this off and in the middle of a town with several thousand residents?* Checking his list, he spied the name of Henry P. McNutt at the Grand Lodge of the Oneida, on the north side of the settlement.

The address did not resemble the previous taverns. Instead, a two-story house was situated on a block with other residences. There was no welcoming sign for weary travelers, or any indication this was a place of business.

Charles resolutely climbed front steps to a small landing and knocked at the door. He heard the sounds of children running inside.

The door opened. A gray-haired woman faced him, wiping her hands on a yellow apron. The short, puffy-faced lady could easily have been someone's grandmother interrupted from an afternoon's baking.

"Excuse me, ma'am. Is this the Grand Lodge of the Oneida?" Charles put forth.

She smiled. "I'm sorry, the Freemasons no longer gather here. They now hold meetings on the south side of town."

Charles rechecked his list. "This is puzzling. I was told I could find Mr. Henry McNutt at this address—"

"Oh, Mister McNutt still comes 'round every week," she remarked. "He should stop by tomorrow. I'll tell him you were here, Mr—?"

"Richard Hudson. Yes, I've an important message for him," Charles replied with the trace of a frown.

The woman seemed satisfied with his explanation. "Please, come inside. Let me offer you some refreshment. Have you come a long way?"

Charles crossed the threshold to be immediately confronted by three boys and a girl, all under ten years old. Behind them, older youngsters worked busily within the room, cleaning, straightening and disappearing into the kitchen.

The dowager intervened with a hint of sternness. "Run along, children. Let the gentleman be."

"My, you have a large family, madam. Are you related to Mr. McNutt?" Charles inquired.

"Oh my, no. I just look after the children. They're homeless, parentless foundlings abandoned for one reason or another." She sighed.

Charles was surprised. "For some reason, I expected to find a tavern here, instead of this—"

"—Masonic Orphan Asylum at Watertown?" she finished. "Yes, the Masons donated this house to the town six months ago. It was little enough to gain the town's favor after our churches expelled those in the congregations who did not renounce Freemasonry. There's still a lot of suspicion toward the Masons since the Morgan affair."

A waif, no more than six, tugged at Charles' sleeve. He glanced at an upturned face and torn red shirt, and stooped to ask the boy's name.

"David, sir. Have you come to take us with you?"

Charles smiled and shook his head. "No, lad. I'm here to see Mr. McNutt about some hunting equipment."

The caretaker raised an eyebrow. "Hunting equipment? The master keeps his tools in the basement. Would you like to see them?"

He nodded.

She led the way to a door at the end of a long hallway. Taking a set of keys from her apron, she unlocked it and allowed him to proceed down the steps while she guarded to prevent the children access.

"There's a lamp on the work bench. Feel free to look around."

Light cast within the confines revealed an orderly workshop. Saws and hammers hung over numerous barrels and wooden crates labeled salt, nails and leather strips. Nothing suggested an armory. He was about to leave when a curtain over the rear wall caught his eye.

Pushing it aside, he discovered another door. It had no lock. He stepped inside a second room and faced familiar stacks of musket containers. The weapons were all there; another depot awaiting the *Patriotes*.

Charles stared at the weapons. *Why didn't they move them?* Overhead, playful footsteps of the children echoed the answer. It was a perfect hiding place. Lord Stewart would not expect him to blow up an orphanage. Even if the place were evacuated, its destruction would leave the orphans without a place to live.

He began to leave, but stopped. *Was it too late to sneak out without alerting McNutt?* He had already announced his presence as Richard Hudson. If he bypassed this cache, it might mean death for hundreds of people; perhaps even the governor. Bloodshed would be on his head. For all he knew, these arms might make the difference between provincial independence and economic hardship for the entire population. And, after the destruction, surely the townspeople would rescue the poor homeless tots from winter's cold.

Maybe there was another way. He could sneak back here at night and somehow disable the rifles one by one…

Voices filtered down from above. The old woman talking to someone.

"Why Mister McNutt, we expected you tomorrow. A gentleman is here to see you. He's down in the basement."

William clenched his teeth with exasperation. The secretary sitting in front of large double doors leading to Lord Howich's office in the *Palais Episcopal* remained intransigent.

"You cannot see the Minister without an appointment."

"No, it's his aide, Lord Stewart whom I must see," William repeated.

"You do not have an appointment."

"No, but, I have important information for him," he growled once more.

"Every matter in the Ministry of Defense is important."

William threw up his hands. "The future of the entire Province is at stake!"

"I can squeeze you in three weeks from today," she responded, unimpressed.

He wrung his hands, fighting an urge to close them around her neck. "Look here, I'm a British citizen with Parliamentary connections. Is there any way I can see him today?"

"I'm sorry," she countered with a perfunctory smile. "Most of the offices are closed today. Governor Aylmer's niece has just arrived from London. Many of our diplomats are preparing for tonight's ball at the *Chateau de Callieres*. Everyone will be there—"

"Thank you," William replied curtly.

There was little reaction to the announcement of William's entry into the Grand Assembly Room of Chateau de Callieres. His name was unfamiliar and of no consequence in the midst of notable members of Provincial society such as Lord Aylmer, his Council Members, the Honorable Cullivier, Mr. Nelson and the Honorable Debartzch.

William admired the spacious ballroom. White columns surrounded a floor crowded with couples in evening dress and black ties. A cacophony of conversations nearly masked orchestral music emanating from a second floor balcony at the far end. Bright light cast by twenty chandeliers created a blur of colorful silk dresses, white gloves, black jackets with ruffled shirts, and legs covered with ivory colored stockings.

Red-coated servants moved purposefully through the assemblage, carrying trays of crystal glasses. Country dancing took up three-quarters of the room and around the perimeter, elderly guests looked on.

William was impressed at the elegance so far from London.

He passed numerous participants catching snatches of conversation.

"Wasn't long ago Papineau would have attended these functions."

"Yes, Governor Aylmer used to be considered a friend of the *Patriotes*. Papineau even entertained the Aylmers at his country estate back '31."

"Didn't he once offer seats on the Executive Council to both *Patriote* leaders Louis-Joseph Papineau and John Neilson?"

"They both refused. They knew the Legislative and Executive councils and the echelons of civil service are dominated by Anglophones, unsympathetic to the demands of the Assembly."

"It was that business with those three French-speaking Canadians shot by British troops during the '32 election in Montreal. Aylmer refused to intervene in the judicial process when Papineau requested a military inquiry."

"And there's always the money. Who controls provincial revenues, including those reserved for the Colonial Office? Lord Goderich instructed Aylmer to submit a pared-down list of estimates to the Assembly and a permanent civil list preparatory to a surrendering this year's crown revenues. The Assembly refused permanent salaries to any officials and Goderich's proposals were rejected by 42 to 9."

"Yes, and anger of the *Patriote* party was fuelled by the cholera epidemic which so far has killed more than 7,000 people in the colony. Aylmer prepared for the outbreak by persuading the legislature to establish a quarantine station at Grosse Île and a board of health at Quebec. But, the Assembly criticized him for issuing funds without its approval and for failing to control the influx of immigrants. So the Assembly passed a supply bill making no provision for a civil list, which the Legislative Council felt compelled to reject."

After taking a tour around the main room and not finding any sign of his wife, William discovered adjoining rooms also occupied. Inside these smoky chambers, he heard more government officials discussing politics of the British Foreign Office and the latest rumors from Parliament.

With the help of a servant, Lord Stewart was pointed out.

A large gentleman sat in the corner of a spacious parlor under the painting of General Wolfe. He gestured forcibly at two other distinguished gentlemen involved in a heated dialog. His booming voice dominated the repartee, interrupted now and then by servants exchanging empty glasses for new drinks.

William edged closer, trying to appear a disinterested bystander. However, when he came up next to the participants, Stewart abruptly fell silent.

Their eyes turned to William.

He swallowed. In a matter-of-fact voice, William addressed Howich's Aide. "Excuse my interruption. Lord Stewart, might I speak with you for a moment? I've a message from a mutual friend."

The other officials harrumphed, clearly annoyed that anyone but the highest ranked would dare to intrude. Lord Stewart, however, sensed the seriousness of his request and excused the other two.

William sat down onto a large upholstered chair.

"Thank you, sir. I'm William Darmon...."

Lord Stewart's eyes narrowed. "Aren't you a member of the *Patriote* movement?"

"I'm a British citizen, sir. My family and I have been victimized by that evil organization. I won't detain you with the details, but I've come with important information that your agent has learned from the conspirators."

Lord Stewart leaned forward. "Tell me, what is the name of this agent?"

William spread his hands. "I've just come from Sherbrooke where Charles Bagwell informed me that the *Patriotes* are assembling several thousand Americans for an attack on Montreal and Quebec. They intend to kill the Governor and his Cabinet."

Lord Stewart straightened. "They're going so far? When will this assault take place?"

"A month hence," William whispered. "At the Champlain celebration in Fort Saint Louis. They plan to burn down the Governor's Chateau with Lord Aylmer inside. As to the rest of the Council, I don't know when such attempts will begin."

The official's face reddened. "Let's call them out, here and now!"

The Aide waved to a servant. "Bring Lady Darmon to me at once."

William's pulse quickened. At last, he was about to find out who was really leading the *Patriote's* band. *Could it really be Elizabeth as Charles implied?*

Lord Stewart reached for another drink from a passing servant. The two men waited without further discussion. William nervously sipped his glass, wondering what he would do if the woman turned out to be his wife. Either way, the idea of confrontation in these surroundings was distasteful.

A rustle of fabric stirred the air behind him. An unfamiliar voice cut through William's pensiveness. "See here, Lord Stewart, I'm not accustomed to the beck and call of British errand boys. What's this urgent business?"

William rose to his feet. He turned and gaped at the woman. Her appearance did not at all remind him of Elizabeth, and there was a discomforting intensity about her, unlike the warmth of his spouse.

She paused upon seeing his smile disappear into a look of disdain. She was at first curious, then indifferent.

Lord Stewart observed the encounter with interest. "Mr. Darmon, allow me to introduce Madam Catherine Cazeau, who, despite her fondness for your wife's name, despises all that is British within the

Colony."

Madam Cazeau flinched. After a sharp intake of breath, she managed to recover her composure. "Not without just cause, my dear Stewart."

William's impatience with the woman grew to the point where he could no longer hold his tongue. "Madam Cazeau, you have done my family such a disservice that I will not rest until you're brought to justice for the crimes of kidnapping, attempted murder and extortion. Your utter disregard for people who meant you no harm makes me eager for the time of retribution you deserve."

The lady's expression became more hostile. "Sir, you'd better look around you when casting blame for your inconveniences. I suspect your precious, sanctimonious British government is more at fault than you believe it to be. As for acts of violence, the Americans have demonstrated such is the path to freedom from tyranny and injustice."

Lord Stewart jumped to his feet. "Enough! Madam Cazeau, I've just been informed of the *Patriote's* plot to remove the Governor. This act of treason will be dealt with in the severest manner. Tomorrow, I intend to ask the Colonial Office for military reinforcements. Once the insurrection is put down, the public will know the price of Reform Party government. You'll all be turned out of office for good."

The woman's alabaster complexion flushed red. For a moment, she glared without speaking.

"Your effort will be of no significance. The path to a free Canada cannot be blocked by old men in power who ignore Quebecois *inhabitants.* Soon, British imperialism will be driven from North America forever."

She turned and stomped away.

Lord Stewart relaxed a bit. "Thank you, Mr. Darmon. I hope this exchange will prevent the *Patriotes* from making a mistake they will forever regret. After the rebels have been dealt with, we shall sit down and sort out your family's imposition. For now, please excuse me. There are preparations I must see to."

William bowed slightly and returned to the main room.

He rubbed the back of his neck, disconcerted by the encounter. He faced the dancers, while carefully surveying the room for Madam

Cazeau and hoping to avoid any further intercourse. *How could Charles have surmised that this shrew was Elizabeth?* A stiff drink provided some consolation. He sighed, his mission was now complete, but there would be no pleasure for him the rest of the evening.

If only Elizabeth had been there. He tried to remember the last time they enjoyed a party together. If she was in Quebec City, surely this is the place she would come if she still tracked the *Patriotes*. He prayed the Cazeau woman had not caught up with her again. More likely, she had fled the city after altering her appearance.

All three women were missing.

Shortly after midnight, William prepared to leave for his hotel when a woman rushed into the Grand Assembly room. "Come quickly! Is there a doctor here?"

The music stopped. Several persons charged after her as she ran back into a side partition. William followed out of curiosity.

Inside the room, a growing mass of guests clustered around two leather chairs. He attempted to squeeze by the tightly pressed bodies, hearing words of concern. Finally, he reached the oversized burgundy seats. Two gentlemen bent over a figure, whose head slumped forward onto his chest. One was taking a pulse, and the other felt under the victim's nose for breath.

"What's happened?' William asked.

The pulse taker looked up. "Poor fellow seems to have had a heart attack. He's lost it. The Council will be hit hard by this. Someone send for the Governor and tell him that Lord Stewart is dead."

A collective murmur spread among the group of witnesses. The other gentleman straightened. "I'm afraid it wasn't a heart attack. This discoloration of the finger tips and the rigid jaw muscles suggest poison."

He looked around and retrieved a glass which had rolled under the chair. After smelling the empty vessel, he handed it to the other man.

"Yes, there's a faint, but peculiar scent," he observed. "I think it is time to send for the Constable."

Numerous conversations burst forth from the bystanders. William turned to look for Madame Cazeau and spotted her just entering the room. As she approached, their eyes met. Her mouth was drawn up in a determined expression.

She held out a finger pointed directly at him. "There he is! He is the one I saw put something into Lord Stewart's glass!"

Several heads turned towards William. Hands reached out and grasped his arms. William's jaw dropped in disbelief.

"He's William Darmon," she accused contemptuously. "The brother-in-law of Richard Hudson, one of the founders of the *Libertine* faction of the *Patriote Party*. They vowed to do away with the Executive Council, and here's the evidence of their handiwork!"

William struggled to free himself. "It's not true. She's casting blame to cover up her own killing!" he sputtered.

A gentleman near William's ear gave him a scathing look. "Why would you accuse Madam Cazeau of such a thing? Who are you?"

William nodded in a desperate attempt to put down their rising hostility. "I came here to deliver an important message to Lord Stewart, to warn of a *Patriote* plot and expose her treachery. She's the person behind this murder."

Another man stepped closer, clutching William's shoulder with disdain. "From whom did you receive this message."

"Charles Bagwell. He's on a mission to assemble the proprietors of American hunting lodges who hold the weapons for their demonstration," William answered.

"Charles Bagwell? The renegade who escaped the hangman's noose? You must be joking!"

The gentleman released his grip and put his face six inches from William's. "You'd better think twice about mentioning his name in the same breath with Lord Stewart. The Minister would have had nothing to do with his kind."

The enraged crowd shoved him into the other chair with looks of scorn. Madam Cazeau cast him a scathing glance, then left the room while a number of male guests forced him to remain seated until the Constable arrived.

Emily, Victoria and Marcque searched the waterfront in Quebec City, hoping to find the fugitive Bagwell.

At Quebec Port, there was no record of any ship scheduled to depart for European destinations within the month. They questioned proprietors of taverns near the wharf and even approached the local constabulary. To Emily's relief, the authorities of Quebec were not conducting any sort of manhunt. They seemed disinterested in bringing Charles to justice. Perhaps it was because of law enforcement's British heritage, or because they were presently overwhelmed by the city's internal problems. Even a reward of one thousand *piastres* posted by the Trois Rivieres Prison commandant had not brought noticeable activity among the populace.

After a week in the city and resigned to having pursued a false lead, they boarded the steamboat, *Canadien,* bound for Montreal.

On February 17, three weary trackers disembarked at the Port of Montreal. From the docks of the newly incorporated city, they proceeded up *Rue de la Commune*. Well-kept rows of stone houses, wide streets and busy carriage traffic testified to a prosperous community. At *Rue Notre Dame*, they stopped at the *Restaurante Ethier* before checking into the *Hotel Du Canada*.

"How are we ever going to find him?" Emily moaned.

"I suppose it's off to police headquarters once more," Victoria offered.

Marcque sighed. "If he's gone into hiding, we may never uncover the man. Our hope is if he's entangled with his benefactors for some larger purpose, we might then read about their cause in a local newspaper."

As they trundled through the hotel lobby, Marcque paused when a conversation between two well-dressed businessmen met his ears.

"Have you heard that a large party of armed Americans has been seen crossing the St. Lawrence?"

"Yes, I read this morning they estimate that one thousand of them are coming this way on the north side of Lake Erie. The paper said they intend to create a demonstration for Canadian independence."

"This is outrageous! It's an act of war!"

"They say the local militia's being called up."

"Hah! They've not seen action in twenty years. I doubt they can find any volunteers who aren't ill-trained and sedentary."

"These Americans are nothing more than a bunch of discontented trappers stirring up trouble, blaming us for their problems."

"They never understand why we don't sever ties with England."

"I think they still want to add our provinces to their collection of states."

"No, I read that one of their rabble-rousing leaders may be out for revenge against our justice system."

"Why?"

"He's the outlaw who was sentenced to die for his crimes at *Trois Rivieres*."

"Well, I hope these renegades are dealt with quickly. I've enough to do just to keep my business above water."

"I think it's time for a holiday abroad."

"You know, it might be prudent."

"Who is this rebel anyway?"

"Charles Bagwell."

"Charles Bagwell?"

"You remember, the one who did the Fort Chamby killings."

Marcque rushed over to Emily.

Upon hearing the news, she stumbled forward. Victoria and Marcque caught her in a dead faint. Carefully, they cradled her arms and helped her up to their room.

Chapter Fourteen

Images of Richard Hudson's anguished face floated in front of Elizabeth as her horse plodded through a white wilderness. At first she paid no attention, drifting in and out of contemplation, hardly aware of anything beyond numbing cold. Now, she was losing hope, certain her struggle was about to end in a frozen world far removed from her homeland. Someday, across time and space, her life would be a footnote in the annals of the exploration of British North America. A death written off as another payment to the cost of mankind's settlement of the planet.

"My outlook is becoming as bleak as the weather," she remarked into frigid air. "I must set my mind on more positive thoughts. Newcastle is within reach. I can do this."

Returning to her memory of their last encounter, she still could not understand why Richard reacted in such a way. She assumed the guilt of his betrayal caused him to leap from the Citadel. But why did he act as if her presence in Quebec meant the end of everything? After all, the two men with him had no compunction about doing away with her. She was beginning to question if it really was suicide. Perhaps Richard fled to the Citadel expecting sanctuary and someone there decided to get rid of him. But, who knew he would come running through the grounds? Of course, his death could have been an accident, a miss-step as he tried to climb down the cliff. *Would anyone ever know what really happened?*

The horse halted abruptly, sending Elizabeth lurching forward.

Immediately in front of her, three growling dogs edged out from behind the trees. The gray fur and pale blue eyes were unlike any canine breed she remembered. On reflection, she concluded they had to be wolves.

Her horse started to back up, raising its head and snorting. Six more animals emerged to join the pack. Their curling lips displayed wicked fangs as they crept closer, matching the horse's retreat. A chorus of howls scared Elizabeth out of a concern for the weather.

She yanked the reigns hard to the right to urge the horse toward a patch of firmer ground. The steed plodded laboriously through the deep drifts, panting furiously with each step into two foot thick drifts.

The wolves moved closer, nipping at the mare's legs while it strained to lift its buried hooves. One of the animals leaped up at Elizabeth. In a flash, it bit into the back of her boot, and teeth sank into her ankle. She shrieked, kicking at the determined attackers, but they grew bolder with each advance. She leaned forward in the saddle, trying to help the horse achieve better balance, but the poor equine was close to exhaustion. It reacted less and less to their charges.

Elizabeth's gaze frantically searched the area for a way out. Ahead, she sighted a copse of oak trees that might provide obstacles for the scavengers. Her horse seemed to sense her thoughts and lunged toward the refuge with the wolves close behind. They entered the dense grove, and she spotted a thick branch a foot above her head. Her arms stretched above as far as possible, and gloved hands closed around the limb, pulling herself from the horse's back as it continued forward. All but one of the pack trailed after the mount, leaving her dangling precariously from the limb. The mare moved a little faster now and quickly disappeared from sight with wolves in close pursuit. Elizabeth glared down at the single lupine creature below, which sat, staring intently through hungry eyes at the suspended prey.

"Go away! Shoo!"

Her pleading seemed to make the animal even more interested in her predicament. Minutes passed. Her arms ached with the effort of holding onto the branch.

"How much longer can I hold on?" she moaned. *Perhaps I can work my way hand over hand to the trunk.* But her arms felt so weak, she dared not let go with either hand.

The panting canine looked about, sniffing the air. At last, the mangy creature slunk off into the woods.

Elizabeth dropped to the ground and leaned against the base of the tree, gasping for breath and fighting back tears of anguish. Her sore arms would not stop shaking. She dared not wait too long, either the horse would escape or be brought down by the predators, and the wolves might return. With a pounding heart, she began trudging out of the grove.

What chance do I have on foot? She hunched her coat tighter about the neck, rewrapped her scarf and hiked out into an open space. With concentrated effort, she tromped one hundred yards through the deep snow before collapsing against another tree. Snowfall seemed to be letting up, and distant hills became clearer. Breath caught in her throat when searching eyes settled on wisps of smoke rising over a ridge of trees in the distance. *A campfire or a cabin!*

The source of smoke turned out to be a log house.

An Acadian man, his wife and two small children jumped back when the unexpected visitor staggered through their doorway and collapsed onto the floor next to a fireplace.

An hour passed before Elizabeth was able to rise onto an elbow and consume a small bowl of hot, hand-fed soup.

She slumped back. Weariness overcame her.

Two days later, Elizabeth entered the familiar office of Constable John Thomas in the town of Newcastle. The lawman chided her for continuing on to Quebec following the loss of his deputies. Despite his misgivings, however, he expressed amazement at her survival and grudgingly acknowledged the perseverance.

There had been a little progress in identifying the kidnappers. Thomas received news that the stable hand, Peter McDougall had ties to the Provincial government of Quebec. At one time, he served as a courier for the British Colonial Office, delivering messages between the Executive Council and the Legislators in Montreal. The reason for his presence at Hudson's lodge had not yet been established, but the Constable also learned that the dancehall girl visited Quebec City a month prior to the shooting.

Elizabeth bit her lip to stifle disappointment. No further word had filtered down concerning her family. She informed the Constable her husband and sisters escaped their captors, and her brother-in-law, Charles survived the ambush. She added that Richard Hudson had been freed as well, but later, died in an accident. Thomas confirmed hearing that Charles Bagwell fled from execution and became a hunted man. Elizabeth wondered if Marcque and her sisters were also the subjects of a manhunt for helping him to get away.

Constable Thomas leaned back in the chair behind his cluttered desk.

"So, from your account, we must conclude these events were set up by Mr. Hudson to extort money from you and your husband. Both his map of Lake Champlain and his reaction to you incriminate him. He must have hired thugs to maroon your family, and used this imposter to complete the job of extracting money from your accounts."

Elizabeth nodded. "It appears that way. But I still don't see what was in it for Richard. I mean, the lodge was worth more than any ransom he could raise."

Thomas fumbled through some papers. "Unless that wasn't part of the original plan. We've confirmed it was Miss Canceri 's body found in the Acadian cabin. Both she and Peter McDougall appear to be responsible for the fire and the murder of four servants."

"What was their motive?" she countered.

He shrugged. "We may never know; the perpetrators are all dead. At least, it saves the Colony a hanging. Without another lead, we have to presume the case is closed. I hope you can recover the rest of your family, but there isn't much I can do about Charles Bagwell. Maybe it's best if he just gets out of the Provinces as quickly as possible."

A month passed without further news.

As the days elapsed, Elizabeth despaired of ever finding her husband or rejoining her sisters. Constable's deputies no longer offered help; they had better things to do than worry about the problems of waylaid tourists. Amos never returned from Quebec; a message finally arrived saying he had left to seek his fortune further west.

With Victoria missing and her husband dead, Elizabeth wondered what would become of their property, especially the timber mill up on the Saint John River. If the business had been shut down, she expected a loss of jobs and the subsequent loss of income to the community would be a topic of discussion among townspeople. However, villagers seemed unconcerned, and no one would talk to her about Richard Hudson or his mill.

She approached the lawman once more.

"Constable Thomas, does Hudson's Mill still run without Richard's supervision?" she asked settling into the visitor's chair in front of his desk.

"Yes, I believe it still operates. Although, in winter the mills close down."

She scratched her head. "But who oversees the work without an owner?"

"I've heard that his brother, Walter John has stepped in and continues production," he replied absently.

Her mouth gaped open with surprise. "His brother? Victoria never mentioned Richard had a brother."

"Well, he does. He owns a hunting lodge in New York near Plattsburg."

"Is he up at the mill now?" she could hardly contain her excitement.

"No, I would imagine he's out in the woods with his logging crew. Winter is the best time to cut trees," he related. "Sap is down this time of year, and snow makes it easy to slide logs to the river. Until the ice melts, however, there's no way to get wood down to the mill. I'm sure John has the place locked up 'til spring."

She stood to leave. "How soon before the mill resumes operation and he comes back to the site?"

"I imagine it'll be another month or so before spring thaw begins on the river. Then, the crew will return to prepare for a new season."

March brought some improvement in the weather, and Elizabeth eagerly prepared to leave Newcastle. She secured necessary supplies and a horse to negotiate muddy roads not yet passable by buggy.

The day before her planned departure, a river barge from points along the Saint Lawrence docked at Newcastle. Elizabeth stepped out of the general store and paused when one of the Constable's deputies sprinted up to her. He said Thomas had important news for her, and she rushed over to his office.

An expression on the Constable's face quickly dispelled any hope of good news.

A deep furrow creased his brow as he read several pages spread out on the cluttered desk. Her heart pounded with dread. He waved Elizabeth to a chair.

"Mrs. Darmon, a company of Americans has invaded the British Province of Quebec. It may be an act of war."

Elizabeth raised a hand to her mouth. "Those scoundrels! Are we to have another conflict with the Colonies?"

Constable Thomas rubbed his forehead. "The attackers call themselves *Patriotes* and *Sons of Liberty.* Several hundred of them have crossed the Saint Lawrence and are streaming into Montreal. They found little resistance. Many French *inhabitants* welcomed the action, and the local militia fled for their lives, completely disorganized."

"Those blackguards! Can't we do something?" Her voice rose with anger.

"The invasion was applauded by many City leaders. They claim it's a show of support brought on by Parliament's disregard for their grievances over the past decade. Some are demanding a declaration of independence."

Elizabeth gaped at the lawman. "Quebec is revolting?"

The Constable shrugged. "Governor-in-Chief, Matthew Aylmer has directed the enlistment of a British regiment outside Quebec City in order to launch a counter attack."

"Will the American President send more troops to fight our men?"

"I don't know," he rubbed his chin. "President Jackson has repeatedly denounced American involvement in Canadian politics. He said any American caught crossing the border to incite violence against the British government would be imprisoned. It's likely this act of terrorism will be condemned by both governments."

She sighed her resignation. "Well, I intend to keep far away from any conflict north of the Saint Lawrence. Once I see Walter Hudson, I'll be on my way home."

"Ah, yes, Mrs. Darmon, but there's one more piece of information. It seems that one of the leaders of the invading army is Charles Bagwell, your brother-in-law who was supposed to have been hanged up at *Trois Rivieres*."

Charles Bagwell was no longer a man to be trifled with. His success at spreading the word to rally the Americans was growing each day. Despite the coincidence of his arrivals at four of the hunting lodges just prior to the destruction of their arms caches, he had come to be regarded as the reveler for mobilizing separatist forces. Fires were blamed on other spies working within the organization. News of those sabotages arrived at the remaining depots and Americans quickly emptied their storehouses.

As his status rose, Charles began using his real name instead of Richard Hudson. The other identity led to unpredictable responses, especially since the man had visited several sites on prior occasions. Besides, the name *Charles Bagwell* gave the pretense of a British outlaw, and thus a *Patriote* ally.

His arrival was anticipated with increasing popularity. He enjoyed the respect of Americans, who wanted their neighbors to share the hard won freedom they earned. Somewhere along the way, it became a task for other Stewart agents to carry out the cache destruction, and Charles began to wonder why one should choose allegiance to the British flag. It had always been a game of chance to predict which side would win and, hence, reward his activities with a pardon.

His increasing fame swelled the ranks of enthusiasts accompanying him on a path to glory at each subsequent lodge. By the time he arrived at the ninth tavern, Big Bear Lodge, fifty armed riders were at his side and, to Charles' surprise, over one hundred *Patriotes* were already camped on the grounds awaiting his message. Handshakes and backslapping thrust him into celebrations that made it easy to forget his family. It felt like he was being carried along like a leaf on a fast flowing river, his freedom disappeared, and he was never left alone.

Only once following his visit to the Royal Coach Inn did he

uncover another agent attempting to bring an end to the demonstration. Their brief conversation unsettled him; the spy announced that their only option left to divert the attack was to assassinate *Patriote* leaders. Charles, if not a leader, at least had become a symbol for the movement.

Shortly after leaving Big Bear Lodge, they were joined by a regiment of two hundred men from remaining outposts to the west, completing the recruitment. Six trappers took charge of daily operations. They discussed military strategy, more often than not, when Charles happened to be away from their presence.

Riding north, the rebel band crossed the Saint Lawrence fifty miles northeast of Kingston. The crossing itself took two days, men and horses ferried aboard flat-bottomed boats. They encountered no interference as scarcely any water traffic ventured on the Saint Lawrence at this time of year.

The scruffy bunch of invaders kept in good spirits, singing and laughing away nights around various campfires. The men expected little opposition, and no resistance had been put forth by local law enforcement. Once into Lower Canada, the brigade of horsemen stretched nearly a mile along a path paralleling the north shore, creeping forward less than twenty miles per day.

Early spring saw the caravan passing through snow-covered farmlands occupied by French *inhabitants,* who waved enthusiastically and invited them to stop for food. Occasionally, new recruits were added along the way. These volunteers were treated as heroes joining a noble mission to save poor peasants from the chains of tyranny. The *inhabitants'* zealousness perplexed Charles for if the army actually succeeded in driving out the British, poor French Canadian farmers would undoubtedly revert to a *signeural* system of servitude. It was debatable which option could improve the lot of the *Quebecois.*

Buildings of Montreal came into view and scouts hurried ahead to assess potential routes and possibility of conflict. By mid-afternoon, the army of Yankee trappers was poised outside the west end of town, ready to ride through streets, proclaiming liberation of the city's dwellers.

Their invasion went unexpectedly well with little gunfire. The local constable remained inside his office, while few pockets of militia resistance proved easily dispersed. Success surprised the attackers considering that a year earlier, violence broke out during a local election and British militia shot six Sons of Liberty protagonists. Today, however, reformers had the upper hand. There was no sense in razing buildings and creating enemies among the residents, so only the local British Foreign Office was burned after its occupants had long since fled the premises.

Buoyed by their triumph, Charles rode into town. With the city under *Patriote* control, he calmly entered a corner tavern and began drinking ale with three Frenchmen. He grinned, now certain he had made the right decision by joining the separatists. The most difficult task still lay ahead of them, their demonstration in Quebec City, but his many comrades never failed to remind him of the humanity of their cause. For a brief instant, he thought of William on his way to warn Lord Stewart and wondered if he found his wife. When his American "troops" finally arrived there, Charles hoped his family would join his side, given the inevitability of a *Patriote* victory.

Commotion outside interrupted his reverie. Two trappers shouted, and angry, insistent voices of several women reached his ears.

One of his men barged up to Charles' table. "Excuse me, Mr. Bagwell, there are two ladies here who request to see you."

Charles nodded for them to be brought inside.

The women marched inside dressed in plain costume. One appeared tall with long blond curls. The other seemed younger and nearly a foot shorter with short dark brown hair. Charles rose as the quite comely females approached. He waved for them to sit at his table.

Their expressions of impatience gave way to smiles. The taller woman closed to embrace him. "Charles, it's you, at long last!"

He hesitated while she kissed him fervently and buried her face in his chest. The other lady frowned at his look of bewilderment. He pushed the first woman away and bowed stiffly. "I'm sorry, a gunshot wound destroyed nearly all of my memory. I presume you are related to me?"

"Charles, it's Emily, your wife!" the tall woman said, gaping at him.

He shook his head slowly. "I am sorry. I don't remember you." His voice trailed off, seeing Emily fight tears burning her eyes.

"It's time to go home and recover from this ordeal," she managed. "You've been through so much. We thought you were dead..." Her voice broke at the last word.

Charles shifted uneasily at her distress.

He nodded. "It has been difficult, to be sure, but I must complete my mission or I will be a hunted criminal for the rest of my life."

The shorter female looked perplexed. "But Charles, what you're doing is treasonous. The British army will put down this insurrection and you'll be hanged."

"Only if we fail," he reassured her. "The *Patriote* cause is noble. A demonstration will benefit all French Canadians by showing Parliament that problems within this Province can't be ignored." Charles paused. "Please sit down. You are then Mrs. Hudson?"

"Victoria, your sister-in-law," she replied evenly.

"You, of all people, should have sympathy for the *inhabitants*, considering what your husband did on their behalf. I am here, because Richard and other proprietors provided the means for an assault on the Governor's manor."

Emily shook her head, staring at her husband with blatant disbelief. "How can you talk like this, Charles? We are all British subjects!"

"We knew Richard was involved in the kidnapping," Victoria uttered uneasily. "Now you're suggesting he was behind this rebellion, as well. I just want to know why he did it."

Charles hesitated. "He was helping to raise money for the *Patriotes*. He pretended to be William, which I found out later from the *real* William Darmon."

Both women's jaws dropped with sudden excitement. Their words tumbled one over the other. "You've seen William! When? Where? We've not had word of him since he left us on Lake Champlain."

Charles held up a hand for silence. "We met in the basement of a hunting lodge—a lodge much like yours, Victoria. We narrowly escaped death from an explosion. Afterwards, he left for Quebec City to find Elizabeth and inform Lord Stewart of the coming attack."

He smiled ruefully, remembering how he once helped the British authorities.

"Oh, Lord," Emily groaned. "Elizabeth left us to return to the Lodge and search for William. She hasn't been in Quebec City for months."

"Yes, not since some cowards abducted her and dyed her hair blonde," Victoria hissed. "I can't believe there's a woman running around impersonating our sister."

Charles held his silence for a moment.

What a fool he had been to work against his own family, believing Madam Cazeau was actually Elizabeth. Yet, his intentions were honorable. He firmly believed in the *Patriote's* cause. "It's just as well she left. That city will be no place for an Englishwoman when our men liberate the townspeople."

Emily shifted uncomfortably. "Charles, think about what you're doing," she pleaded. "Let's leave now and return to London. This isn't our fight."

He shook his head. "It's everyone's fight, Emily. You go back if you must. I, on the other hand, know of no place other than these territories. William said there's a ship leaving for the Isles in three weeks, the *Oceana*. Stay here until the fighting ends, then make for Quebec docks. He will meet you there. The ship will take you all home."

"But Charles, what about you!" Victoria objected. "You're still a wanted criminal!"

The Englishman grinned. "Don't worry about me. After our victory, my men and I will be heroes. I've become a symbol as a British outlaw fighting for the inhabitants. I wouldn't be surprised if they ask me to become Mayor of Quebec City."

Chapter Fifteen

William glared defiantly at the gentleman seated opposite in the jail cell.

"Sir, I challenge you to find anyone this side of the Atlantic who has greater loyalty to the Crown than myself."

He wrinkled his nose at the person's unpleasant demeanor. Portly, with a receding hairline and sagging jowls, his visitor fidgeted as if to free himself from a brown, wrinkled waistcoat and rumpled shirt.

Once more, conversation was interrupted by an uncontrollable coughing spell.

The gentleman dabbed a wadded handkerchief at the corners of his mouth, then proceeded to smooth the cloth on top of his knee before folding it and returning it to his pocket to wait for the next bout.

"This may be true, Mr. Darmon, but you're purported to be a close friend of Charles Bagwell, whose loyalties have recently come into question. There's also the problem of an eye witness to your poisoning Lord Stewart."

William spread his hands. "Mr. Moffat, I assure you that whatever Charles' actions appear to be, the last time we spoke he had every intention of preventing an attack on the Governor. It was his information that I gave to Lord Stewart."

His interrogator hacked violently once more and wiped his brow with the rumpled kerchief. "Yes, well, we now have some doubt about its veracity, given the fact he's leading several hundred *Patriotes* against the authorities in Lower Canada."

William jerked his head up. "I can't believe he's changed allegiance. He suffered memory loss and on occasion demonstrates a naive acceptance of appearances, but he would never knowingly abandon his status as an Englishman."

"All I can say is that if he proposes to gain a pardon for a role in preventing this insurrection, he's chosen an odd path," the agent observed.

"This is madness! Charles doesn't care about Canadian politics."

William rose and crossed to look out a tiny barred window.

Moffat remained unruffled. "According to reports, these men hold him in high esteem and he shares their enthusiasm for independence."

William slammed a fist into his palm. "If only I could talk to him, I'm certain his motives would become clear. No matter how misguided his plan, underneath it all his loyalty is as sound as yours or mine."

"I'd like to give you the opportunity, but there's a small matter of your being the prime suspect in Lord Stewart's murder," the agent added curling his lip.

"You know as well as I who was responsible for the crime. The accusation was a ploy by the Cazeau woman to divert suspicion from herself. I was the perfect dupe and she seized the opportunity."

Moffat expelled into his handkerchief. "Governor Aylmer and I believe this may be the case, but we have no proof. Mr. Bagwell, himself, could be the key to bringing down the *Libertines* if he would testify against her. You need to convince him of his duty."

William's eyes bore into the official. "Give me the chance and I'll do everything in my power to bring that organization to justice. They've cost the life of my brother-in-law, separated me from my family, and taken my bank account."

Lord Stewart's man held out his hand. "Well then, we're agreed. You may be surprised to learn we have an idea how it might be done."

William reclaimed his seat, looking at the man intently. "How?"

Moffat began to pace the small expanse. "We'd like you to join a regiment being assembled here in Quebec City. I have a letter from the Governor authorizing your enlistment as a scout. It will give you the freedom to maneuver behind enemy lines. Our latest report suggests the rebels are preparing to leave Montreal. Our brigade will march south and be ready to confront the invaders in three days at *Trois Rivieres*. You will go on ahead and extract this man from the traitors before he gets himself killed."

William's heart pounded. "Wait a minute. You want me to be the first to encounter the American ruffians? I've had a bad experience with those hostage-holding revolutionaries."

The agent shrugged. "You would prefer to be hanged for Lord Stewart's murder?"

William settled back thoughtfully. "What if Charles refuses to come with me? With his memory loss, the man is sometimes unpredictable."

Moffat sighed. "Mr. Darmon, I know this is a terrible risk to take, but what other choice is there if you two are ever to be pardoned?"

William rose and squeezed his hands around the bars of the cell door.

He nodded with resignation. "I can't believe the irony of this. Two best friends, both facing a hangman's noose, leading opposing forces into battle against each other."

Moffat put his hand on the prisoner's shoulder. "The Governor has given me authority to escort you to the regiment of Colonel Wetherall."

"Let's get on with it," William muttered.

The 104th Royal Regiment of Foot Infantry camped just outside the Citadel on the Plains of Abraham. Four hundred Colonial Regulars or 'Fencibles' under the command of Lieutenant Colonel F. A Wetherall marched over grassland, back and forth in separate formations. Mobilization of the so-called 'Sedentary Militia' occurred in record time after news arrived that American raiders reached Canadian soil. Uniforms uncrated, volunteers recruited, and weapons distributed, yet the battalion bore little resemblance to corps originally formed in New Brunswick twenty years earlier.

Two newly outfitted soldiers conducted William and George Moffat between rows of canvas shelters to Colonel Wetherall's tent, where their papers were reviewed and the mission discussed. The Colonel expressed reservation about Moffat's plan, but did not question his authority. Eventually, he saluted the agent, and a trooper escorted Moffat from the compound.

Wetherall summoned another officer, Captain Colborne.

While they waited, the officer turned to William. "Mr. Darmon, I don't envy you this task. Captain Colborne is one of my best officers.

You'll find my men disciplined, however, it's no secret you're accused of Lord Stewart's murder and, if Charles Bagwell is your friend, I recommend you keep it to yourself. My men think you to be a traitor, so watch your backside."

William swallowed. It had not occurred to him these former Englishmen might regard him as an enemy.

"We'll try to get you free of the battalion as quickly as possible," he went on. "In the mean time, you're responsible for your own well-being. Once the battle is joined, I advise you and your friend to get out of the area quickly. Take a boat downriver. Until then, you could be shot by either side."

William's anxiety reached new heights. He would be jumping at shadows for the next few days, and then face muskets of the *Patriotes*.

Captain Colborne entered the tent.

Wetherall briefed him on William's assignment. The young officer regarded the other with cold formality. They asked William to step outside for a moment.

William bowed, stooped to exit through the low doorway and retreated several steps from the tent.

Beyond temporary barracks, throngs of red-coated infantry maneuvered under an afternoon sun. Men were divided into groups of thirty, practicing different forms of combat, while others marched in unison.

William watched the hasty preparations. It reminded him when he once observed soldiers in Kent near the town of Langdon preparing for great battles on the continent. He glanced to his left at the distant Saint Lawrence. Somewhere beyond the horizon, Charles was marching steadfastly toward them.

Suddenly, an object flew out of the sky. Before he could duck, it struck his right cheekbone. He yelped in pain and dropped to one knee as a jagged rock bounced away.

The two officers came out of the tent and helped him to his feet.

Blood oozed from the wound and ran down his face, covering his right hand as he tried to wipe away the mess. The officers quickly scanned their surroundings, but the men nearby were busy doing their best *not* to pay attention to the incident.

"Come with me, Mr. Darmon. I'll take you to the infirmary," Captain Colborne urged. "We'd better get you into a uniform and decide on a temporary identity to help you get through the next few days."

With his wound treated, William followed his escort to the supply tent to be outfitted in appropriate dress. By the time he finished mess call, the rest of the encampment had retreated to their tents to prepare for an early wakeup.

William shared a tent with three other soldiers younger than himself. They seemed unaware of his identity and paid him no attention. He loathed the idea these men might consider him a traitor and refused to go into battle without comrades. There was no choice but to try to draw them out and gain some measure of friendship.

He lay on his bedroll looking up at the canvas ceiling. "Does anyone know what's in store for us tomorrow?"

"Jes' a stroll in the woods, friend," a grizzled infantryman on the nearest cot answered. "Them Yankees will learn better than t' mess with a Regiment of Fencible Infantry. It's time ta dust off the lessons of 1812."

"I say let Frenchies farm their seigneuries," another voice added. "They don' care two hoots about independence. These trappers need ta mind their own business."

"I'm goin' ta get me a few souvenirs for the missus," the remaining occupant contributed.

"Have any of you been in battle before?" William asked.

The man nearest William laughed. "I doubt anyone in the regiment's fired a musket for military purposes, except maybe Harlan here on parade day last year. There was some target practice at the south end today, but there's not been time for much shooting."

"I've heard those Princess Victoria's Royal Irish Fusiliers are good," another soldier remarked. "They just arrived. They'll know what to do, but them laddies keep mainly to themselves."

The brigade broke camp at daybreak. Men quickly closed ranks to begin their march to *Trois Rivieres*. Sixty cavalry rode ahead of the main infantry, which quickstepped in two columns stretching two hundred yards. Three horse-drawn cannon accompanied by Fusiliers brought up the rear guard.

In the cool, clear air of spring, the procession of red and white uniforms made a colorful spectacle against greening banks of the blue Saint Lawrence. No other travelers appeared on the road, winding its way westward next to the river westward. Despite the absence of onlookers, the soldiers did a good job of maintaining formation, creating an impressive entourage that masked their inexperience.

William rode with the cavalry; his mission required the fast pace of a horse. He felt awkward under the uniform's heavy coat and pack. Much to his embarrassment, straps kept slipping off his shoulders and catching on his arms. He planned to discard the disguise once in sight of the enemy and move through undergrowth without obvious colors. The enemy! He gazed at the fast-flowing river, wondering if Charles and his band of ragtag fanatics knew what faced them ahead. Of course, Americans knew how to hide and shoot against an orderly procession of infantry. He had no reason to assume the Fencibles would prevail, in spite of their appearance.

Eight hours of forced march brought the regiment to within two miles of *Trois Riveries,* where they broke ranks to set up the night's camp.

Hudson's mill was actually built on a tributary of the Saint John River.

Elizabeth admired the barn-like structure at water's edge as her horse meandered closer. Overhead, puffy white clouds filled a breezy spring sky between fluttering evergreens and budding ash trees.

A hundred yards from the building, Elizabeth dismounted. From a bend in the river, she could see its' water facing façade. No activity could be seen around the mill. Sizable chunks of ice still floated near shore.

The Constable of Newcastle predicted it would be a few weeks more before operations resumed. Much of the work would be directed at 'squaring' the logs in preparation for floatation down to the Bay of Fundy and subsequent transport abroad.

After tying her horse to a nearby tree, she stood for a moment, considering how to find a way inside the building.

The mill appeared to be completely closed up with a large bar and padlock securing the single doorway. There were no windows in its sloping roof, which extended nearly to the ground. At each end of the barn, a ramp attached to a square opening ten feet above the water. These shoots extended all the way down to a frozen river surface. Unfortunately, the openings displayed a cover of rough wood planks nailed into place.

On the riverside, however, a small opening sat near the top of a long, sloping pile of waste pieces formed by bark and irregular splinters congealed into a tall mound. Much of the pile entangled within a latticework of support beams, forging a barrier against river current. Only a simple canvas hung over the lofted opening, apparently left to protect the interior against weather, rather than intruders.

Elizabeth maneuvered her way along a frost-covered bank to the south end of the mill and carefully stepped out onto the latticework. She clung to the wet boards, while trying to avoid touching the ice encrusted water. With some difficulty, she worked her way out, only inches above the floe and reached the woodpile. From there, she gingerly climbed up the mountain of soggy wood fragments to the tiny portal. Panting foggy breath, she arrived at a precarious perch next to the canvas flap and needed no encouragement to scramble inside.

Beneath the ceiling, an empty trough extended horizontally from her position and angled downward thirty feet to a platform ten feet above the floor. She knelt down inside the sluice and crawled hand over hand further into the darkened interior. Tiny dust motes filled the air, illuminated by sunlight streaming through cracks in the sideboards. No sound came from within the building, except for scuffling noises from her boots as she pushed to reach the far end.

From the platform, she gazed down at a large empty room.

In one corner, a partition separated a narrow causeway from the area, complete with door and a small glass window. She imagined a senior foreman conducted business there, while isolated from the clamor of timber passing through the blades of the saw. Elizabeth concluded if any answers were to be found, they must be inside the enclosure.

She climbed down the ladder.

On the main floor, old wallboards creaked with buffeting breezes outside.

For some reason, she felt a need to move quietly despite the deserted surroundings. She tip-toed awkwardly over planking strewn with wood chips and sawdust in order to peer through the office window.

A small desk stood against the opposite wall under a shelf holding an oil lamp, lead and box labeled Sauria's Friction Matches. Elizabeth recalled that William had once referred to these new devices as 'Lucifers' and warned not to breathe phosphorus fumes when they were lit.

Papers littered everywhere within the tiny room. Elizabeth was amazed at the number of sheets covering every surface. The desk itself was buried under inches of bills of lading and receipts. In front of the wall to her right, a bureau with overstuffed drawers stood sandwiched between stacks of paper two feet high on both sides. Other parchment pieces scattered over the floor under messages tacked to every square inch of wall space.

She went around to the door. It was unlocked.

After lighting the lamp, she began scanning the mountain of paperwork. She was not sure what to look for and it was going to be a formidable task to paw through the mess. Her eye was drawn to three drawers on the right side of the desk, Unlike those of the bureau, these were not ajar. She pulled on them, but they would not yield.

Locked drawers could mean hidden secrets. Her excitement soared.

Prying them open was another matter. She could not budge either one enough to create a gap and no tool showed itself to give her leverage.

She glared at the piece of furniture.

There was no need for timidity. If necessary, she could drag the desk outside smash it with rocks to get at the truth. She tried to think logically facing the mocking container. The desk was constructed of soft pine standing on tapered corner legs, and the bottom drawer positioned six inches off the floor.

Bending over, she gripped the bottom of the desk and lifted until it crashed onto its backside, sending papers scattering in all directions. The unfinished bottom surface suggested the lower part of the drawer might be its weakest element, so she turned and kicked at the base with the heel of her riding boot. It cracked, then splintered around a jagged hole.

Satisfied, Elizabeth carefully stuck her hand inside the irregular opening and felt a bundle of letters. She withdrew the neatly-tied stack and sat down on the floor to inspect the correspondence.

The topmost envelope displayed large, sprawling handwriting, addressed to Richard Hudson at the mill.

She removed its' letter and read:

Dear Richard:
Your accusation of September 2, suggesting that I had something to do with boycotting your mill offends me greatly. As an outsider, you knew local timber companies would regard your purchase as unwanted competition. Hearing your difficulties saddens me.

I was surprised to learn you had to pay fifteen shillings a day for immigrant workers. Small wonder your indebtedness now exceeds eight thousand pounds. If the mill does not become productive in a short time, others will build down river and your project will fail.
Yours faithfully,
Walter
30th day of September 1831

Setting that letter aside, she opened the next.

Dear Richard:
I was relieved to learn that you found a benefactor to offset a portion of your indebtedness. The offer of three thousand dollars Halifax Currency for implement storage is intriguing. I would be interested in securing a similar arrangement with Madam Cazeau here at the Royal Coach. I wish I could be of more assistance, but I fear, short of selling the Inn, there isn't any more money.

Perhaps it's too late, but have you considered an insurance policy against the annual production of the mill? I have a friend who's a subscriber to Lloyds at the Royal Exchange in Cornhill. He might be interested in underwriting your holdings. Lloyds traditionally provides marine insurance, yet possibly there's an underwriter who would endorse such a policy.

Closer to home, an idea came to me that we might consider forming our own corporation of insurance, much like the Pennsylvania charter of 1768. The company would be an association of tavern and lodge owners across Canada, and here in America. Such an association could provide mutual protection against business losses, risk by fire, loss of life, etc.

Under this scheme, each depositor would be liable to his fellow members for losses in the amount of his deposit plus half more. Interest on funds raised would belong to the company, while the principal could remain the property of the depositors, subject to payouts for business losses. After a term, losses and company expenses would be determined and new policies issued. Thinking of such a plan, I'd be surprised if we couldn't secure deposits of at least fifty thousand dollars in the first year alone.

I will think more on this idea and keep you informed of its potential as a solution to your difficulties.
Yours faithfully,
Walter
27th day of October 1831

Another letter was also enlightening:

Dear Richard:
The Union of Hunting Lodges now has a membership of twenty-five with the addition of the Wild Fox Inn at Cleveland. Cost of the policies is presently set at one thousand five hundred dollars, a small investment for piece of mind in the unsettled territories. Aside from damage payment made to Big Bear Lodge, assets in the Bank of Quebec now exceed sixty five thousand dollars. For appearance sake, I urge you to secure separate policies for both the Mill and the Lodge.

Your visits to the lodges on behalf of the Directors have been greatly appreciated and Madam Cazeau's offer to the proprietors for safekeeping rifles was mutually beneficial. There are many in

American communities who support the cause of Canadian independence. Our plan ensures that blame will be cast on political motive, while providing her with money for the Patriotes.

Take heart, brother, for I feel certain we will soon realize prosperity far beyond what might have been derived from the sale of your business.

Yours faithfully,
Walter
13th day of August 1832

Elizabeth swallowed hard, aghast at the plot they had set up.

The last letter implied Richard's Lodge was burned in order to collect insurance money and cover his poor investment. Her family had been kidnapped to make it look like a political action and, in return, the *Patriotes* got extortion money. Poor Victoria! What a devious man she married. He destroyed the lodge and four servants were killed to perpetrate an insurance fraud.

She bit her lip, realizing her brother-in-law was not the only culprit. With Richard out of the way, Walter Hudson stood to make off with the association's fortune. She did not know this Madam Cazeau, but concluded she must be a person of influence among the French Canadians.

Elizabeth unfolded the remaining letter.

Dear Richard

Preparations are on schedule. M. Cazeau has hired men for the abduction at Dawes Creek. She requests you proceed with her to the Bank of England before the hostages are transported to the island. That way if additional details are needed, William will be on hand. I will meet you on the 30th to file our claim at the Bank of Quebec. I'll be staying with an old friend, Captain Louis at the Citadel. The facility is largely undermanned these days, so I should have no difficulty securing accommodation.

Remain steadfast. The end is in sight.
Yours faithfully,
Walter
17 July 1833

Elizabeth dropped the paper, remembering her pursuit of Richard. Walter must have been at the Citadel that night. Richard might have fled there to inform his brother of her presence in Quebec. Maybe they argued over what to do and Walter killed him, knowing he would inherit the insurance claim.

Suddenly, she thought of Charles. He was said to be leading a force of Americans, presumably armed with weapons stored in these hunting lodges. But, why would he do such a thing? Perhaps it was a condition imposed by the Cazeau woman to reveal the location of her hostages.

She resolved to take these incriminating letters to the authorities. If Walter Hudson were apprehended and Madam Cazeau put to flight, maybe then they could all return to England and be free of the entanglements.

Elizabeth carefully gathered up the missives and examined the remains of the desk. She wondered if other drawers held further revelations. She leaned over to inspect the splintered hole, but sighed, reluctant to continue dismantling the piece. After all, she had what she needed. Peering through the opening to the next drawer's bottom surface, she did not hear the outside door of the mill quietly open.

Chapter Sixteen

Charles awakened in darkness. A hand shook his shoulder.

It took him a few seconds to remember the Inn at *Trois-Rivieres* where they bivouacked and events about to unfold. A final march to Quebec City would begin today. Unless they met formidable resistance, the Americans would reach the Governor's Palace in three days, exactly on the appointed day of Champlain's anniversary.

"Mr. Bagwell, wake up!" a young recruit stammered. "There's been a change in plans. We're due at Molson's Wharf in one hour. A ship called *Lord Melville* has been commandeered to take the men down to Quebec Port."

Charles brushed away last vestiges of sleep. "What? Why aren't we marching into the city like we did in Montreal?"

"Justin thinks we'd be met by a counter attack before we covered the distance. We have to strike before their spies give warning. We'll leave the horses here with a few men and pick them up on our way back."

Charles sat up, reflecting on the plan. It could save a day's ride and avoid the exposure on a long march downriver. With an extra day, he might slip away and give William a message that Emily and Victoria were on the way to meet him at the docks for their final departure.

Lord Melville pulled anchor at dawn. Charles watched from the bow as the four hundred ton ship quietly glided out from port and crossed to the south shore of the Saint Lawrence, thereby reducing the chance of notice by any defensive forces. He sighed at the thought that even if spotted, it was a good bet the ship could outrun any land troops chasing them to Quebec City unless they were detected within ten miles from the destination.

Morning light gave rise to clear, unseasonably warm and sunny weather. Their vessel overtook a steamboat and several flat-bottoms passing inlet settlements. Sails and a swift current combined to speed them downriver at twenty knots while most of the three-hundred-man invasion force remained out of sight below deck.

Charles smiled. The invasion was going as planned. Unless the city stood on full alert, an unscheduled arrival of *Lord Melville* should not cause great concern. Trappers would then merge with street traffic before a military response could be assembled.

They would all find their way to the Governor's Chateau at Fort Saint Louis and blend in with the crowd awaiting Lord Aylmer's speech. According to Justin's plan, a disturbance was to be staged to distract the guards while a party slipped inside and upstairs to attack the governor. The end result would be a tragic fire, leaving Quebec without foreign oversight and enough chaos to allow *Patriotes* to take control.

Within a few days, after remaining resistance was extinguished, the reformers could claim independence at last. Word would be sent to major nations that a new country had been formed with autonomous leadership. Madam Cazeau predicted other provinces would soon follow and, by the time British Parliament responded, reprisals would be too costly to enforce.

Charles waved at some children playing among the rocks. At last, he found a place in the scheme of things. He no longer cared about a forgotten past.

Just before noon, a scout returned to the loyalist regiment.

An approach by a single rider at full gallop signaled important news. The messenger quickly passed through milling soldiers and headed toward the Colonel's tent behind officers' portable shelters at the rear of camp.

William hurried toward a cluster of converging leaders. By the time he came within earshot of the discussion, shouts rang out passing an order to form ranks.

"What is it, Colonel?" William asked breathlessly, drawing up next to Wetherall.

The officer turned with a frown. "We've just received word that the Americans have boarded a ship headed this way. Given the current, *Lord Melville* should be here within an hour."

Commands echoed directing the troops to do an about-face for a fast march back to Quebec City. Orders were also given for a small artillery crew to set up three cannon at the water's edge, near the narrows thirty miles north of *Trois Rivieres.* From that vantage point, the Saint Lawrence extended only two miles across and cannon fire might reach the vessel as it sailed by.

William decided to wait with the Fusiliers. He was determined to reach Charles and see if the ship were stopped. If the cannon missed their mark, he still had time to make a long gallop to the harbor and arrive not long after the raiders disembarked. The scout mentioned *Lord Melville* was not armed. William muttered a soft 'aye', relieved they could not return fire.

By the time the merchant ship was sighted, all traces of the regiment had disappeared. A small grove of trees hid the guns, allowing the ship to come within range before it could perform any evasive maneuvers.

Cannoneers stood silently by their weapons, anxious to commence fire.

On a wooded cliff some distance away, William steadied his mount in anticipation of the loud reports. The ship heaved clearly into view. Bulging sails of the fast approaching craft suggested they would be lucky to get off more than one round apiece.

Only two or three crewmembers could be seen on deck. There was no sign of an army of trappers. William began to question if this was the right ship.

The vessel drew up even with his position.

Three loud thumps of cannon fire shook ground under William's horse, which whinnied and lunged backward. He clutched at the reins to regain his balance, watching puffs of white smoke follow the projectile launches.

He waited patiently for seconds to pass while the fusiliers quickly turned to reload their guns.

A column of water erupted directly in front of the ship's bow as it floated past. A second cannonball hit the merchantman near mid-ship sending pieces of wood scattering from a hole just above the waterline. A third missile smashed into top deck at the stern, dispersing a cloud of debris into the river.

The fusiliers cheered.

William observed passengers crowding onto the deck. Distant figures ran toward the damaged sections in a flurry of activity. He could only hope Charles found a safe spot away from the incoming barrage.

Cannons fired a second volley as the vessel's aft section began receding from view. One shot scored another hit, breaking the mizzenmast several feet above its base and toppling it into the current.

The disappearing vessel listed to port. William could only imagine frantic efforts taking place on board as men tried to keep the ship upright for as long as possible. Perhaps his Fencibles would make it back ahead of them after all. There was no time to waste. He urged his mount onto the road and galloped off, hoping to reach town within hours of their landing.

Outside the Governor's Palace, impatient *Quebecois* milled about in crowded streets. The mid-morning address by Lord Aylmer had been postponed until afternoon, and word circulated he had retreated to another refuge. A sea of faces filled the central square. *Inhabitants* of all ages, men women and children, stood shoulder to shoulder gazing up at the five-story edifice.

Charles and his men moved unhindered from the waterfront to the Upper City. *Lord Melville* had barely escaped cannon fire at *Trois Rivieres*. By the time the ship made port, it listed thirty degrees, and Justin ordered the captain to ram it directly into the wharf. Remarkably, no one was injured, and the trappers scampered off before the port authorities arrived.

The plan proceeded. Justin assured the Americans that regardless of whether or not the governor was present, worthwhile attention could be gained simply by razing the ancient Chateau and, if the Governor chose to flee, he would not hinder their efforts to seize control of the city. As to the members of the Executive Council,

Madame Cazeau's people would take care of that business.

When the invaders arrived at the central square, the crowd was already seething, growing tenser by the minute as *inhabitants* waited for the Governor to answer their many complaints. Pushing and shoving were commonplace within the predominantly French audience. Some of the rabble became unruly and political disagreements broke out everywhere. A formal announcement was long overdue. *Patriote* supporters mingled within the crowd, taking part in the discussions and reacting on cue to the rumored invasion. Meanwhile, the trappers merged through the morass, elbowing their way toward the aging stained blocks of Montmagny Palace.

Charles managed to squeeze his way around to the rear of the decaying monument. Already, three of his fellow invaders confronted two uniformed guards at the back entrance. Space behind the building proved to be less overrun and, while the sentries were distracted, Charles slipped inside.

Relieved to be out of the commotion, Charles found himself within a long room packed with dignitaries. A few soldiers moved between well-dressed gentlemen, but they paid him little attention. He presumed these were lesser-ranking diplomats, voicing concerns over schedule changes handed down by higher-ups. He absently touched small bags of gunpowder tucked within the pockets of his long coat, reminding him of his next task. He spied a hallway at the far end of the room, leading to a staircase.

Taking a deep breath, he walked purposefully toward the passageway.

Halfway up the first flight of stairs, a gentleman in regal attire descended to meet him. "Who are you? No one's allowed upstairs without my authorization."

Charles froze. He looked squarely into the official's eyes and pressed his breast pocket. "See here, my good man, I've come with a message for the governor from his Lordship, Ian Stewart."

The man stared back for a moment, eyes wide with indignation.

Slowly he nodded, averting his glance as if entertaining a distracting thought. He absently waved Charles to pass and continued downward.

Charles exhaled relief and quickly completed his climb to the second floor. Unlike the one below, this hallway appeared deserted. Closed doors lined a causeway on both sides. Cautiously, he crept down the passageway, stopping to listen at each room.

Near the far end, a door stood partially open.

Charles peeked and found an empty office. He stepped inside and shut the door.

The ten-foot square room held three large upholstered chairs facing a blond desk positioned before two windows. In one corner, a small brocaded Ottoman sat next to the grimy stone walls. He stepped over to it and unloaded his parcels. Carefully, he stacked the bags into a pile on top of the cushion and spread some black powder over the mound. From there, he backed toward the door, spilling a trail onto the musty brown carpet.

Squatting near the entrance, he retrieved a flint and struck it.

The door burst open.

Two soldiers, followed by the person Charles encountered on the stairs charged into the room with guns drawn.

"Shoot him!" yelled the official.

Charles dove to the carpet as muskets fired. He rolled over against a window.

The soldiers dropped their weapons and started after him, while the other man leaped toward the fast burning fuse.

Charles groped for the sill, but hands rudely pulled from behind, flinging his torso backward. His head struck the wall. Pain stunned his mind. Disoriented, he could do nothing but watch the two soldiers pummel his bruised body. Their actions seemed to slow in a dreamlike motion, sounds became muffled—until the room exploded with a searing flash. Instantly, time sped up and the room filled with piercing sounds of chaos.

The guards crashed against the desk. A scream resonated behind them. Charles turned to see their comrade engulfed by fire.

From somewhere deep inside Charles' psyche, an image of his manor's parlor in Surrey swam before him.

Emily! Our house is on fire!

Time sped faster. Frantically, he lunged past the soldiers and leaped across the flaming carpet. Heat became suddenly unbearable. Smoke poured into the hallway as he staggered out and came face to face with four soldiers rushing to the entry.

Charles held up shaking palms. "My wife! Have you seen Emily?"

The first sentry cast a puzzled glance toward his partner. He reached to restrain Charles, but screams from inside the room convinced him of a more desperate need. Instead, the red-coats piled into the burning office.

Coughing and sputtering, Charles careened down the hall. Another gentleman bolted out of a room into the cloudy corridor and smacked against the Englishman.

"Where's my wife?" Charles demanded. "Have the servants gone for help? Why are these soldiers in my home? We must get everyone outside!"

The man picked himself off the floor and ran to the stairway, yelling, "Fire! Fire!"

Charles chased after him, but, instead of going down, he climbed stairs up to the third floor. People were pouring out of their rooms, creating a mob heading toward the stairs. The crazed bunch shoved Charles backward when he tried to squeeze past, leaving him pressed against a window before they disappeared down the steps.

Recovering his balance, Charles charged down the hall, desperately throwing doors open, calling for his wife. *Why were all these people in my house?* In a frenzy, he worked his way through every room while smoke billowed up the stairwell, creating an ever thickening layer of fumes just under the ceiling.

"Emily!" he shouted hoarsely. "Emily!"

He staggered over to an office window. His brow furrowed in confusion at the sight below. Ugly buildings and streets holding a morass of bodies had replaced his palatial gardens and well-kept courtyard.

While staring dumbfounded at the crowd, he heard a crackling sound from the hallway. He spun around to see flames spreading along the ceiling out in the corridor. Tongues of fire shot inside his room. Within seconds, the chamber became an inferno, forcing him out the window onto a narrow ledge.

Upturned faces within the melee below were cheering at the sight of the flaming building, but Charles barely heard them. A searing pain attacked his neck. His coat caught fire, and flames climbed to his hair!

Terrified, his gaze searched the throng below. Many of the intruders were backing away from the burning structure, leaving a twenty-foot open space directly under his position. It was a terrible distance to fall but the alternative was worse.

He spied a similar ledge on the next floor below. If he could lower himself to the next level, he might be able to work his way down. He crouched facing the building and clutched the edge while swinging his legs over the side. His grip slipped under the weight of his body and he dropped. His feet landed for an instant on the lower ledge, but the impact prevented gaining his balance. His body tipped backwards, and the flailing figure bounced away from the wall.

A woman in the crowd screamed as Charles plummeted twenty feet to the ground. He landed feet first, fell forward onto his face and rolled over onto his back. For a moment, he lay motionless, staring up at the sky. Over pain in his legs came a memory that he was no longer in his homeland. He was in Canada.

The fully engulfed Montmagny Manor formed a fiery backdrop and a huge column of thick black smoke rose hundreds of feet above the building, darkening a midday sky. The sight gave him some satisfaction. He was the one who created the pyre, symbolizing the death of an evil administration.

Charles struggled to sit up and shed the smoldering coat as the crowd closed in around him. Numerous hands reached down to lift him onto sore feet. Even at twenty-feet, he could feel intense heat that forced the throng to retreat further from the Chateau. Hands patted him on the back, He turned to see members of his American gang, mingling among the cheering *Quebecois*.

Charles suddenly remembered his instructions. When the conflagration ended, he was to return to the Palace Hotel and meet with Madam Cazeau. He paused for a moment, again, his brow knitted in confusion. Strangely, he felt as though he had been transported from another world. He had been sure that the woman he met in Montreal was somehow trapped in the Governor's mansion. *What was I thinking?*

A shot rang out. He swung around. Shouts echoed throughout the crowd.

In the distance, swarms of red-coats were streaming into the square from adjoining streets. They *inhabitants* were trapped. Pride in his work was now replaced by the anguish of realizing his message to Stewart must have gotten through. William warned the Governor in time to prepare for the assault. He would now be responsible for the capture and hanging of countless Americans.

Soldiers pressed inward, firing muskets into the air and pushing the crowd back toward the raging flames. Shouts of desperate *Quebecois* filled the air. Many pressed together in a large groups as they tried to resist confinement by the increasing pressure.

Suddenly, the Americans had had enough. Rifles appeared from under coats, and a chorus of gunfire halted the diminishing perimeter. Several red-coats pitched to the ground. Upward directed muskets became leveled at the crowd. Shots exploded everywhere.

Charles watched the furor through disbelieving eyes.

Terrorized participants fled in all directions, colliding with one another, and trampling helpless victims felled by musket balls. Bullets whistled through the crowd, collapsing bystanders in their tracks. Others fled toward the streets, heedless of a wall of thrusting bayonets.

As the throng surged outward, a portion of the troops was carried off. Those escapees that evaded muskets ran for their lives, leaving a thinning courtyard strewn with abandoned dead and wounded. Around the Manor, an inner ring of *Patriote* supporters continued to fire at the regiment, but the militia closed in from all sides. The number of fallen Americans outnumbered those left standing.

Charles crouched behind the melee. He had to get away. If he were not shot, he would be hanged as a leader of the lawless bunch, as well as for his prior crime.

A frantic gaze scanned the perimeter. *Inhabitants* still darted between shooters and their targets. Some limped away, others tried to carry their children to safety. He took a deep breath, said a silent prayer and jumped to his feet.

He bolted with head down toward a thin section in the converging ranks. He ducked behind a burly young man and his wife who ran toward a gap in the line of red-coats created by sentries reloading their guns.

"Halt! Stand where you are!" one soldier shouted.

The trio stumbled to within ten feet of the perimeter before soldiers again pointed their bayonets. Recklessly, the threesome dashed between thrusting bayonets.

At the last minute, Charles threw himself sideways into one of the guards. The collision sent the man flying backward, allowing Charles to tumble onto the cobblestone street. Two sentries charged after as he hauled himself to his feet. A sharp, piercing pain exploded in his side as he turned to see the escaping Frenchman smash into a pursuing militiaman.

Charles staggered onward, running blindly past storefronts as he tried to flee the commotion behind. A bullet nicked the building, just above his head, spurring him to an even faster pace.

He rounded a corner and disappeared down a narrow lane ten blocks away from the battlefield.

Chapter Seventeen

A soft creak startled Elizabeth. She was not alone in the building.

Rising on silent feet, she leaned over and blew out the lamp.

A second snapping noise sounded closer. She retreated to a corner, between the small window and the doorframe, and pressed her back against the wall. Frantic eyes scanned the room for a weapon of some kind, but not so much as a wooden board met her gaze—and there was no place else to hide. Her heart began to pound wildly in her chest. The door would open within seconds. There was no other way out of the room.

Breathing came in short gasps as footfalls grew louder.

The door slowly swung inward, blocking her view of the intruder. A man's heavy breathing whispered only inches away on the other side of the barrier.

After what seemed like a lifetime's hesitation, a dark form slowly moved beyond the edge toward the lamp. She grimaced, pulling the door closer to cover her presence before light hit the room.

Elizabeth barely breathed while sounds came from the newcomer rifling through papers strewn across the floor. A sudden cracking of wood told her that he discovered the hole in the desk. She considered flinging the door forward to catch him by surprise, but it would be impossible to get around and out the entrance before he grabbed her.

A full minute passed. She began to smell a scent of oil. The fragrance was joined by the telltale odor of smoke.

Elizabeth peeked around the end of the door. The visitor's back was turned, but a flickering light beyond his broad shoulders increased in intensity. He started a fire! Her surprise caused a sharp intake of breath. He whirled towards her. She froze, paralyzed with fear. In the glowing light his features became clear.

The man staring back was Peter McDougall.

They stood, eyes locked as hungry flames consumed papers and crept up the wall. Smoke filled the air. Heat became unbearable. Peter started toward the door, and Elizabeth followed with no thought of attempting to stop the blaze. They raced from the office to the mill's main entrance and scrambled outside.

As if by mutual consent, they mounted their horses and galloped upriver toward Petit Sault.

An hour later, the two riders stopped to catch their breath in a clearing along the Saint John River. They dismounted and sat on a mossy riverbank. Peter leaned against the trunk of an ash tree.

Elizabeth could no longer contain her curiosity. "Peter, I thought you'd been killed in Petit Sault. Constable Thomas told me so."

He took off his hat and gazed at the river. "The man they found in the hotel room was registered under that name. The deputies had no way of knowing it wasn't me."

She watched matted brown curls spill down the back of his neck. "But who was he, and why was he using your name?"

The young man retrieved a neckerchief from his pants pocket and wiped perspiration off his face. He looked at her, deciding he owed her an explanation. "He was an agent, like myself, working for Lord Stewart in the Quebec Assembly."

Elizabeth frowned. "You're some kind of spy?"

He grinned. "Yes ma'am. Peter isn't my real name. It's Edward, Edward Flannery."

"Well then, Edward, please tell me what happened the day the Hudson's Lodge burned down," she demanded.

He hunched forward, crossed his legs, and began to chew on the end of a long stalk of grass. "Well, I suppose there's no harm in telling now. Some months ago, I met Beatrice, I mean Miss Canerci, in Petit Sault. We got to know each other pretty well. She told me she was working for some bureaucrat named Moffat in Quebec City. She said the Provincial government was concerned about a secret society enlisting volunteers in New Brunswick and the American territories.

"Anyway, Moffat got word Richard Hudson had been approached by these conspirators and sent Beatrice to keep an eye on things. She asked me to seek a job at his Lodge. They knew that guns were being secreted to Hudson's place and wanted someone on the inside to keep track of who came and went."

Elizabeth nodded, thinking how she foolishly treated him as a stable hand.

Edward watched large chunks of ice crowding the river slowly float downstream. "When I hired on, the other servants didn't tell me much. They kept to themselves. One day, I found a partially written letter from Mr. Hudson to his brother talking about burning the place down. I sent word to Beatrice and, a week later, she visited the lodge. She informed me that the servants were part of a French gang plotting to overthrow the government. She said they would kill Mr. Hudson if he tried to set fire to the place."

He hesitated. "I didn't know what to do. After she left, I told Mr. Hudson I had seen the letter. He said he didn't care about the *Patriotes*, only their money. If Moffat wanted the guns destroyed and Mr. Hudson could get fire insurance cash they would both win."

"But what about the servants?" she asked.

Edward nodded. "Since the they were watching Hudson, we agreed I would do the job."

"You were to burn down the lodge?" Elizabeth gasped.

"It was planned for when your family was away. The trip to Grand Falls had already been planned for the abduction, it seemed like a perfect set up for the fire. Except, when you stayed behind, I thought you might be an agent of some kind. For all I knew, you being English and all, maybe Moffat also sent you; so I waited.

"After the empty carriage came back and you took off after your family, I lit fires all over the place. I was ready for the servants. Each time one of them came out I shot him. They weren't about to stay inside."

"Oh, Edward!" she cried.

He grimaced. "When the job was done, I headed out to Petit Sault to meet Beatrice, but found Mr. Bagwell instead. He was in awful shape, so I took him with me to find a doctor. "Beatrice got mad and said because of Bagwell, we'd be blamed for everything. She wanted to do away with him, but another agent tried to stop her. She killed him right there, and we left his body in the room. She said it was for the best, since I'd be suspect, being the only servant missing from the Lodge. Once the sheriff found the body, it might close the matter. Trouble was, we discovered Mr. Bagwell had escaped. Beatrice told me to go on to Quebec and tell Mr. Moffat what happened. I never saw her again."

Elizabeth whistled softly. "She's dead. We found her in a cabin north of town."

Edward's features sagged with remorse. He stood and shoved his hands into his pockets. "About a month ago, one of Mr. Moffat's men came to my room and offered me ten pounds to burn down the mill. He said this militant band was about to start a war and the Hudson places were part of it. So, I took the money and here I am."

Elizabeth could only feel sadness at the tale.

"I'm beginning to understand this now. According to some letters from Richard's brother, they intended to burn down the lodge to collect insurance money. They and other lodge proprietors had already collected money to store guns for the *Patriotes*, and Madam Cazeau arranged with Richard to kidnap my family and withdraw our funds."

Edward turned to her. "So, what are you going to do now?"

She took his arm as they walked back to their horses.

"Well, it's been months since Richard's death, but I'm going to check with the bank of Quebec to see if an insurance payment was made to Walter John. The payment, together with these letters," she said patting her bodice where the letters were saved, "should convict him of fraud. Mr. Moffat might also appreciate information confirming Madam Cazeau's involvement in the extortion."

The door to the French woman's suite was partially open when Charles arrived at the *Hotel de Palais*. He knocked softly, then, pushed it all the way inward.

An empty foyer opened to a sitting room and, beyond lay a bedroom. From the entrance, he could see the back of a man sitting on one side of the bed. There was an eerie silence within the place. Charles quietly proceeded across the sitting room.

He paused at the bedroom doorway.

Madam Cazeau lay on the bed, her eyes were open in a lifeless stare and her complexion as white as a sheet. The gentleman leaned over and took a glass from her hand. He wiped it clean with his handkerchief.

"What have you done to Madam Cazeau?" Charles blurted.

The man jerked in surprise. He bolted to his feet and whirled to face the newcomer. His short, fine-boned frame, thin, rimmed glasses, and banker's suit immediately identified him to Charles. It was Walter John of the Royal Coach Inn.

Charles' anger intensified. Madam Cazeau's death was a blow to the freedom of every French Canadian.

Instead of answering, Walter John threw the glass at Charles and darted toward the door. The Englishman dodged the object and jumped on the culprit as he tried to wiggle past. They both sprawled on the floor, with Charles on top.

Charles rolled Walter over and pinned him down. The murderer looked up at him through wide, fearful eyes. He squirmed, fruitlessly until it was evident he could not get free.

"I repeat, what have you done?" Charles said through clenched teeth.

His captive stammered at first, then the words spilled from his mouth in a torrent. "She did it. She and that other one, they ruined us! She killed my brother and burned down the lodges. It's over. It was small payment for our loss!"

Charles relaxed a little at his captive's apparent resignation. "Sir, if you do not explain why you've done this, I shall punch you until you do!"

"My name is Hudson," the captive admitted defiantly. "Walter John Hudson. My brother Richard and I were trying to save his business. How I wish we'd never met that devious woman!"

He began to sob, making further inquiry difficult.

Charles suddenly remembered. "Richard Hudson? You're Richard Hudson's brother? I remember you from the night we set fire to the arms cache in your barn at the Royal Coach."

"Yes, my brother seldom told anyone he had a sibling. I guess he never forgave me for spying on their soldiers during the war. I sided against our homeland and helped the Americans counter a major military thrust from the St. Lawrence down to Lake Champlain.

"His property in New Brunswick was a chance for us to mend fences. I convinced him to come to Canada and buy the mill, but local businessmen resented him. He was going broke because no one would stay with the mill."

Charles let him sit up.

Walter brushed off his sleeves. "We had this idea to form an association to insure our businesses. I was the principal holder of policies for over twenty lodges. We planned to burn down his place and collect the insurance."

"But why didn't he just sell his lodge and mill and move out of Canada?" Charles asked, perplexed

Walter adjusted his glasses. "No one would deal with him. He was disliked for favoring the Acadians and, when he came to Quebec to find a buyer, no Frenchman wanted to move to New Brunswick. It was hopeless."

"So, what happened?" Charles questioned.

"Everything was going fine until Richard met this Cazeau woman. She offered an arrangement to store weapons. We posed the deal to the other lodges as an association benefit. When Richard's place was burned down, his family was to be taken away for ransom. She would get this money to help the *Patriote* cause and we would get the insurance. It all went according to plan—until this Elizabeth Darmon showed up here in Quebec City."

"The real Elizabeth Darmon," Charles added.

Walter nodded. "Yes, I was meeting with Cazeau at the Citadel to discuss the transaction when Richard burst in on us. He said Mrs. Darmon was in town. He wanted us to stop the whole thing, no insurance, no ransom, no more killing. Madam Cazeau was furious.

"She wanted to get rid of the Englishwoman and the hostages to prevent interference with her insurrection plans. They argued so loudly, I thought the entire barracks would be down upon us, but then this Frenchman, Jacques, showed up, panting like he'd run a mile. He grabbed Richard and dragged him outside. Madam Cazeau told me that if we proceeded with the plan, no harm would come to me or Richard, so I agreed to go along."

Charles frowned. "You didn't know what this fellow Jacques was going to do with Richard?"

"No. I was scared, so I left for my place in Plattsburg first thing the next morning. I figured it was better to wait a while before laying claim to the insurance."

Walter John hung his head. "Then, you showed up at my Tavern and burned down the barn. We learned that all the lodges were being burned down. Don't you see? It ruined any chance of my laying claim to the Association's fund to pay for Richard's place. The best we could hope for was to get back our original investment."

"So, what did you do?" Charles inquired.

Walter nervously wiped his brow. "I had to stop the destruction before it was too late. So, I came back to Quebec, figuring it was someone trying to stop the *Patriote* plan by destroying the weapons caches, British Colonial Office agents working undercover. There was this huge party for the Governor. I worked my way inside and nosed around. Sure enough, Lord Stewart was behind the counter attacks. I took a chance and made certain he couldn't wipe out the rest of the lodges."

Charles blinked, stunned. He began shaking. His voice rose, trembling with rage. "You...you killed Lord Stewart, as well?"

He grabbed the little man by his throat. "What have you done, you weasel? He was the only person who could give me a pardon. You fool! You've done in the two persons who could have forgiven me for the crimes I was to be hanged!"

Charles released him and slumped back into a chair.

Walter struggled to his feet and rubbed his neck. He tried to straighten disheveled clothes. "Don't be too concerned. With all the commotion you and your American friends have created, I doubt much attention will be paid until law and order is restored."

Charles sighed. "And I suppose you poisoned Madam Cazeau, because you blame her for Richard's death at the Citadel?"

He shuffled his feet nervously. "I hadn't heard anything for weeks. I thought she might be holding him until the plan was finished. When you showed up at the Inn claiming to be Richard Hudson, I began to suspect foul play. Why would someone claim to be my brother, and then attack my Inn?

"When I came here and read in the newspaper that William Darmon was blamed for Lord Stewart's poisoning, and that he was the brother-in-law of recently *deceased* Richard Hudson, I checked back into old editions and found an account of his death at the Citadel.

It was clear that Jacques had thrown him over the wall."

Walter John shrugged. "I decided to visit Madam Cazeau. It wasn't difficult to find her here at the hotel. She received me, thinking I came back to claim the insurance. The woman was in a terrible mood, half-drunk, raving about Quebec being free for only a few hours before the Governor had the militia ambush their demonstration. All her work resulted in only a minor disturbance. When I mentioned Richard's name, she laughed at how she'd used the poor fool; that he got what he deserved—."

"Wait a minute!" Charles interrupted, backing up a bit. "William was accused of murdering Lord Stewart? I was the one who sent him to the Minister. Good God, what's become of him?"

"I suppose he's in prison awaiting trial," Walter replied. "I doubt they've transported him to *Trois Rivieres*, what with the fear of invasion from the west. A large troop encampment moved out to stop the rebels two days ago."

Charles' responding smile was caustic. "Yes, we outsmarted them for awhile, but now Justin's men are dead or scattered."

Charles shook his head slowly. "What have I done? All for the sake of a cause led by a ruthless assassin. I've served two people, and neither of them can vouch for my good intentions."

Walter closed his eyes, drained of emotion. "What shall we do?"

Charles thought for a moment. He stepped over to the window and gazed down on the deserted streets. Finally, he turned to the little man, his mouth set in a grim, determined line. "We go to the local Constable's office and find out where William is being held. You will go inside; my face is too well-known. Perhaps we can then effect a rescue of my brother-in-law and leave this Colony when my wife and sister arrive on Saturday."

Walter turned white. "Me, go into the local police department? Are you crazy? I might get arrested!"

"Listen, you little wharf rat," Charles sneered. "If you don't talk to them, I'll kill you myself for the trouble you've caused!"

Chapter Eighteen

Governor Aylmer placed Quebec City under martial law.

William's regiment arrived in Upper City shortly before the battle ended at the Governor's Square. They moved quickly to secure the streets. Redcoats manned corners, and soldiers milled about avenues, stopping citizens at random to check their papers. A few surviving infiltrators managed to escape following the razing of Montmagny Manor. They fled east, finding their way home without returning to Montreal. It was not a good time to be an American tourist in Lower Canada.

Suspect apartments were searched and known *Patriote* affiliates had been arrested. Charles and Walter narrowly missed apprehension when the militia barged into Madam Cazeau's headquarters and found her body. No assassination attempts occurred, leading to speculation that Cazeau's death had spared the Executive Council.

Headlines in *Le Quebecois* announced that on Friday, five days after the incident, His Excellency, Lord Aylmer would address people of the city to officially declare an end to the insurrection. The speech in Montmagny Square was scheduled to take place prior to the hanging of Justin and three other rebel leaders seized during the conflagration.

In spite of the appeasement, *inhabitants* maintained an ugly mood. Most poor farm workers and merchants tacitly approved of the *Patriote* efforts, and a growing number of sentries in the streets emphasized their lowly status in the British Empire. The city seethed with resentment at the wanton murder of ninety-three innocent participants in the Champlain celebration, and consequently, the highly visible guards often dodged well-thrown missiles from anonymous passersby.

Charles fumbled with his stocking cap, pulling it down to cover his forehead, but not far enough to create a suspicious mask. He and Walter Hudson quickly left the hotel and began walking along city streets to the closest magistrate. Charles frequently had to shove his captive to keep him moving, while attempting to avoid suspicion from officers patrolling the *rues*. The redcoats were easy to spot, but their positions on main thoroughfares made it necessary to travel in back-alleyways, greatly lengthening a half-mile trek.

Walter slowed again. He was leery of entering police headquarters and looked everywhere for a chance to run. He knew that Charles could not prove he was guilty of Cazeau's murder, but it would not be difficult to establish his role in storing arms for the rebels.

Dusk settled over the city by the time they stood on a corner opposite the *Palais de Justice* on *Rue Saint Louis*. The District Courthouse loomed before them, an immense, gray building occupying most of a city block. Virtually all of Quebec's legal transactions were processed at the central location.

Charles watched from the alley next to *Ye Olde Tea Shoppe* as Walter crossed a busy boulevard and disappeared inside the courthouse. From there, the *Patriote* could observe the comings and goings of visitors without notice.

An hour passed. Gathering darkness added cover for Charles, but a strictly enforced curfew also made him vulnerable. He was one of the invasion leaders still at large. He watched militia arrive at the Courthouse, often escorting former *Patriote* acquaintances into the Constable's Office. Twice, he retreated further into the shadowed lane as pairs of soldiers ambled by on the main road.

By 10:00 PM, the streets appeared deserted. Lights within the building at the late hour suggested a busy time of prosecution. For some reason, Walter still remained inside. Charles wondered if he had slipped out a rear door, leaving him to do his own dirty work. Once more, he felt rising anger toward the varmint.

A carriage rounded the far intersection and pulled up to the front steps.

The main doors of the *Palais* opened. A policeman emerged, escorting a woman down steps to the waiting vehicle. Charles squinted at the figure. She looked like the individual he had helped to imprison in the house on *Rue Grande Allee*—the woman William thought to be his wife. He smiled. *Certainly, she will know William's location.*

The carriage sped off and flew past him toward buildings on the next block. He glanced around anxiously for any sign of soldiers. A person seen running after dark would likely be shot without question.

He started after the conveyance.

By the time Charles arrived at the next corner, the carriage was already three blocks away and turning south. He ran as fast as he could up the avenue, keeping close to storefronts and avoiding street corner lamps.

Three blocks later, he stood panting at curbside with no carriage in sight down the narrow cobblestone road. He caught his breath and continued down the avenue, looking both ways as he passed cross-streets.

Eight blocks later, a carriage was just pulling away in front of a tall building up the street to his right. Roads had been deserted up to this point, but two sentries guarded the entrance to what appeared to be a formidable hotel.

He edged up the street and, a moment later, saw a light flicker on in a third floor window. Retracing his steps, he approached the living quarters from the rear. No door was visible, but trees adjacent to a stone wall provided the means to reach a second floor ledge. Charles scrambled up the sturdy growth and gingerly stretched his leg to the point where he could step onto the narrow platform. He worked his way along until he found an unlocked window and climbed into a darkened room.

His foot caught on a rug, causing him to stagger into a bureau. The collision jarred a small object, which fell to the floor with a loud crash.

A sleepy occupant sat up in bed. *"Qui est-il? Que voulez-vous?"*

Charles leaped for the door. After fumbling with a key in the lock, he ran out into the hall, ignoring shouts behind him. He fled to the stairway and vaulted up to the next landing. The lodger would surely alert the hotel clerk and a search would forthcoming. He must find Elizabeth quickly. He strode purposefully toward the door at the far end of the third floor hallway to the room where light had come on and knocked softly.

"Who is it?" a woman's voice asked.

"Charles Bagwell."

A latch clicked and the door swung open. Immediately, the woman yanked him inside, closed the portal and enveloped him in a fierce hug. She clung desperately, as if he would fly away. Tears ran down her cheeks as they parted.

"Charles, Charles, I was hoping you would find me. Walter Hudson came into the courthouse just after I had shown his letters to the constable. They immediately arrested him. He broke down and confessed everything, including the murders of Lord Stewart and Madam Cazeau. He said he had a message from you, but wouldn't tell us where you were. You can imagine how interested the police are in finding the man behind the rebel insurrection!"

Charles shook his head. "My part's been greatly exaggerated, Elizabeth. I was more of a symbol than a participant. For some reason my escape from the hangman's noose made me attractive to both the *Patriotes* and Lord Stewart. Now I'm simply hunted prey."

Her sympathetic eyes probed her brother-in-law's face. Charles shifted uncomfortably.

"Tell me," he broke an awkward silence. "Have you seen William? He'll be greatly relieved Stewart's murderer has confessed."

Elizabeth walked over to the window. "No, but he's here in the city. Once the troops returned, he was taken to Lord Aylmer for consultation. I haven't seen him yet."

She turned back to him. "So, how did Emily and Victoria get you out of *Trois Rivieres*?"

"They didn't. I was rescued by Lord Stewart's men," he replied with a smile. "They wanted me to infiltrate the *Patriotes*. Emily and Victoria caught up with me in Montreal. We all agreed they would come here in three days."

She brightened. "Do you mean it? Thank God! Aren't you overjoyed?"

Charles bowed his head, staring at the floor for a long moment.

He sighed. "I have no reason to be overjoyed, Elizabeth. I've lost my memory. Nothing comes to mind before I woke up near Dawes

Creek with a gunshot wound. The bullet grazed my temple, but it was enough to take away all recollection of Emily, Victoria, William—and you. You are all strangers to me. The others tried to help me, but..." He shook his head in confusion. "Half the time, I don't know right from wrong."

Elizabeth frowned like an impatient parent addressing a misbehaving child.

"So, this is why you led the Americans against our Colonial Office?"

"They convinced me it was a just cause," he said defensively. "I have no history; no beliefs or loyalties to trust. I did only what was expedient."

"Charles, you must stay here until the Governor's address. We can go over your past in the meantime. Once the Governor declares an end to this chaos, I'm sure William will be freed, and we can sneak you aboard a ship headed for home."

He nodded. "I intend to write down my entire involvement with the *Patriotes* and Lord Stewart. I'll leave it for the Governor. Maybe one day, after we're long gone from Quebec, the Colonial Office will no longer consider me a criminal."

On a bright morning of the Governor's address, Charles and Elizabeth ventured into the streets. He wore a hooded coat and avoided looking at strangers.

By the time they entered Montmagny Square, a crowd of several thousand had gathered. In the center, ugly blackened remains of the Chateau loomed, a monument to hatred expressed by the rebels. In front of the tower, a hastily erected platform stood awaiting Governor Aylmer's speech. A second, larger scaffold, fifty feet to the left held four dangling nooses.

Charles shuddered, remembering how close he came to a similar fate—one which might yet claim him. He looked closely at people crowding the stage. Most of the individuals were a poor lot; men, women and children dressed in tattered, dirty clothes.

As Charles and Elizabeth edged closer to the dais, foul odors, rude bumps and vile curses impeded their progress. He overheard conversations spoken in French, condemning the *Patriote's* suppression and blaming both the Governor and his Executive Council for the city's ills. Scattered among the audience, signs displaying crude lettering and occasional French flags poked above swaying heads.

"Aidez le pauvre habitan!" "Retirez les oppresseurs!"

At precisely 10:00 A. M., Lord Aylmer and seven distinguished looking gentlemen escorted by ten uniformed militia climbed onto the stage. Charles elbowed his way forward, leading Elizabeth to within ten feet of the podium. He studied each of the diplomats and discovered one smiling at them. Quickly, he glanced downward, fearing his disguise had been blown. No alarm sounded.

Governor Aylmer stepped forward. The others stood five feet behind him, anxiously scanning upturned faces between guards positioned at each end of the rise.

He reflected on events leading to this crowning moment.

Matthew Whitworth-Aylmer, 5th Baron Aylmer was both a British military officer and colonial administrator. At age twelve he entered the 49th Foot as an ensign. He became a lieutenant in 1791 and a captain in 1794. In 1798 he participated in an abortive British raid on Ostend, Belgium, was captured, and spent six months in a French prison. Adjutant general to Lord Wellington's army, he commanded a brigade in major battles of the Peninsular War. In 1814, following service in the French Revolutionary Wars and the Napoleonic Wars, he was appointed adjutant general of British forces in Ireland until 1823.

In 1830, he was named commander of British military forces in North America as well as Governor General of British North America and Lieutenant Governor of Lower Canada.

In his own words he was a perfect stranger to all that related to the country and had never served as a civil administrator.

In the beginning, he was known as a francophile, and spoke French with ease and elegance. Wishing to convince French Canadians of his benevolence, he defended the seigneurial system and sought permission to grant seigneurial lands under crown control to French Canadians who could not afford to purchase on freehold tenure.

Unfortunately, Lower Canada politics did him in. The Assembly would not be appeased regarding suspicions that on critical issues for the *Quebecois*, he spoke only for London and the Colonial Office. In return the Assembly refused to vote supplies and passed 92 resolutions of grievance, including one demanding the governor's recall. Asserting that the resolutions were tantamount to a Declaration of Independence, Aylmer argued that British influence in Lower Canada must ere long be paramount and that French Canadians must finally reconcile themselves to a fate which cannot be averted.

He warned Sir John Colborne, lieutenant governor of Upper Canada, that when the king's Subjects are spoken of as Foreigners and the Canadians as a Nation held in subjection by another Nation, it should alert the constituted Authorities to be on their Guard.

He became convinced that so long as the Assembly was composed largely of French Canadians the Constitution of the Province could never work beneficially. He blamed the *Patriote* Party for promoting a list of sham grievances.

"My fellow *Quebecois*! I've come here this morning to announce an end to this unlawful conspiracy. Through gallant efforts of our militia, we've put down a *coup d'etat,* which threatened our people and assaulted the sovereignty of our government. Never again will terrorists challenge the rights of English Colonists."

Several disparaging shouts came from various places in the sea of onlookers. Once more, Charles could sense tension building in the crowd.

"...restoration of order and a civilized process of government will enable you *inhabitants* to return to productive lives. We abhor the violence thrust upon us. The destruction behind me stands as evidence of the *Patriotes'* wanton disregard for property and lives of the good citizens of Quebec. I shall express gratitude to Parliament for choosing not to execute reprisals for this dastardly attack on British soil. These radicals will be punished for disregarding their benevolent treatment."

Curses in French echoed within the thong. Fists rose into the air.

Charles shook his head in disbelief.

He took hold of Elizabeth's sleeve. "Why doesn't the governor address the populace in their native tongue?"

She nodded. " At least, he should have offered an apology for the loss of innocent lives."

The administrator staunchly proceeded.

"I deliver today, four of these villains, and one man falsely accused in the death of a loyal aide to the Executive Council. The gentleman to my right is William Darmon to whom I offer a pardon. He helped prevent the attempted *coup,* giving us vital information. We now have the true villain in custody; a villain who without conscience took the life of His Majesty's noble servant, Lord Stewart, an unfortunate casualty of this misguided rebellion."

Charles returned William's grin. For the first time, he could knowingly look upon his old friend. At least, *he* was free of the hangman's noose. Charles almost felt sorry for Walter, who, along with his brother perpetrated fraud and became a catalyst for the insurrection. Many died as a result, and justice would be served.

"... I now give you the culprits who invaded our land, destroyed our buildings and murdered our children. Let their execution be a testament to right men everywhere, who uphold governments unhindered by greed and selfish lust for power. Today's retribution should remind us of the need to remain steadfast to my program of orderly administration and the necessity to maintain an effective militia ready to protect our borders. Further, we must put an end to these ideas of reformation and return to the time-honored methods of government handed down from the motherland."

Shouts of protest accompanied more contemptuous remarks from hecklers.

Thirty redcoats marched forward, conducting wretched prisoners to the gallows. Four guards and a hangman stepped onto the platform, while other soldiers formed a cordon around the structure. Each captive was forced to step onto a small rise under individual nooses. Before their heads could be inserted into the ropes, several young protesters pushed their way through the guards and jumped onto the stage. They leaped at the attending soldiers. Fists flew, knocking three guards tumbling off the platform into the watching horde.

Shots rang out. Two of the charging youths fell. Another received a bayonet from behind.

Onlookers screamed. The redcoats surrounding the platform raised their weapons, but the crowd pressed in on them. Hundreds of protestors' bodies swarmed against the officers. They beat the uniforms, throwing them down and trampling their torsos underfoot.

Enraged *Quebecois* continued pushing forward on the executioner's platform. Bodies streamed over the stage and pulled down the gallows. The freed prisoners jumped into crowd to be welcomed as heroes.

Governor Aylmer watched his men disappear under the wave of humanity. Horrified, he turned to summon more of his infantry.

Behind the podium, fifty additional uniformed guards edged into view, their guns leveled at the crowd. Bodies pushed Charles and Elizabeth forward in crushing press as the teeming mob converged— five thousand *inhabitants* opposing one hundred militia and the governor's quaking staff.

Fearful sentries threw down their guns and tore off red jackets before diving into the cheering horde. Menacing hands reached out toward the governor's stand. Lord Alymer clung to his swaying dais as if on an island about to be washed over by a stormy sea. William leapt off the perch and into the turbulence without much notice. Two council members did not fare as well, when malicious clutches dragged their bodies away.

Charles jerked around in abhorrence at what was happening. He had to act! His name was synonymous with the insurrection. Struggling free from the distracted throng, he managed to climb up next to the governor and threw off his hood.

Several inhabitants directly in front of the platform recognized him. "Look it's Bagwell! Leader of the *Patriote* Rebellion! It's him!"

Gradually, shouts in front settled down. News spread rapidly back through the crowd as a rippling wave of upturned heads and calming focus.

Charles raised his hands as noise slowly subsided. He swallowed twice, trying to relieve his suddenly arid mouth. The morass of faces stared at him, ready to tear down what was left of English rule on the continent upon his command.

He took a deep breath.

"People of Canada...People of Canada, hear my words! We stand at a crossroads, facing the choice of violence or compliance to an imperfect government. We are *Canadiens*, but we must not sever ties with our European heritage. French, English, Irish; our varied culture is our strength. It's our link to a civilization man has labored to build for thousands of years.

"His majesty, Parliament, and the Executive Council do not wish to interfere with your future settlement of this vast frontier. Resources of this colony can serve all mankind and, by doing so, we shall leave our children a better place for our presence.

"Yes, may injustices have been imposed, challenging our right to lead productive lives. Children are dying in the streets from cholera, but will killing these men save one single baby? It is the midnight hour of our oppression, but mark my words, London will yet address your grievances.

"In a few months, Joseph Papineau and others will carry a new list of resolutions to Parliament. Our grievances are just. We are honest men and women seeking a life of promise, sharing a commonwealth created by our fathers. Let us honor their legacy and find a peaceful solution...."

A face in the crowd caught his gaze. Emily stood next to Victoria. Suddenly, a vision came of their ship on its voyage to Halifax...

His attention to the message waned.

The mass of humanity waited patiently.

He rubbed his eyes, trying not to lose concentration.

"....People of Quebec, I implore you, do not strike down these men! We shall see if our injustices are righted, and we shall say to Parliament that the action of the *Patriotes* was a warning, a warning that we are resolved to seek a better government."

Another image formed, a sprawling estate in Surrey. *His estate!* It was as if he were two people, one speaking and one listening. *What was this speech about?*

Charles stared at the people. What should he say? What did they expect of him? Suddenly, he knew. "We offer this proposition: heed our grievances or suffer rebellion. Let us not forget today! Each one of you say '*Je me souviens!*'"

Charles saw Emily standing at their front gate. Their manor stood behind her... His attention no longer found the crowd. Participants began talking among themselves and repeated the chant in growing numbers. The rising chorus brought Charles out of his reverie.

He raised his hand once more to quell the voices.

Turning to look at Lord Alymer, he scowled. "We offer this compromise, Governor. Pardon the rebels, and we'll lay down our arms and return to our homes."

Aylmer stepped forward and surveyed upturned faces. The audience no longer seemed so hostile.

"My fellow *Quebecois*, let us declare an end to the insurrection. I hereby pardon all who have taken part, and promise to do everything within my power to ensure your complaints receive a fair hearing. We shall show the world that Canadian Provinces can achieve equitable solutions for its problems."

Applause signaled an end to the turmoil.

Lord Alymer shook Charles' hand.

Those near the edge of the assembly began to leave. They stopped, however, when two men climbed onto the platform and lunged at the Governor. One grabbed his arms, while the other pulled a knife from his belt.

Charles pointed to the attackers. "Stop them! They're Cazeau's agents, Jacques and Frances!"

Several demonstrators mounted the podium behind the two Frenchmen, but they paused when Jacques held the knife to the official's throat. More individuals jumped onto the platform, surrounding the assailants, but they, too, stopped as Jacques moved the blade to carry out his threat.

"What do you want?" Charles demanded.

"This man must die. He is an enemy of freedom."

Charles scowled. "It's over, don't you see! Cazeau's methods are finished. You have no hope of escape."

Jacques glanced anxiously at the encompassing Frenchmen, but saw no sympathy in their eyes. At last, the weapon slipped from his fingers, and the defenders pinned the attackers' arms to their sides.

Charles shook his fist. "These are the men who killed Richard Hudson! They're the ones who should be hanged! Tie 'em up!"

Jacques' eyes widened. "*Mais, non! Non, Monsieur, pas vrai!*"

While the crowd stopped its retreat to watch the confrontation, captors again looked at Charles uncertain whether to carry out an execution.

Another voice came from the crowd.

"The Frenchmen didn't kill Richard Hudson."

A short, dark haired man moved to the fore. Charles looked at the person in bewilderment. William and Elizabeth edged forward. The latter's jaw dropped open in amazement. "Deputy Amos! I thought you went west!"

Charles reached down and gave a hand to pull the lawman onto the platform. William helped his wife up to join them. She hugged the deputy.

"What happened to you on the river?" she asked.

He smiled slightly. "Aye, when the storm finally forced me ashore, I discovered you'd been washed overboard. I wasn't sure if you'd drowned, so I sent the canoe back downriver just in case. Then, I made my way over land to the city and started asking questions at the docks about new arrivals."

Elizabeth's own forehead furrowed with confusion. "But how did you find Richard Hudson?"

"I tracked the kidnappers to a house out on *Grand Rue Allee*. I watched the place for a few days until this fellow Hudson came running out. He stopped in the street and waited for a woman to join him. I followed their carriage to a hotel and listened at the door. They talked about how they had enough information and were ready to hit the bank."

William scratched his head, staring up from below. "So, you knew about their plan even before Elizabeth got to town?"

The deputy nodded. "I stayed on Hudson's tail for a week, then I got the idea to throw a little scare into him. One night, I slipped a note under his door saying the *real* Mrs. Darmon was in town, ready to point him out to the police."

He paused before turning to Elizabeth.

"The very next night, I watched from across the street when he and his two French buddies here bumped into you and he took off like a scared rabbit. I saw you first and then this one here, Jacques," he glanced at the Frenchman, "start after him, so I took off as well.

"At the Citadel, while you stood in the open yard, I ran into the barracks. I found Hudson and Jacques. They spotted me and ran outside before splitting up. I chased Hudson to the wall. When I caught up with him, he swung at me, so I hit him in the stomach. He lost his balance and fell."

"I never saw you," Elizabeth remarked, wrestling with memories of the events.

"There was nothing more I could do, so I went back to the house on *Rue Allee*. When I got there the place was empty."

Charles whistled. "I guess this finally clears up what happened to Richard, but these two are still guilty of murdering one of Lord Stewart's agents in a back alley near the docks."

Lord Aylmer gestured for the prisoners to be taken away.

With help from remaining bystanders, Emily and Victoria joined them on the stage. Charles turned to his wife with a happy smile of recognition and embraced.

Chapter Nineteen

Sunlight glinted off many waterfront windows facing Quebec Harbor as the *Oceana* sailed smoothly from port onto the Saint Lawrence. On board, five passengers stood at the railing, watching the sight with differing emotions.

Elizabeth pressed close to her husband. "Do you think reformers will continue to cause trouble here?"

William did not take his eyes off the receding coastline. "For now, I expect the city will stay calm, perhaps even attend to local problems with renewed energy. Contentment is precarious, however, and many colonists remain anxious about the list of ninety-two resolutions to be carried to London later this year."

Elizabeth bit her lower lip. "I wonder if French Canadians will ever achieve independence."

William returned waves of some children at water's edge. "It's a question for the ages. Most Canadians of English descent still choose to remain a part of the British Empire. Yet, New France has no less legacy for the French Canadians. We may rule, but their voice cannot be suppressed.

"Parliament realizes its dependence on these territories. Our Colony's resources are needed to sustain England's economy, but they also understand that a portion of the revenues must stay within the province to improve life within the region."

Charles shifted uncomfortably. "If Parliament cannot afford to administer the colonies, then the Provinces deserve self-determination to solve their problems. I fear there'll be more rebellions until the situation is resolved."

William shrugged. "England has invested lives, property and money to colonize this district. Should we now abandon the hard work and have to barter for the fruits of our labor?"

Charles squeezed the railing until his knuckles turned white. "Conversely, should unfair government practices be ignored? Why not let the Canadians compete in world markets? It could only strength both countries' economies."

"Perhaps, a compromise will have to be made," William said with a sigh. "Maybe some degree of independence is the only solution."

Emily took her husband's arm. With her other hand, she pulled Victoria close. "Such a beautiful place, your cabin at Humphrey's Valley. I shall never forget the countryside. It's a wondrous land, Canada, with scenery unlike any we knew back home."

"Yes, Richard and I found it so. There's an excitement about frontier living that I'll forever miss," Victoria responded wistfully.

She absently turned her wedding ring as she watched the islands pass. Her right hand held a letter from the bank manager, confirming that a buyer had been found for their properties. It assured a substantial return on her husband's investment, once their debts were settled.

Charles pulled a piece of parchment from his pocket and gave the pardon—granted by the governor—another appreciative look. A small wooden carving emerged with it and plopped onto the deck. He reached down and picked up the crude shape of a black bear.

"What's that?" Emily asked.

Charles smiled. "It's a present from a young lad who lives near Watertown. David wanted me to have it as a remembrance of my brief stay at his home."

Elizabeth frowned for a moment, looking at her husband again. "Tell me, William, will the impact of losing twenty-five thousand pounds be devastating to our businesses?"

"We'll have to do some belt tightening to be sure. I suspect we shall live quietly without lavish balls. It's a high price to pay for a holiday, but considering all we've been though, it's been the experience of a lifetime."

Grosse Ille passed by on their left. Elizabeth's features saddened. "That's one experience I never want to relive. Such misery and despair. What an awful welcome for those immigrants after enduring a long, grueling voyage from their homeland."

She turned her back to the railing and regarded her family.

Elizabeth smiled at Charles. "I must say, you did an awful job of dying my hair. I will not forgive you until my appearance has been completely restored."

He stared at her with a blank look. "Huh?" He stepped back. "Who are you people? Why am I standing here with a bunch of English strangers?"

For a moment, they hesitated at his remark, then his boyish grin relieved their anxiety. Emily punched him not so playfully in the arm, and the others laughed.

They were on their way home at last.

THE END

Thomas Thorpe was the Project Manager of NASA's highly successful Mars Global Surveyor Mission – a spacecraft that orbited Mars for nine years, returning two hundred thousand images of the planet and relaying pictures from the Mars Rovers.

Mr. Thorpe has written six historical mystery thrillers in the Darmon Mystery series about a couple from Kent that solves international crimes during the 1830's. These novels include: *Message of the Pendant, The Forth Contention, The Patriote Peril, Fair Wind to Bahia, Desperate Crossing* and *Without Redemption*.

© Black Rose Writing

CPSIA information can be obtained at www.ICGtesting.com
Printed in the USA
LVOW081004230112

265146LV00004B/19/P